T0130207

Praise for RETRIBUTION by Anderson Harp

"Tense and authentic—reading this book is like living a real-life mission."
—Lee Child

"Want to see what the military's really like? Harp knows his stuff. *Retribution* proves that the scariest story is the true story. Here's the real intelligence operation."
—Brad Meltzer, bestselling author of *The Fifth Assassin*

"I seldom come across a thriller as authentic and well-written as *Retribution*. Anderson Harp brings his considerable military expertise to a global plot that's exciting, timely, and believable. His characters are exceptionally well-drawn and convincing. If you like Tom Clancy's work, you'll love *Retribution*. Harp is very much his own man, however, and to say that I'm impressed is an understatement."
—David Morrell, *New York Times* bestselling author of *The Protector*

"Anderson Harp's *Retribution* is a stunner: a blow to the gut and shot of adrenaline. Here is a novel written with authentic authority and bears shocking relevance to the dangers of today. It reminds me of Tom Clancy at his finest. Put this novel on your must-read list—anything by Harp is now on mine."
—James Rollins, *New York Times* bestselling author of *Bloodline*.

"*Retribution* by Anderson Harp is an outstanding thriller with vivid characters, breakneck pacing, and suspense enough for even the most demanding reader. On top of that, Harp writes with complete authenticity and a tremendous depth of military knowledge and expertise. A fantastic read—don't miss it!"
—Douglas Preston, #1 bestselling author of *Impact*

"*Retribution* by Anderson Harp is a fast-paced, suspenseful thriller loaded with vivid characters and backed by a depth of military knowledge. Top gun!"
—Kathy Reichs, #1 bestselling author of the Temperance Brennan and Tory Brennan series.

The Will Parker Thrillers by Anderson Harp

NORTHERN THUNDER
BORN OF WAR
RETRIBUTION
MISLED

Killing Mercury

Anderson Harp

LYRICAL UNDERGROUND
Kensington Publishing Corp.
www.kensingtonbooks.com

LYRICAL UNDERGROUND BOOKS are published by

Kensington Publishing Corp.
119 West 40th Street
New York, NY 10018

Copyright © 2020 by Anderson Harp

First Electronic Edition: November 2020
ISBN-13: 978-1-5161-0977-7 (ebook)
ISBN-10: 1-5161-0977-5 (ebook)

First Print Edition: November 2020
ISBN-13: 978-1-5161-0981-4
ISBN-10: 1-5161-0981-3

Printed in the United States of America

Chapter 1

The Outskirts of Zinjibar, Yemen

War is a prologue to revenge.

The sun's setting caused the shadows from the torn and broken buildings to paint a jagged picture across the street. Dresden had no less damage after the B-17s and Lancasters of World War Two had leveled the city. The thousands of tons of explosives that shredded the German town overlooking the Elbe River seem to have done the same damage to the small Yemen coastal town of Zinjibar. Here it was the constant barrage of rocket propelled grenades, mortars, and Chinese-built machine guns. Empty shells of buildings, jagged walls scored with bullet holes the size of grapefruits, outlined what was left of neighborhoods. The smell of spent gunpowder, burnt wood, melted tires and death lingered.

Zinjinbar's streets had become only winding pathways through mounds of fractured cinderblocks, shredded wood scraps, burnt out shells of cars, piles of shredded clothes, a bloody shoe tossed on the heap and the broken evidence of the death and destruction caused by a series of battles. First, the Houthi rebels had attacked, then the government, and finally, al-Qaeda had taken control of the small town. The shadows left long, sharp knife-like marks of the gloom that stretched over the remaining ruins. As the machine gun fire stopped, those remaining came out of their shelters and cleared access for their mule carts, motorcycles, white Toyota vans, and pickup trucks. A small boy missing a leg bore his light weight on a makeshift crutch as he made his way down the street and disappeared into the wreckage of a home. On the backstreets of Zinjibar, rows of mud- and clay-roofed villas, connected together in tight lines, survived the brunt of the destruction.

One sign of what the town once was still stood, oddly: a gigantic soccer complex, the Al-Wihda stadium, just outside the town center. Now, it was the shell of what once was. The ghosts of past football games only haunted its field. The structure, disfigured by the constant barrage of shelling, seemed more like an old man's mouth of jagged teeth, with some broken, some missing.

The town of Zinjibar, within a close walk to the waters of the Gulf of Aden, had been the home of small fishing boats, made for centuries of wood, but replaced in recent decades with thin, long fiberglass skiffs powered by single outboard motors. Each was manned by a handful of men. At the end of the day, they would pull their boats on shore and walk into the town to their homes. One such place, buried deep in a neighborhood of brick, clay and cinderblock structures, stood out—at least to a particular observer on the other side of the world.

The two-story structure sat in a row with its neighbors and, on the back side, was connected to a small alley. Two men, dressed in black shirts and green camouflaged pants with their AK-47s on their laps, sat sleepily on overturned oil barrel halves on the flat roof behind parapets that guarded them from the street. The flat roof was an oven. It was a different color as it was floored with a "good hat" made of "nurah" or a heavier lime-based material that held the structure during the rare rains. They used a torn tent to protect them from being spotted from above; however, they were not good stewards of the ruse. Because the tent blocked what little breeze came off of the Gulf of Aden, they hid under it only in the noonday heat. Now, with the sun setting, they came out of their shelter.

One of the guards looked at his watch, a small Timex, and then moved his hands to animate the conversation he was having with his fellow guard. He pointed down at his sandals, seemingly complaining of a past injury to his foot.

The observer could not hear what was being said between the two AQAP soldiers but she saw each and every detail of the men from the unpiloted aircraft that soared more than forty-eight thousand feet above Zinjibar. The drone watched its target from well beyond the sight of those on the ground. The MQ-9 Reaper's camera lens was like the eyes of a hawk, only better. While a hawk's eye was eight times more powerful than the human eye, the Reaper's camera could see the man's watch and tell time from it. It even saw the flies that circled the two men as they swiped them away with their hands.

The other man had a finger missing on the hand he was using to hold the stock of his rifle. The drone's camera even picked up the scar tissue that had built up around the old wound.

The targeted building had been under the watchful eye of the Reaper's Operation Center at Shaw Air Force base in South Carolina for days now, and with good reason. It was thought that its occupant led a cell of one of the bloodiest groups in the world of international terrorism. AQAP, al-Qaeda in the Arabian Peninsula, as it was called, extended a long reach from this dusty, arid town. It had caused the slaughter at the office of the French magazine *Charlie Hebdo* and attempted a grander attack with a failed bomb detonation in Times Square in 2010. It was AQAP that had blown a hole in the side of the *USS Cole*, killing several seamen asleep in their bunks. It had even prompted the killing spree carried out by an Army recruiter in Little Rock, Arkansas. AQAP took pride in its slaughter of the innocent. It had murdered fifty-six innocent doctors, nurses, and patients in a hospital raid in the capital Yemen city of Sana'a. Women and children in beds, healing from injuries suffered in past attacks, were torn to shreds by the assassin's machine gun fire on the hospital wards. AQAP also had taken hold of Zinjibar, lost it, and then regained it multiple times over several battles.

* * * *

"Definitely AQAP." The Reaper's pilot in South Carolina focused in on the guards from the drone's perch in the upper troposphere. The house had caught the attention of the eye in the sky by the most innocent of mistakes. A child with a basket full of bread had visited there a week earlier. She'd knocked on the door while the guards above were asleep in the midday sun. A hand had reached out, taken the loaves, and handed her some money. It was a man's hand. The child had left with an empty basket. A Reaper had been on random patrol over the town for weeks. Later, analysts had noticed that two men were standing guard on the house's roof under the thin cover of a tent.

And now, three small white Toyota trucks appeared in the alley behind the house. They stopped only briefly. Two armed men jumped out and entered the rear of the structure.

"Gonna call this in." The pilot sat up in her chair as she spoke to the senior airman sitting on duty next to her. The two, assigned to the 50th Attack Squadron, sat side by side in twelve-hour shifts. The Reaper hadn't come from Shaw—it was only controlled by the crew there. The constant communications that guided the aircraft came via satellites, but the aircraft's home was a secret base called Camp Baledogle. "B-Dog" was in Somalia and kept the Reapers on duty by refueling within striking distance of the home of terror—Yemen. B-Dog's airfield had been built by the Soviets during their past efforts to win over the Somali Air Force. Later abandoned, it was taken over by the Department of State's Africa Peacekeeping Program—which, when translated, meant the U.S.'s war against al-Qaeda. This Reaper was one of four that were rotated on duty above the target. As one became low on fuel, another drone would take off from B-Dog and relieve the other. The surveillance remained constant with the stateside operators swapping out. It was this crew that brought the action.

The RPA pilot keyed her microphone to the operations center. The officer in charge passed the call up the line to the White House operations center, through the CIA and Pentagon; in a matter of minutes, the video from the Reaper's eye had reached the higher-ups.

"Pilot, what's the armament on this bird?"

She had placed the communication on speaker. She didn't recognize the voice. Her sensor operator glanced at her, her stare showing the tension in the room.

"I'm sorry, sir." She hesitated to answer the question.

"This is the Chief of Staff of the White House."

"Oh, sorry, two GBU-thirty-eights" The Reaper continued to circle above the target with a five-hundred-pound bomb under each of its wings. The craft was an improvement over its younger brother, the Predator, with the ability to reach higher into the heavens—nearly fifty-thousand feet—and carry more payload. Each GBU-38 contained five hundred pounds of explosives that could be guided into a car window. The terrorists might still be able to hit so-called soft targets—the children at malls or theaters—but they had to live with the constant fear that every small glimmer they spotted on a clear, sunny day could obliterate them and their families in an instant.

"What's your rank and name?" asked the man who had identified himself as the chief of staff.

"Yes, sir, Lieutenant Isbell here." Her voice sounded too young to be manning a machine that could cause the death of a covey of terrorists with the pull of a trigger. She had the slight tinge of her southern Arkansas upbringing in her voice. Shaw was a long way from Helena on the bank of the Mississippi River.

"Tom, do we have recognition on the two?" the chief of staff asked someone in the room with him.

"Just confirmed from Hawaii. The second one is Jamal."

The drone pilot in the ground cockpit had a small poster in her cubicle showing photographs and names of the principals above her in the chain of command. "Tom" was the Director of the Central Intelligence Agency. Lt. Isbell felt her heart beating as she realized the Reaper's eye had caught something that had pushed this matter to the top of the pile. She had been trained from her first day at the Air Force Academy for what was next likely to happen.

"Okay, let me get the boss."

* * * *

Jamal had not seen his wife and young child for more than a month. He kept his family in this most protected safehouse available, not allowing anyone to visit, come or go. It had been stocked with everything the occupants needed until the next move would be made. This visit wasn't meant to happen; however, Jamal's child had been ill for several days with a high fever and constant diarrhea. The heat had caused her mother to use up nearly all the water. Jamal feared the worst. Cholera had taken the lives of other children by the hundreds. He felt the child's forehead. She was hot and dry. Her lips were parched. The diarrhea had stopped only when the little body had nothing more to give. Her eyes continued to stare out into space. Jamal had seen it before. Only medicine could save the girl's life.

He would not let their only child die. They had tried to have a baby for years. The men were jealous of his wife's beauty, but she was frail. Jamal had married her when she was only fourteen. She came from Sana'a, was a good mother and obeyed all of the teachings of Mohammad.

"We'll get her some antibiotics." He promised the mother. "And more water. Clean water."

She provided a slight smile that didn't remove the worried look from her eyes. Jamal used one of his cell phones to call the nurse who had helped the wounded after the battle that had retaken Zinjibar. He tried never to use the cell. Messengers only. But urgency forced him to take the risk.

He hoped the call, so brief, would escape the eyes and ears of the Americans. Swift destruction of the chip after the call should stop the trace.

The cell rang, and rang. He pressed it to his ear, waiting for an answer.

"She needs to drink." He called another number. Again, it rang and rang. "Do you have some clean water?"

"Yes." The mother held up a plastic bottle of water. "This is it. But she won't swallow."

Now Jamal knew that his daughter needed both antibiotics and an IV. Barely three, she continued to stare into space with a blank look, as if her father was not there.

"I'll get help." He redialed the number. Spending this time on the phone was the last thing he wanted to do. He knew that the Americans followed every conversation and used their powerful systems of surveillance to home in on targets.

"Yes?" The nurse's voice finally answered.

"Lala is very ill."

"Cholera?" The nurse's voice did not seem surprised that another young child was desperately ill. It was framed as a question that needed no answer.

"Do you have something that can save her?"

"Yes."

"Bless Allah, I'll be there shortly."

"Is her skin dry? Hot?"

"Yes."

"Don't try to move her. The sun will kill her."

Jamal kissed his child on the forehead. He squeezed his wife's shoulder, looking back at his lieutenant near the door. A display of affection would not sit well with his men. He stopped, pulled the chip out, and broke it in half. Then he grabbed his AK-47 and headed to the door where he stopped, looked back at the two huddled in the corner of the small, starkly empty room, and waved at his wife to reassure her.

"It's Allah's will that she be spared." He spoke the words to comfort her more than anything. *The calls took too long,* he thought as he turned and paused at the door. The sky was clear, but he knew it was no indication of what lurked out there.

I'll need to move them quickly, he thought as he stood in the door. *As soon as I can get something into Lala.*

"Another safe place nearby?" Jamal asked the man at the door.

"Yes." The man that rode with him had been a good lieutenant from the beginning. "On the other side of the stadium."

"We need to move them as soon as we come back with the medicine." One risk to avoid another…a chance he had to take.

* * * *

"So, you have Jamal?" The president's voice was recognizable to the pilot as soon as he spoke. Like a celebrity who was always on the television, his voice had a positive timbre and fast pace that she'd often heard on various news channels.

"Yes, sir, but he'll be gone," said Tom. "He's a killer that who has to be stopped. This is the first time in years we've even had a chance. The guy hides well."

"Okay, let's go down the checklist." The chief of staff had taken back control of the conversation. "I got the PPG in front of me."

The chief was speaking of the top-secret Presidential Policy Guidance for direct lethal action against a terrorist outside of the United States. It was the guidebook for when a kill would receive a green light. Even POTUS had to be sure that a Congressional hearing a year from now would be satisfied, particularly when a city block might be leveled.

Isbell's hand felt the chill of sweat as she held the Reaper's stick. The slightest touch caused the bird's nose to rise. The pilot kept the drone in a slow circle over Zinjibar and the sensor operator kept it focused on the building. The two guards on the roof were standing, now facing the alley at the back of the house. Their attention had been drawn to three trucks in the alley. They seemed animated, as if talking to one of the drivers who had gotten out of the truck and was standing guard.

"Are we confirmed that this is our HVT?" The chief of staff seemed to be reading from a checklist as he spoke.

"Absolutely," said Tom. The Director of the CIA didn't hesitate.

Isbell knew that Jamal had been on the high-value target list since the *Cole*. "Absolutely" meant that Jamal was beyond being captured and they were certain the target was Jamal. "Our counsel agrees."

"The surrounding buildings?" It was the voice of the president.

"No, sir, this area is a ghost town. Nothing left on this side of Zinjibar." The Director of the CIA certainly seemed an advocate of what was going to happen next. The PPG required that nearby non-combatants be at little risk. So, if Jamal had made any mistake, it was locating his safe house in a remote part of the blown-out city.

"He's been on our nominated list for some time," Tom spoke again.

"So, Tom, you're telling us this will be isolated." The chief of staff remained stuck on the list. It was not a casual question. A bomb that leveled a house would outrage the world if scores of other innocents were killed and the footage hit CNN that night. APAQ had become skilled at ensuring that the bodies of dead children were uploaded to the internet after an American bomb strike.

"Yes, sir." Confirming the target was isolated. "And with regard to the PPG. If we don't do this, American lives will always be at risk."

"This guy was behind Arkansas and Paris," the president said.

The RPA pilot sat up in her seat when she heard her president speak. The Arkansas attack had reached deep into her home. It had happened years ago, before she'd even left for the Academy, but the death of recruiter Private William Long proved that any man or woman who wore the uniform of their nation was always at risk. Little Rock was not thought of as a place APAQ could reach. But it had.

"Yes, sir." The chief of staff showed no sign of hesitation.

"Okay, let it go." The president's voice seemed heavy with the decision. There was a long pause.

"Your last one," the CIA chief noted. The changeover of administrations would occur within days.

"I won't miss this," said the president.

His heavy responsibilities would soon be passed to the next man to sit at the head of the table.

A short time later, the Reaper rose abruptly as it lost five hundred pounds of cargo. At the altitude of the aircraft, the bomb would take some time to reach the ground. The order was given. The bolt of lightning had been sprung from the clouds.

Isbell's speaker went silent.

* * * *

"I'll be back shortly." Jamal waved to his wife and child as he turned and ran with his lieutenant toward the trucks. He almost stumbled on the scattered rocks that covered the back yard. His sandal twisted under his foot but he regained his step, his lieutenant on his heels. He reached the middle truck and tossed his rifle through the back window.

A blinding flash of light struck just as his saw the rifle land on the truck's back seat. It seemed that the world went instantly into slow motion.

The blast lifted Jamal up and threw him across the bed of the truck. Like a large fish pulled in by one of the local boats, he flew through the air. The wave of heat singed everything. The concussion blew out the windows and lifted the truck up on one side.

The air was sucked out of Jamal's lungs for a brief moment, his vision blinded by stars as he gasped for breath.

Some moments later, Jamal pulled himself toward a nearby wall with his arms. His ears were ringing with a loud shrill. His legs did not seem to work. His left side felt burnt. One side of his face, his left arm and his leg were all singed. Jamal looked around for his lieutenant, who had been directly behind him when the bomb struck. The man had disappeared. Blood and fragments of a body coated Jamal's shoulders and the wall that he pulled himself up to.

He felt a warm liquid drip down his cheek, and brushed it with his hand. The red tinge dripped onto his clothes. Jamal brushed his ear only to see his hand drenched with more blood.

The driver of one of the trucks was standing over him. The man's mouth was moving, but he didn't seem to be saying anything. He was pointing to the first truck in the line of trucks. The third truck was on fire. Jamal's Toyota was resting on its side. Somehow the first truck remained unscathed.

"My wife? My child? My Lala?" He spoke the words but heard nothing. His mouth moved but nothing came out. Tears furrowed through the dust caked on his face.

The man slung his AK-47 over his shoulder and reached behind Jamal, lifting him up. Jamal looked down to his motionless legs.

The man's mouth continued to move. There was fear in his face. Jamal knew that a strike would be followed by another if they had any doubts about whether the target had survived.

The driver dragged Jamal to the first truck and lifted him up into the bed.

Jamal lifted his head and looked back at what had once been the building where his wife and child lived. It was now a gaping hole in the ground.

As the vehicle started to move, Jamal screamed out with all of his might. All he heard was silence. Tears ran down his face and blood dried on his skin and a yellow cloud of dust engulfed the Toyota as they pulled away. Soon Jamal could barely breathe or see the sky. All was dark. The dust cloud at least served one purpose. It gave cover for the fleeing vehicle.

He raised his fist upward and cried, *"Antiqam! Antiqam!"*

Again, his mouth moved, but his scream was silent to his ears.

Chapter 2

A cabin near the Susitna River, Alaska

"Got to go back to Georgia."

Will Parker put his cell phone in the pocket of his parka. His voice was somber. It had been some time since he had returned to his farm in the south. The snow storm had finally stopped after days of trapping them in his cabin north of Anchorage. The sun lit up the drifts of snow in such a blinding way that one could only glance outside. An early fall meant sudden storms, but the weather had quickly cleared as a brilliant blue, cloudless sky opened up and the sun's rays overcame the temperature.

"What's up?" Karen Stewart came up to Parker, who towered over her.

"I lost a man."

"What? Who?"

Will Parker took the loss of one of his team no less than the loss of a member of his family. He didn't lose his Marines.

"Shane Stidham."

"Oh."

"A drunk driver came across the center line on the interstate south of Atlanta." Will had spent many a night deep in Kuwait where none of them thought they would ever see home again. The small team of Marines had been dropped well beyond the front lines with the mission of calling in air strikes. They were designated as ANGLICO, or an air and naval gunfire liaison company that used its radios and lasers to drop fire upon the unsuspecting 1st Hammurabi Armored Division. The fear of death had never left their minds. But they'd survived. Now, on some empty interstate highway, Shane's luck had run out.

"Both trucks were moving well above the speed limit." He paused. "In opposite directions." The few times he had ridden with Shane, the pickup truck stayed at nearly a hundred miles an hour. Shane had lost his license more than once. And more than once, the police had let him go with another warning. It was known in the county that Shane had served his country well. His driving never hurt another. The same could not be said for the man who had crossed the highway.

Karen waited in silence.

"He never had a chance." According to the caller, Stidham's pickup truck looked like an accordion that had been crushed into a single piece of metal. Two objects moving fast and on a collision course were beyond the ability of any reaction time to move out of the way. "The body had to be pulled out in pieces."

"Oh, god. I'm so sorry, Will. When will you leave?"

"The runway won't take an hour." Most who lived this far into the wilderness had aircraft that landed on river banks or open fields. Parker had one aircraft that was an exception—a jet that needed a runway. He'd have Coyote Six's auxiliary power unit warming the engines of the HondaJet in its hangar so that as soon as he had the runway cleared, he'd be airborne. His truck had a plow that would clear it quickly. All he needed was a narrow path for the landing gear.

"Do you want me to come?" She stood at the door of the aircraft.

"Thanks, but there's no need."

"I can put off the trip north." She'd had a month-long scientific trip planned for months to a village north of the Arctic Circle, where there had been sightings of bears coming out of hibernation early and acting strangely. Bears never left their caves while snow was falling. Dr. Karen Stewart's expertise was the spread of rabies in the north country.

"Go. Go back to your Georgia."

It was his home. As a prosecutor well in the past he would have put the drunk driver in prison for the homicide. But he wasn't a prosecutor any longer. Nor was he an active duty Marine. He did missions that no one could talk about. Missions so classified that they would never see the light of day. And in all of that, he hadn't lost a man from the team—his Coyote team. Until now.

"Did you see the news?" She was trying to change the subject in an effort to allay his grief.

"No."

"They killed the terrorist that hit the *Cole*."

"Good." Will needed something to turn the day around. It would be a long few days ahead. Shane's wife was as much a member of the team that had survived the combat tours as the men who made up the ANGLICO unit. She had been pregnant during their last tour, when they'd been well behind the enemy's lines, calling in air attacks from a pile of rocks above a valley. Will and Shane shared a space between the rocks so small that their faces almost touched. Will recalled Shane debating names for the baby while they radioed in two-thousand-pounders from the B-1 above. When the bombs struck, they were thrown against the rocks like ping pong balls bouncing off a wall, but they had survived.

Shane had told Will about his daughter often. She was everything Stidham wasn't. He was built like the runner who'd pushed through the defensive lines of NCAA Division I football teams, whereas his daughter was a fifth of her father's size. He'd struggled with books and school, while his daughter had gone on to become a medical student at Duke. Shane had also struggled with the tuition debt. Duke was far from cheap. The funeral would be hard.

The HondaJet lifted off well before the sun started to set over the Alaska frontier. Will Parker would, with favorable winds and a refuel, arrive at his farm in south Georgia by daylight.

The survivors of his Teufelhunden team would be waiting upon his arrival. They liked the German term, a translation of *Devil Dog*. In the battle of Belleau Wood during World War I, the German soldiers had given this name to the relentless attack dogs that came across the wire and through machine gun fire. Coyote dogs became a shorthand nickname for Will's team.

Chapter 3

The White House

"Finally!" Elizabeth looked up from her cell only to realize that everyone in the room had seen her reaction to the text. She quickly put her phone into her pocket. Her mother, the First Lady, gave Elizabeth the stare that she was known for. The meeting in the office in the East Wing was for the outgoing First Lady's staff and Elizabeth had been invited to sit in the back. The topic was the transition plans for the new administration.

Elizabeth sidled to the back wall, then, when everyone's attention returned to the subject of the meeting, pulled her cell out and covered it with her hand as she texted a quick reply: *prw*, for "people are watching," meaning she was in the back of the room of another boring meeting.

A quick reply came.

She giggled as she typed *fofl* and hit send. She didn't really fall on the floor laughing.

The First Lady slid her glasses down her nose and gave Elizabeth that same look.

wru

Elizabeth got a reply of where he was, slid the phone into her pocket and quietly moved through the door. She got in an elevator and took it down, deep below the White House.

She was headed for a storage room in the subbasement across from a small room kept for a dentist. The White House was equipped for much more than the public knew. Fortunately for Elizabeth, the dentist rarely visited. For the last two years, the storage room had become their meeting place.

"Okay, oh crazy one." The man waiting for her wore the "Charlie" short-sleeve uniform of a Marine. The silver railroad tracks of the rank of captain were on his collars and the gold pilot wings were above the ribbons of an officer who had done a tour in his fighter jet over the mountains of Afghanistan. Michael Kerr stood on eye level with the president's only daughter. In comparison to their friends, she was tall and he was short. He wore a Devil Dog's close-cut haircut that showed little of his amber hair and a face with a sprinkling of freckles that ran back through his family tree to Scotland. Elizabeth's tight body fit well in his arms. Her Secret Service detail gave Elizabeth, code-named "Mercury," a reprieve from their constant scrutiny when she was in the White House—and especially when she was with the Marine.

"Thank God this is over." Elizabeth was as pleased with the conclusion of her father's term in office as anyone. It was a breath not of fresh air, but free air. She was tired of hiding her relationship with the young officer. She was exhausted by the endless scrutiny.

"Okay, Merc. Boston?" He had shortened her codename to their own private call sign of "Merc." He was referring to her going back to school.

"Why, you worried?"

"Hey, the next president has some seriously good-looking daughters."

At his verbal jab, she pushed him away. "They're from the other side."

"Oh, I know." He waggled his eyebrows for effect.

"Besides, did you see who's the chief of staff?" The news of the next president's selection didn't sit well with Washington. Even those in the other party had misgivings. His nickname was derived from a well-known DuPont nonstick cooking product due to serious trouble that had narrowly missed him on more than one occasion.

"Yeah." Kerr's job was to obey orders and he tried to remain apolitical.

"Dad tried to give the new president a piece of advice: *Don't hire him.*"

"Probably the wrong thing to say."

"Oh, yeah." She smiled. "He hired him the next day."

"D.C.?"

"They're pulling off my best buddies. I'm down to two." She squeezed MK—her own pet codename for her lover—meaningfully. The reduction of the Secret Service detail to only two was a major improvement over her restricted life of the last eight years.

"Two agents to keep up with Mercury?" Her father had come up with the name used by the service.

"That's right." She smiled again at the thought of less scrutiny. "And they suck at skiing."

"Okay, okay." He looked directly into her dark brown eyes. "And yes, I'll keep flying to get that flight pay." Kerr's one approved escape from White House duties was to catch up on his flight time.

"So that is the only reason for Boston?"

"Absolutely!"

"Tomorrow." She pulled away from him.

"What?"

"When I go back."

"Okay."

"Me and the caravan." Her disdain for the crowd that followed her everywhere wasn't well-disguised.

"Okay, it will all be over soon. Before you know it, you'll be an Amy Carter. Only on the front page when you get arrested."

"Gee, thanks." She paused. "Maybe I'll do something crazy?"

"I'll get up to Beantown next month." He looked at his watch. It was a Timex Waterbury chronograph that she had given him for Christmas.

She sighed. "I may be there." Elizabeth was known to take pleasure in not being predictable.

"Sure." He paused. "Gotta get some run time in our new toy."

He had recently been away for a month to launch the Marines' conversion from the AV-8B Harrier to the newest aircraft in the Corps' arsenal—the F-35 Bravo. The F-35 Bravo had been configured to lift off and land from nothing more than a helicopter pad. The jet fighter was a sophisticated flying computer that could harness the energy of the turbine to move up and down on command, and fly very fast.

"Okay?" After eight years living in a house that had more generals and admirals for dinner than any other place in the world, Merc understood the need for a pilot to stay ahead of the curve to have any chance of getting promoted. He had to continue to fly. He'd joined the Corps to fly. It was in his blood to take multi-million-dollar machines into the air. But she had her own plan for him and it didn't necessarily include a military career. His degree in economics from Brown made the Corps a brief stopping off before a career on Wall Street or perhaps even politics. Despite the scrutiny of a life in the big house, even the life of politics was not something she would reject. And all fliers must come to the ground one day.

"I'll see you in a few weeks."

"Let's go to Vermont." Elizabeth had first crossed paths with the new officer assigned to the White House during a brief trip to Aspen. Kerr's skiing skills made the Secret Service team look lame. At Brown, he'd spent as much time as possible with the Brown Outing Club on the ski trails of Vermont or ice-climbing in New Hampshire. He had all the skills necessary to compete in the biathlon and had won a race or two.

And it was the biathlon that had caught her eye at Harvard. She couldn't escape being the president's daughter unless she excelled in something else. Admittance to the U.S. Olympic team in the biathlon was, as she saw it, a ticket out. And Kerr would help her reach that goal.

Captain Kerr, like all Devil Dogs, could shoot. Merc couldn't.

With his boss's help, he was able to get a small part of the skeet range at Camp David laid out for a fifty-yard rifle range. He showed up one Christmas with a slightly used Anschütz 64 rifle. With its .22 cartridge, it had little kick. But that wasn't the problem—it was hitting a small target without a scope and between beats of a heart racing at 180 beats per minute that made biathlons so difficult. The sport had been invented in Scandinavia by hunters accustomed to chasing game over the snow. It was famously brutal, like running up the stairs of the Washington Monument and, upon reaching the top, trying to thread a needle. And in this game, a miss meant doing another lap.

Their first adventure had ended poorly. He'd had her run the loop around Camp David and then fire at the five small targets. She'd missed them all.

"That would be five more laps." Kerr had been trying to get the message across. The accuracy with the weapon was as important as one's skill in cross-country skiing.

When Camp David had caught a snowstorm, she'd begged her father to allow her to visit the base. There, she and MK had used the trails to ski a short loop and then circle around to the range. Again, she had missed each target, while MK struck the small discs every time.

* * * *

"Not sure about Vermont." He laughed at the thought of such an exotic escape. "Plus, I'll have a new boss."

Kerr's official job at the White House was coordinating the use of the president's fleet. He served within the White House Military Office as the junior man in the Presidential Airlift Group. Every aircraft of the executive fleet was essentially owned by the president and the President alone. It was little known that even the vice president had to request the use of an aircraft from the Oval office. The president rarely got involved; it was Kerr's office's responsibility to ensure that there were never any conflicts. He and his boss, an Air Force colonel, had a busy several weeks ahead as the new administration would need to learn how to use the air fleet. Plus, it would be a change of political parties, which meant that all of the new kids on the block would be putting in requests for rides.

"Okay, well, get in your hours. Don't want you to get rusty." She mostly meant it in earnest. She didn't want to lose MK through some avoidable flight mistake. Especially in the unfamiliar jets he'd be piloting.

"Got it."

"Probably going skiing anyway with Jenny." Merc turned and started to walk away. Her roommate at Harvard had been raised in Burlington. They had been randomly assigned together but hit it off instantly when Jenny had showed up with her cross-country skis at the dorm.

"Sure," he said, "but if you really want this, remember: Bailey never took a day off." He shouted the reminder after her.

Lowell Bailey had become a hero to anyone dedicated to the sport. For two decades, the biathlete had been the best hope for America's chances at a winter gold medal.

"Yeah, I know."

Chapter 4

Al-Mahfid, Yemen

"Are you sure?" The man from Sana'a sat across Jamal in the small café on the outskirts of Al-Mahfid. The man was the treasurer of APAQ. Both would stay no longer than was necessary. And Jamal would leave mid-sentence if the conversation took more than a few minutes. It was this repeated practice that had keep both alive this long.

"Yes." Jamal leaned towards the man with his right side facing the visitor. The burns had started to heal but still gave the appearance of a bad sunburn on his dark skin. Even now, he had to turn his right ear toward the speaker. "His security will be lessened now that he is out of office."

The argument was persuasive. The killing of a president would achieve exactly what they wanted.

"Not all agree." The treasurer, it seemed, had taken the pulse of the leadership.

"What?" The question reflected both what was being said and his need for it to be repeated. He turned his good ear toward the words.

"Perhaps it will bring too much attention."

The Saudi bombing of Yemen had been relentless, but there seemed to be a crack developing in the Americans' support of the endless war here. It had become, again, a question of whether America had been caught in the middle of a bloody civil war or was taking part in a righteous attack against terrorism. So far, it had only cost America the bombs and weapons that the Saudis dropped on their land. Another Yemen-sponsored attack might change the public's view.

"It is my cause."

The treasurer shrugged and dropped the subject. "Here is what you need." He handed Jamal a manila envelope. The treasurer had served the leadership of the Sunni group well. The funds of AQAP were flush after he had successfully pilfered more than sixty million from Yemen's central bank. He was a graduate of the École Normale Supérieure of Paris in the field of economics and far brighter than the thick glasses or pudgy face indicated. He was also the source of whatever was needed to pass across borders unsuspected—passport, airline tickets, driver license, etc. "There will be a man in Togo who has made this journey before. He will help. But be wise, my friend, be wise."

Jamal looked around the café. It was empty but for his two guards. Jamal struggled with opening the envelope and, as he did, several packs of crisp new fifty-dollar bills fell out along with several debit cards loaded with funds. Other papers and passports fell onto the pile. Several drivers' licenses from the United States fell out as well. They covered several states. Another small packet contained several white pills. He picked up a passport and looked at it.

"Photo?" Jamal asked skeptically. There was a picture of a clean-shaven man who looked somewhat like him.

"It doesn't matter. No one will look that closely." The treasurer was known to be perfunctory and direct.

"Ammon Mahmoud?"

"You're an Egyptian." The treasurer said.

"I like the name." *Ammon* had special meaning.

Jamal leaned over the table and looked at three small cell phones. He picked one up, but didn't activate it.

"In case of emergency." The treasurer said it quietly.

Jamal knew that meant only one thing—the cell was to be used if there was a need for more money. The treasurer was not generous with funds, but this was an exception. The mission proposed only had a small chance by both coordination and funds. They had agreed that the mission was worth it. As it was Jamal's life on the line, he didn't expect resistance from the treasurer.

"And these?" Jamal knew what the pills were. He had used them before in the battle of Sana'a.

"If you're in battle."

The pills would make him indestructible. Or at least feel that way.

"You need to get to Addis Ababa."

"Yeah."

"No later than tomorrow."

Jamal's face showed some hesitancy.

"Problem?" The old man leaned over as he whispered the question.

"No." A skiff could cross the short twenty miles of the Red Sea to Africa. One had to avoid the shipping traffic and the many guardian ships, but a small Yemeni skiff traveling at night could make the crossing to the shore town of Assab undetected. Jamal's father was a fisherman from the Yemen and Red Sea village of Al-Hudaydah. As a small boy, he'd spent days on his father's skiff, pulling in the nets full of catch. Jamal was not unfamiliar with the waters of the Red Sea. "Getting across Yemen quickly may be the worst of it."

Jamal considered the risks. He knew well the other risks of the Reapers overhead.

"A skiff up the coast may work best," he said. He would return to Zinjibar and used a boat to make the journey. They would bring cans of fuel and travel all night. When the boat neared the gateway to the Red Sea, they would stay close to the shore. It would be the safest way.

A cell ringer sounded in the treasurer's pocket. He rushed to pull it out and silence it.

"Forgive me."

"That'll kill you."

The man could only lower his head. He tried to change the subject.

"We have someone in Eritrea who can help once you're there." A shorter path would have been through Djibouti but there were too many American eyes there. Once in Eritrea, a long, hard ride and a dangerous border crossing into Ethiopia would get him to Addis Ababa and the airport. Ethiopian Airlines had hundreds of flights that crisscrossed the African continent and it was easy for a man to hide in the crowds of passengers.

"Good." The treasurer had the broad outlines of the plan, but much would depend on Jamal. "You're an Egyptian seaman."

"Yes?"

"The son of a fisherman from Abu Qir."

"Do I know the place?"

"A village near Alexandria. Since you were a child, you've helped your father catch mullet in Abu Qir Bay."

Jamal nodded. It made for good cover, given his upbringing.

"You need to be in Lomé by noon the day after tomorrow." He handed Jamal another piece of paper.

Lome was on the other side of the continent, but Addis Ababa was not just the capital of Ethiopia. It was also the base of Ethiopian Airlines, which covered much of Africa.

Jamal smiled as he looked at the ticket the treasurer handed him.

The plan moved quickly. Jamal wanted nothing less. Any delay only caused the chance of the Americans to catch up. Especially when Jamal left the safety of Yemen and the territories which AQAP controls.

"You know you're dead." The treasurer said it with a smile.

"What?" Jamal held up his hand to the ear. The aching had not stopped.

"The world media are reporting that you were killed."

"Allah wasn't ready yet."

The treasurer nodded. "You've got a window." He played with a china cup as he spoke.

"Togo?" Jamal asked as he scanned the travel documents. Lomé was the port in the small African country and the site of much shipping on the west African coast.

"It's your fastest way to make it across." The treasurer hesitated. "And stay alive." He pointed to a place on a map.

"What's this?"

"You'll meet another there who will take you further."

The treasurer looked at his watch. It was a gold Rolex Daytona chronograph. The luxury stood out in this bleak world; however, he had become too important to be criticized. He saw Jamal stare at the watch.

"This was a gift." He waited for a response. When none came, he added, "The emir gave this to me himself."

Usama Bin Laden had rarely given such gifts.

"I met Ayman on the same day." The treasurer spoke of the surgeon, Ayman al-Zawahiri, the new commander of Al Qaeda. "You know our Osama was ethnic Yemeni and had twenty sons. They can kill many, but we will still have warriors that will take up the sword!" They were thought of as members of the same tribe. The desolate, rocky country had produced, by its ancestry, several of the most hated men in the history of mankind.

The treasurer had a nervous look in his eyes. Probably because of how much he knew about Jamal's mission. Knowing too much was a dangerous commodity in this part of the world.

Jamal stared at the man and assessed him one last time. Without the treasurer and the few Iranians that still hated the Americans more than they loved Rolexes, AQAP could never have reached out across the seas. Jamal's daughter would have died from a lack of clean water but for the American bomb. The cost of the watch alone would have saved many. But the packet in front of him meant that much would be tolerated. Still, the treasurer's life was no less at risk. A photograph taken by the cell of one of Jamal's guards would be held as insurance. If it appeared on the internet, the Israelis would ensure that his Rolex would have blood on it. And Jamal knew that the treasurer suspected as much.

"Allah be with you." The treasurer gave Jamal a hug and kiss on each of his cheeks.

"And with you."

"Good luck. If you succeed, it will be as grand as the emir's efforts."

The journey had begun.

Chapter 5

A church on the outskirts of Cusseta, Georgia

The white-washed, cement block country church with a chocolate-tinted rusty metal roof stood on a dirt road just off of Georgia Highway 27 and south of the town whose name had been stolen from the Creek Indians. Cusseta was a group of gas stations, a Bojangles fried-chicken drive-through, and an abandoned hardware store. Beyond the gas station, a sign with the paint peeling off marked the church. Piles of pickup trucks—some still loaded with tool boxes, chainsaws, and bales of pine straw—were parked in front, jammed together, as men came out of the trucks with rarely worn dark suits and ill-fitted ties. Women dressed in white, with their children, young girls also dressed in white, were entering the church.

At the door to the church, four young Marines, dressed in their blues, stood at an awkward attention as the people walked up the steps. Some of the older men, who had spent their lives in back-breaking labor in the fields and on the log trucks, hobbled up the stairs, stopping to whisper "semper fidelis" to the honor guards.

Will Parker, Gunnery Sergeant Kevin Moncrief, and Staff Sergeant Enrico Hernandez dressed in their green, business-like "alpha" uniforms, walked towards the church. As the Marine guards saw the three approach and saw the many-colored ribbons on their chests, they stood at stiff attention. The four saluted the officers.

"Barely fit," Moncrief whispered as they climbed up the steps.

Parker, like his teammates, kept the uniform to be used rarely. It meant a high and tight haircut and every detail perfect. The men would not dishonor the corps by anything other than perfection. They would not dishonor their brother by doing anything less. Moncrief's complaint was false humor. The three had the same size and shape as when they had last left active duty. The uniforms fit well, their black shoes shining like glass.

"Let's do this."

The coffin carried the American flag. And it fell on William Parker as his duty to present it to the wife of their teammate. She was small, frail, and her Asian features showed the pride that went with staying at home when her husband was thousands of miles away, surrounded by men who wanted to kill him.

"Thank you, Will."

The call of rank and use of last names had ended years ago.

A young woman, bearing the beauty of her mixed ancestries and bright brown eyes, sat next to her mother, grasping her arm.

"I'm sorry, Doctor." Will bent over as he whispered the words.

"I'd like to speak with you after this."

Will stood straight, surprised by the response.

"Sure."

* * * *

"Your father saved my life more than once." Will stood at the edge of the small country cemetery just behind the church. It was the ultimate compliment one Teufelhunden soldier could say about another.

"Thank you."

Will had not seen Shane's daughter in years. The child had become a woman. She had become the best of the blend of her parents. She stood at eye level with Will Parker's ribbons on his chest. She had an athlete's build, though not the great size of her father. The doctor was petite, like her Malaysian mother, but carried the shape of someone who competed in Ironman races, returned to the hospital, and did an all-night shift in the emergency room.

"I'm finished with school," she added.

"Yes." Will had kept tabs on her for some time. Stidham had been too proud to take help on the tuition, but an anonymous charity had granted her a scholarship. Its home address was not publicly known, but deep research would have shown it as being a post office box in Anchorage, Alaska. Stidham never knew the source.

"Had more hours in an ER than anyone."

"That's where you want to practice?"

"Sort of."

Will hesitated, waiting for her next words.

"I've got another idea I'd like to discuss." She seemed afraid to address the subject.

Chapter 6

Quito, Ecuador

The director of the National Endowment for Democracy for Ecuador rarely visited the high-altitude capital of Quito. Margarite Zorn favored living in the seaside town of El Arenal far from there. With her computers set up at her seaside villa, the young Ecuadorian of American-German descent could accomplish everything she needed by infrequent visits to the capital. And the political climate warranted her keeping a low profile. In El Arenal, she had more than fifty acres on the beach, with an orchard between her and Highway 489.

The villa was much more than a seaside retreat. Two satellite dishes were well behind the roofline. Beyond the orchard, a wall with shards of broken glass embedded in the cement kept out any foolish casual visitor. A steel gate blocked the entrance and had a small portal that a guard could peer out of if someone foolishly ventured down the dirt road that cut through the fruit trees.

The Chinese had the villa down the beach. The cat and mouse game was always afoot. Zorn's villa was impractical and cost more than preferred by Washington; however, she had achieved success in revamping the American presence after another previously had been found out. The carpet dealer had been expelled, but the damage was the loss of several influential generals. The country was not too inclined to make the National Endowment for Democracy welcome.

Zorn's serious demeanor sent the message that she meant business. She kept her blond hair cut short, and looked more like her German father than anyone else in her family tree. It was never clear as to why her father left Frankfurt, but the timing of his arrival in Ecuador in 1946 suggested the answer. She was the youngest of six. The others had helped on countless occasions to provide the introductions needed. She was tanned, not from the beach, but from working in her orchard. Her reputation with the other wives of the military was as the one who would carry a gift of the ripest and juiciest oranges—Ecuadorian oranges. It always helped the conversations, and conversations were the source. If she could keep a wife talking, she always learned more than anything she might have gotten out of the spouse.

"I need to go to the capital." Zorn looked up from her computer as she spoke to the tall, thin, dark-haired man standing in the hallway. He wasn't particularly handsome or even muscular, and had the olive complexion of an Ecuadorian with both Latin and African ancestry.

"I'll get them ready."

A small airfield at nearby Posorja provided her the transportation she needed. The company allowed a Pilatus PC-12 to be available, which ensured her access to anywhere in the country. It was a short jeep ride from the hacienda. And her assistant served the station well. With his nearly ten thousand hours in turbo prop aircraft, he had flown into nearly every airfield in Ecuador and several remote ones in the country to the north—Colombia.

"I hate that damn city." She lived on the shore line. Quito, at over nine thousand feet, stood as one the highest capitals in South America. Margarite Zorn's problem was something she had picked up as a stupid child in Catholic high school. She wore out a pack of cigarettes a day. Each visit to the north seemed to tax her lungs more than the past.

"What?" His words were brief. He had all of the clearances and had access to everything in the station. Her security guard was trustworthy; however, she had learned long ago that "need to know" had a meaning. If it didn't help the mission, someone else having information only risked a leak. His only "need to know" was that she needed to get to the capital.

"This place is like a sieve."

"Immigration?"

"Hell, yes."

The country's policy of open access had been an invitation for anyone who wanted to go north. And by north, she didn't mean Colombia, or Honduras, or Mexico.

* * * *

"Colonel." Margarite Zorn met the man at his home. She was standing there next to his wife as he returned from the base on the outskirts of Quito.

"Look, José, she brought us a basket of her naranjillas." The officer's wife held up one of the little orange colored pieces of fruit no bigger than a tennis ball. It was famous for producing a sweet tangy juice. The naranjilla could only be found in Ecuador and parts of Colombia. It had become Zorn's calling card. The spiny fruit served another purpose—its barbed leaves worked well as a deterrence for anyone interested in wandering through the orchard or approaching Zorn's villa. Tall trees shaded the plants below giving the appearance of a jungle just off of the beach highway. Despite being on the other side of the country, she was known for her success in growing the fruit. And it seemed to those that received them in the capital that Zorn's were the sweetest.

The man frowned as he stood in the foray of his villa perched on the side of a mountain overlooking the capital. He closed the door quickly and took off his officer's jacket. There was a faint clank of the metals as he hung it on the back of a chair. The day had involved some ceremony that required the more official dress.

"Hello, Margarite, how's your brother?"

Zorn's brother and the colonel had attended Xavier, a private Jesuit school in Guayaquil as children. His tone was chilly.

"Fine, he's in the States, working for an engineering company."

"Mara, Margarite and I will go out into the garden."

"I will bring you something."

The garden was surrounded by a wall that extended up and blocked the view of anyone nearby. He offered her a seat from one of the two wrought iron chairs that were on both sides of a small iron table.

"It is cold." Margarite wore a sweater and pulled it up around her neck.

"The summer is ending."

"At this altitude, Quito always has a chill."

"And what do you want?"

"You know I had to come here."

"Yes."

"No one saw me. I made a point of it."

"The oranges don't help."

She knew what he meant. He would have to convince his wife to make sure no one other than the children drank the juice. Word of fresh oranges meant one thing to suspecting eyes.

"She likes them so." Margarite had brought the first gift upon the birth of their first child.

"And?"

"I saw an intel brief."

"From your company?"

"It seemed to indicate that someone survived a bomb in Yemen." She was saying something that the media in the States would have screamed for. A terrorist that was declared dead yet had survived would be both a danger and an embarrassment.

"His name is Jamal. He's al-Qaeda from Yemen." She didn't mention the cell phone photo taken of two men at a café in Al Mahfid.

"So, your drones aren't perfect?" He had to put in the dig. The Ecuadorian army had known of drone activity over the Colombian-Ecuadorian border for years. FARC was always a potential troublesome group for both countries. The revolutionaries didn't mind taking on any government that paid them too much attention, but FARC generally kept north of the Ecuadorian border.

"If Jamal comes through Ecuador, I need to know that."

"Why would he come here? Why leave Yemen?"

"I have a hunch."

"What?" If one wanted information, sometimes one had to give information.

"His wife was killed. He knew who ordered it."

"Your president, of course."

"Yes, but it is more." She pulled her sweater closer as the setting sun chilled the air further. "The news made a big deal about it being the President's last called strike."

"So?"

"Jamal was meeting with their money man. He didn't need to do that for another attack in Yemen."

"So, in America?"

"Yeah."

"And what does Ecuador have to do with this?"

"You have no borders."

"We don't have the needs that your country has." The colonel had to get another dig in. "Our worry has been more about some of your past efforts." He wasn't talking about Margarite Zorn, but her predecessor.

"All I want is information."

"You know of Guayasamin's helmet?"

Margarite knew well of his reference. The congress building had a massive mural on its wall depicting the history of the country's heroes and its enemies. Almost unnoticed when first revealed, in one corner was the face of a skeleton bearing a Nazi helmet with three letters. The artist had warned of outside interference. The helmet had etched on it the initials of her employer—CIA.

"If you need remind me of that, I need remind you of a Swiss account."

He turned his head, and stared at a small fountain that his wife had built in the garden. The water bubbled up from the center and fell into a basin where it was collected and pumped again to the top.

"Just information." She had played too strong a hand, but knew that it was sometimes necessary. "All I want is information."

"What?"

"If he comes through Guayaquil, I'd like to know." She was doing her job. No one from Washington had directed this. Margarite was smart. She had viewed it like someone who wanted to get into America. Someone determined to sneak in and kill a president. She knew that Ecuador could be the passageway.

Chapter 7

Cusseta, Georgia

"I want to be part of your team."

Will wanted to say, "What team?" But he knew those were false words. "Why?"

"My dad told me everything. I want to be on the next mission." Dr. Kaili Stidham could be just as stubborn as her father.

Will stood there in silence.

"You'll need a doctor." She was making her case.

"There is no mission."

"I know. Just…" She held back for a second. "If you do, consider me."

His face seemed to repeat the question: "Why?"

"He asked me to do it."

The words stuck Will in the gut.

"Why?" He looked her in the eyes. "Why would he ask that?"

"He thought I needed more."

"What? Success? Husband? Children?"

"I don't need that."

"Have you ever been shot at?"

"Yeah."

Will knew what she was talking about. A psychotic patient, stretched out on drugs, had visited the emergency room in Durham with his assault rifle. A nurse and a patient were gunned down near the entrance.

Dr. Stidham had rushed the man with an orderly, bullets ripping through the sheetrock walls of the corridor, and tackled him to the floor. She was half his size, but hadn't hesitated a moment. She was her father's daughter.

The orderly was shot, but survived the gut wound. Kaili had made the national news for a day or two. Will had wanted to hear her say it.

"I'll talk to the others."

It was his way out of the conversation. Too many people Will cared about hadn't made it back from such missions.

* * * *

Parker and his teammates returned to his farm, put their alphas away, and made their way to the fire pit. The sky was clear as the sun sank in the west. The Chattahoochee River, well below the cabin, looked like glass as the fading light glimmered on its surface.

"We can use this." Will pulled out a bottle of Wild Turkey.

"Yeah." Kevin leaned forward in the chair with his glass.

Parker rarely drank. Moncrief and Hernandez could count on one hand the times that the Turkey had been taken out.

"Last time we did this was at end-ex." Moncrief was commenting on the end of their last combat tour as a team. "And as I recall it, Staff Sergeant Stidham got totally shitfaced."

The men laughed as the stars began to come out.

"He would want us to laugh." Will held up the glass.

"Going back to Alaska tomorrow?" Hernandez posed the question.

"No, Karen's well into the north country by now. I'll stay here a while."

"I first met him on the parade deck." Moncrief poked the fire with a long piece of metal. As he did, sparks flew up into the air.

"P.I.?" Hernandez held out his glass for another hit.

"You, on Parris Island?" Will smiled at the thought.

"Stidham couldn't have weighed more than a hundred and fifty pounds soaking wet. No butt, all shoulders." Moncrief poked fun at the man that couldn't defend himself. Stidham had to remain silent on the dig.

"Yeah." Will stared into the flickering logs being consumed as a blue blaze swirled up into the dark sky. "What do you think of Kaili."

"She finished an Ironman with a broken leg." Moncrief had kept up with his friend's daughter. "And then drove herself to the hospital."

"Sounds like someone else I know." Hernandez pulled up his collar. The chill was climbing up from the river valley below.

"Four hours."

"What?" Will asked.

"The drive to the hospital."

"The tornado do anything?" Moncrief asked. A brutal storm had passed through the county a week before.

"Yeah. It cut a clean path like a B-1 strike." Will had passed over the farm and the land to the north as he'd brought the HondaJet into the field for a landing. "I'm going to check out the trail tomorrow."

"How long are you staying?"

"No rush." Alaska was caught between the seasons. The dark, cold winter gave solace. The spring and summer gave Will the chance to fly into the back country. Landing a Piper Cub on a river bank was a thrill for any pilot and what called him back to Alaska.

"Are we done?" Hernandez asked.

"Didn't know we ever started." Moncrief was commenting on the fact that the missions came as needed. It wasn't planned since the North Korean operation had begun it all. But with the success of that mission, the word had gotten out that the hopeless missions were the ones that required Will Parker and his crew.

Will sat there in silence.

Nothing in the pitch black indicated what stood out beyond the light of the fire.

Chapter 8

Togo, West Africa

A constant breeze came off of the water as Jamal sat on a plastic chair at a small beachside food spot just off of the Boulevard du Mono. It was a short taxi ride from the airport to the beach in Lomé.

The sign on the road said "Restaurant Coco Beach" below a thatched roofed hut tucked into a row of palm trees. A colorful painting of a dish of fish called in customers.

Jamal's head was pounding from the long journey. He had given up on his ear. It remained a reminder of the loss of his child and wife. He sat in the center of the chair so it would not sink further into the sand, but his balance was off. The chair tilted again, and he corrected it.

"A bottle of water." Jamal said the words in English as he also pointed to one on a table nearby. As a boy of thirteen and fourteen, Jamal had been schooled in the language inherited from the British colonial rule of Yemen.

The waiter stood there next to the table.

"Fish stew?" Jamal asked. The air had the hint of a sweet, tangy smell.

"The best in the capital." The waiter's line sounded like a well-rehearsed and often used English.

"That too."

A man on a donkey rode past on the beach. Its hoofs splashed water as it continued down the shoreline just at the edge of the water. In the bay ships were anchored as far as one could see both to the north and south.

"Bring some bread."

"Try some fufu." The dish was unique to this part of Africa. Like corn tortilla chips, the dish was served with a plantain that was pounded into a ball and then shaped into a small cup used to scoop up some of the fish stew.

Jamal nodded, adding it to his order.

The chair continued to sink into the soft sand. A breeze came off of the water.

"Brother." A small man pulled up another chair. It was a warm day, but he wore a thin hoodie covering a brown work shirt stained in spots with grease.

Jamal recoiled from the stranger. He was already on edge, in pain still from the injury to his head, tired and hungry. His clothes had a worn, dirty and pungent smell after the journey across most of Africa. He didn't say anything.

"You need to shave the beard and get a close haircut before we make it to the launch. I know the place. It will be safe."

The little man was clean-shaven and had a crew cut. His clothes were slightly cleaner than Jamal's.

"Yeah, I know." His passport showed a beardless man, but with the arduous travel over the last day, he hadn't had a chance to shave it off, let alone get a haircut. The passport examiner at the airport had given him a second look holding the passport, but the customs had too many seamen coming through Lomé to hold up the line for a stricter scrutiny.

"We don't have much time."

Jamal leaned forward, after looking around to see if there were any scant glances. They remained alone on the beach, at a table on the far end.

"Most here are non-believers." Togo had far more followers of voodoo than either those of Christ or Mohammad.

The waiter brought a bottle of water and a bowl of rice with a thick, red stew topped with a large prawn. Jamal handed him several francs.

"Eat quickly. The launch will not wait."

The food burned as it went down, full of spices. He used a large spoon and scooped it up quickly, alternating with the fufu. The bottled water was lukewarm but he swallowed it in large gulps. It was his first real meal in several days.

"Come on." The little man stood up and turned to the roadway. There, he stepped into the road, almost being hit by a taxi before it came to a stop.

The barber shop was near the port. It had been used by sailors often and asked few questions. The man took him to a store on the same block and picked out a heavyweight Dickies cotton long-sleeve shirt, a spare, and some work pants. He handed him some heavy work boots.

"They have steel toes. Got to have them on the boat." The little man's boots were scuffed and well-worn.

They walked across the street to the entrance to the port and stood in line as others going to the launch waited for their papers to be inspected.

"What's your name?" Jamal asked.

"They call me Aabis."

Jamal knew that it wasn't his birth name, but it didn't matter.

"And you?"

"Ammon."

"You speak the truth?"

"My father gave me the name."

"What ships have you served on?"

"I have a list. Not many." Jamal had the paperwork in a small backpack he carried everywhere. Even in the barber's chair, he'd held onto it tightly in his lap.

"Me, less. This is my second crossing." Aabis started walking fast towards the pier. He suddenly stopped, looked around and pulled Ammon in. "We're here for our jihad, yes?"

"Yes."

* * * *

The motor launch pulled away from the pier and headed out to the far end of the bay. Jamal felt the warm salt water on his hand as it moved across the glass-like surface. A small vessel sat high in the water. It stood out thanks to a bold sign painted on its bridge that said "No Smoking". The name *Acca Energy* was painted on its bow.

"It may be a rough crossing." The man who called himself Aabis grabbed the rope ladder as they pulled alongside. He hesitated before pulling himself up the side of the ship. "Call me Reet. I will never remember Aabis."

Jamal smiled. The names and the covers were good, but also easy to forget.

The crew on the bunker tanker was no more than eight. Its deck was covered with pipes and large hoses. A long white crane was affixed across from the bridge.

A man stood at the top of the ladder dressed in a white shirt and dark work pants. He had the same type of boots that Jamal wore. He was strikingly blond and fair-skinned, looking every bit the German he was.

He extended his hand asking for their paperwork and scanned a clipboard.

"Not much time at sea?"

"We work hard." Reet spoke for the two of them.

"Okay." The comment was dismissive, as if they were the two most junior men who would be given the tasks that no other wanted to do. Plus, Reet had said that two crewmembers had become ill and they would be the replacements.

"You two are in the bunk room below. Your chores will be posted on the mess deck bulletin board." The chief engineer pointed to the sign above. "No smoking!"

Jamal nodded a yes.

The ship moved quickly out of port. It stood high in the water, but moved fast. The bunk room was shared with two Englishmen, but the shift was split with them working the night, most often in the engine room. The shift allowed Jamal and Reet to wash after eating, lock the door and do their prayers. They laid down towels turned towards the east when their room mates were below, kneeled and spoke the Fatihah in a quiet voice that only the two could hear. It was important that they spoke the words loud enough that they could hear their own voices, but not loud enough that a passing crewmember would stop. There were five obligatory prayers through the day and the two would steal off from their shifts to quickly do their prayers.

"How long?" Jamal asked when they took a break from the newly set daily routine of scraping off rust and covering it with new paint. When not working the rust, they cleaned the heads and scrubbed the pots for the mess deck.

"Several days." Reet looked out at the calm water. "If we don't run into bad weather."

The next to last day brought the worry that Reet had warned him of. The wind picked up at dusk. The small ship tilted up and down all through the night. Jamal's ruined ear made matters worse. He held on to the bunk, trying to sleep. His head swirled.

At dawn, the waves came over the bow.

Reet woke Jamal up with the bang on the door as he came into the cabin.

"Eat this." Reet handed him some soda crackers. "It may help."

"Allah be praised." Jamal murmured the words. "I could barely offer my prayers."

They had made a point of blocking the door, using a small sink in the room to wash, and making their prayers as best as they could. But the work schedule kept them away at times. It took ingenuity for them to conduct their prayers when their roommates were below in the engine room and upon breaks of their shifts. Occasionally, they would stop, ask for a break, go to the fantail of the ship where they could be alone, and kneel and pray. The time might have been off on occasion, but the prayer was conducted.

"We will be forgiven." Jamal believed that the jihad gave good reason for their missed prayers, whether late or not done, to be allowed.

* * * *

"You must work today." Reet sat on the end of the bunk. "We will stop for fuel in Puerto Cabello."

"Where?"

"Venezuela. If you don't do the job, they will kick you off there."

"Okay." Jamal got up, put on his shirt and work boots. He wasn't going to delay this journey one minute more than necessary. He was dizzy with the rolling ship and could not do his prayers at first light. One roll had flipped him out of his bunk and onto the steel, cold floor. He knew, however, that missing work, especially since he'd claimed to be an experienced seaman, would cause suspicion.

"We've made good time."

"Yes?"

"Crossing in three days less, now." Reet actually sounded happy about serving as a seaman. He had shown no hint, during the entire voyage, of any sea sickness.

Jamal could only think of getting to dry land.

"We'll be in Colon in another day."

Jamal didn't know much about the waters of the Caribbean, but knew enough to know that was the entrance to the Canal Zone.

Chapter 9

Near the seaside town of El Arenal

The hot coffee burned her tongue as she took a sip. Margarite started every day in her compound, looking out over the Pacific as the early light broke out over the horizon. The waves pounded the shoreline. She glanced at her Apple Watch, calculating the time at Langley. This was good duty and what she was meant for.

Margarite loved to put the pieces together. She watched one of the security guards as he patrolled the beach below her balcony. He wore a blue baseball cap, and had a pump-action twelve-gauge shotgun slung over his shoulder. Ecuador was not the best of America's friends, but it was generally safe. She knew that it would not tolerate any attack on a hacienda that was owned by an American, let alone an American with dual citizenship, and particularly with ties to an agency that they tolerated despite disliking it. But the equipment alone required constant security. The satellite communications and scrambled computers were valuable to some of the other intelligence agencies that roosted in the country, so guards were needed. Ecuador, however, left them alone as it likewise did with the Chinese MSS and Russian SVR. They would provide their own security. Ecuador had no interest in picking fights.

Her office was just through some glass paneled doors off of the bedroom. The Sectéra vIPer secure telephone sat on her desk. She pushed the pre-dialed number and it rang only once.

"Operations."

"This is Zorn. Olive, please."

"Wait one."

"Hello."

"Any word on my thoughts?"

The voice at Langley was the one person who would run interference for Margarite. A field officer needed some latitude to follow her suspicions. And headquarters didn't always allow such.

"No one is excited about it."

"Why?"

"If they believed it, it'd mean that we didn't get him."

Margarite knew the politics of what was being suggested. The media had bragged about the death of a ringleader. It would be bad form to say that they missed.

"Okay."

"I'm sending you something now that might help."

"Thanks."

The Agency Data Network computer on her desk required multiple sign-in procedures. The email was waiting once she opened her inbox. It provided what she needed to follow her suspicion.

Another email was from her boss. It required a summary of her most recent visit to the capital. Margarite had always stayed above the curve. She had already written out the report and now attached it to the reply. She still called the Ecuadorian colonel a valuable asset and requested another deposit be made to his Swiss account. It wasn't something that he had asked for. She knew, however, that the extra deposit in his account at the Zurich Cantonal Bank would ease his reluctance to cooperate. She wanted him to return all of her calls. And when pressed, she wanted him to deliver on difficult demands.

"Got it." Margarite logged off, picked up her coffee and went downstairs to the kitchen. The housekeeper would have her breakfast of toast, avocados, and fruit ready. She felt good. More important, she had a feeling that she was on to something.

Chapter 10

Cabin overlooking the Chattahoochee River

The fire pit behind the cabin popped as the split oak logs crackled in the blaze. The sun was setting and a chill rose up from the river. The shapes of the three men could be barely made out in their chairs sitting around the fire.

"So, how'd she handle it?" Moncrief stood up waving an empty glass, signaling that he was walking over to the table that served as the bar near the back door to Will Parker's cabin and implying that if anyone else needed one, he would make the run.

"I'm good." Hernandez sat back in his chair with his boots up on the lip of the stone fire pit.

"She'll be okay." Will Parker was talking about Shane's wife. But he wasn't thinking of her as much as he was of Kaili.

It doesn't matter. He considered her request moot, since their missions were done.

"Shane raised one hell of a girl." Moncrief seemed to know what was on Parker's mind. "I'd want her on my right flank."

Moncrief was giving her the ultimate compliment for a Marine, even though Kaili wasn't one. She *would* have been a Devil Dog if Shane hadn't stepped in and told her that she couldn't miss the opportunity to go to medical school.

"So, we done?" Hernandez raised the question.

"What? Worn out?" Moncrief gave his teammate grief.

"You didn't work the chainsaw," Hernandez shot back.

Will Parker's running trail, as it crossed through a valley that led down to the river, was covered with broken and torn trees. The few that still stood had been shredded halfway up, twisted and looked like a field of broken pencils. One could barely tell that a trail had ever passed through the forest. They had to begin at the edge of the destruction and cut a path through fallen trunks of trees as large as granite pillars. And the trunks, some from trees over a hundred years old, could only be dragged out of the way.

"And *you* did?" Moncrief gave it back to Hernandez.

Will had worked the chainsaw through dozens of trees. He'd had to use several saws that had overheated and become dull. They had only stopped to repair the saws before beginning again. Moncrief had run the backhoe tractor that dragged the cut-up logs to a field nearby. The mound was now larger than a small house.

"At least we've got it open." Will's trail followed the hillside, descended down into the valley and then headed toward the river. "One more day and we'll be done. Thanks, guys."

Clearing the trail had been more of an exercise in grief. It left them too sore to feel bad. The ache of the muscles distracted their minds from the loss.

"What's this?" Hernandez tossed him a small object no bigger than the palm of a hand. The clay piece had large eyes and sharp teeth.

"Where'd you find it?" Will examined it in the glow of the fire.

"Near where that big oak flipped over." The oak stood at the entranceway to the darkest part of the valley. Trees that had been there for well over a hundred years blocked out the light. The storm had let light in where it had not been for generations.

"It's Creek. A coyote." Will started to toss it back, but Moncrief held up his hand to stop the throw. "Keep it."

Will studied the object in the light.

"They were here twelve-hundred years ago," said Will. He fingered the clay coyote, studying it and thinking of the last human who'd held it in his hand. "The Creeks outnumbered every man, woman and child that had come to America from Europe for nearly two hundred years. But the coyote owned much of North America." Will sipped on his drink. "And they were what the Creeks feared most."

"They were killers that worked as a team," Moncrief added. "Our call sign."

"Yeah, our team," Hernandez said.

The ANGLICO team were called the coyotes. In radio traffic, its leader used the call sign Coyote Six.

"Yeah." He paused. "Well, a few more days and we're done." Will's trail would be cleared in that time. "If you guys can do it." He knew Hernandez had a family to get back to.

"I'm in." Hernandez didn't hesitate.

"I've not painted a house in months." Moncrief's painting company had been on hold for some time.

"We can go back to a quiet life." Will didn't see a reason why his world couldn't return to some sanity.

"I don't think so."

Will gave Hernandez a puzzled look.

"You can't go back to dropping supplies to lost hunters in the wilderness," Moncrief added. "I can't go back to painting houses. Not if there's a need."

Will hesitated before replying.

"At least there isn't a need."

* * * *

Moncrief's cell phone rang as they stood there.

"Oh boy." He stared at the phone recognizing the caller ID.

"Hey." There was a pause. "Yea, he's here."

Moncrief handed the cell to Will. It was Alaska.

"Can we talk?" The voice was full of static. He was standing in a hot field and she was somewhere well in the Arctic Circle.

"You got the extra grant?" He knew that she had been trying to get the funding for a study that would take years to complete. And it would mean years well to the north.

"Yea!" She sounded like a child on Christmas morning.

"Good."

Will walked further away from the other two. He stared up into the blue sky.

"Maybe we will see each other in a few months?" She was tied to her work just as he had been with his missions. Both were completely committed to what they did.

"Sure. You will win a Nobel one day."

Her laugh came through the static.

"A few months." He hung up the cell.

"Did you do what I think you did?" Kevin was standing close and had a sense of the conversation.

"What?"

"She wanted that grant for some time." Kevin had been the contact for both. Will stayed away from computers and cell phones as much as possible. Only when it was necessary did he send a text or message. "Five million just doesn't drop out of the sky."

"Mind your own business." Will ended the conversation.

Chapter 11

Colon

"Brakes are on." The chief engineer used his walkie-talkie as he pointed to the two men to help drop the anchor. "Bridge, power is on. Clear below."

The commands of dropping the anchor were being followed.

"Depth is fine."

Jamal pushed up his safety glasses as he stood by to follow the orders.

"Walk out the anchor." The chain rattled as the large links passed into the water. Despite the depth, it was crystal clear.

Jamal watched as the iron slid into the deep. It struck bottom and a plume of silt exploded in the water below.

"It's on the bottom." The chief spoke into his walkie-talkie.

Jamal had become a seasoned sailor by now. He moved quickly over the deck, jumping over the pipes and hoses. He had become used to the constant smell of oil and fuel. It had gotten worse after the fueling in Venezuela. He looked out over the morning light to see ships everywhere, parked with their anchors down, waiting their turns. In the far distance, the land of Panama was green, a green that Jamal had never known. His life in Yemen had been absent of color, its only palette brown and clay.

His memory of the past had been temporarily put on hold. But only temporarily. He remembered why the trip was being made. His resolve was not going to change.

After the anchor settled on the sea floor, the ship swing around and then settled down. Jamal stood near the rail watching the movement on other ships. They lined up like school children waiting their turn for admission to the class. The Canal Zone ran an orderly process.

Some ships needed fuel. The bunker tanker would be on station after another was emptied. Now, the crew would wait.

"You're a good seaman." The chief engineer stood just behind Jamal. "Not your friend."

Jamal turned around.

"He'll not be welcome back."

Jamal wanted to defend his mate, but knew it would gain nothing. It didn't matter.

"You can go ashore for a quick two days."

Jamal nodded.

"Take your friend with you." The implication was that it mattered little if Reet came back.

* * * *

"Gather your things, but leave some." Jamal was carefully folding a blanket that he had used as a prayer rug during the journey. He knew that an inspection of the cabin would be made in a few days after their failure to return. It was important that a few pieces of clothing, a hat, his safety vest, and other smaller items be left so as not to show that there was never any intent on not returning. "Leave the shaving gear. We'll get more."

"Good, I'm ready. I'm sick of this smell." Reet's clothes always were stained with fuel or oil. He was one of those few who could walk by a hose, not touch it, and then somehow be covered with grease. He had closed the door to the cabin as his weather jacket was on a hook.

"We've never talked," Jamal said.

"Yeah?"

"Why are you here?"

Reet hesitated. "I know why *you're* here." Reet spoke as he pulled out a cloth sack he had carried since Togo. He started to put the weather jacket in the sack.

"Leave that." Over the course of the voyage, Jamal had become the commander.

"You talk in your sleep."

Jamal froze for a moment.

"Lala? I can guess."

Jamal didn't answer.

"I'm here because of the same," said Reet. "My family was from Gaza."

Jamal didn't need more to put the pieces together.

"Besides, I have two little brothers still there with their aunt. I'm promised a payment if I succeed."

Jamal nodded, uninterested in money. Nor was he here for the blessing of virgins or heaven. His was a more fundamental need.

"They will take us into the city." Jamal had spent his time on the ship crafting the plan. From Colon and Cristobal on the Caribbean, they would take the train to Panama City on the opposite coast. The trip would take an hour or so. In Panama City there would be a short ride to the port of Balboa. "The last railroad car. We'll get tickets for the last car."

Reet showed a quizzical look.

"They're for the laborers. It leaves at seven. We'll get something to eat, and spend the night in the train station." It was important to keep moving. The last railroad car was packed with the day workers. Two men dressed the way they were would attract little attention squeezed into the last car. The trail would leave as few clues as possible.

"Is a night in the station a problem?" Reet's inquiry made sense.

"No, many of the workers get there late. The police are used to it." A lack of sleep for a worker was little punishment as compared to missing the 7:15 train. Many lived in the city on the one coast and had to be at their job on the other coast.

"Balboa will have a freighter," said Jamal. "It's a busy port with plenty of ships."

Reet nodded, clearly aware that his job had become to follow his commander's directions.

* * * *

The old tramp steamer from Balboa was happy to receive two paying customers. It was a short journey down the coast of South America to their destination. They occupied two bunks that would have been otherwise empty. And the pair looked like seamen looking for another port and another ship. This one did not need more additions to the crew.

"Allah would not feed this to a dog." Reet ate from a metal tray in the small galley with a metal spoon. The serving was a hash mixture of potatoes and some type of canned meat. He scraped the meat aside, unsure of its origin. They were in a corner and the only other crewmembers were men who came in quickly for a coffee, then left.

Jamal gave him the look that spoke the words one was never to mention. Their religion had to be held close. He felt his clean face. They had stopped in a barber shop in Panama City to get both a shave and a close haircut.

He has spent his entire adult life with a full beard and long black hair. It was what his young wife had been most attracted to. The beard that went down below his chin was a sign of leadership. A clean-shaven man was an abomination. He had it shaved in Togo, but much had already grown out. It needed to be removed again. It was, however, a sacrifice that had to be made. Like eating this mystery meat. A beard and long hair would only help the followers on their trail. It had now been gone since Togo but needed a shave again.

Only forty-eight hours had passed since they'd left the bunker tanker on the other coast. By now the chief would understand that they were not coming back. It would not be assumed that the men had deserted, as final pay had not been issued. The chief, Jamal thought, would call the police in Panama City to see if the two had showed up in the morgue. But he'd have no pictures and little paperwork on his two missing crew members. The police would have gotten such calls before. No one would pursue the matter. And Jamal knew that the chief would go ashore to recruit as many new workers as needed. It was likely that the chief would confiscate their wages and split it with the captain. No one would care.

"The water is so blue." Reet looked across the metal table at Jamal. He had just come into the galley after being topside.

The journey's chief difficulty would be the lack of much to do. They would be restless as the ship headed south.

But this would be the last period for some time that they would have little to do. It would be the last time that they would feel safe.

"We will be in port in the morning." Jamal rubbed his face with his hands. "And then we can turn north."

It was north that he had to go.

Chapter 12

The White House

Michael Kerr took a seat in the back of the conference room. He was worn out by the hop up to Westover. He'd had to jump a flight from Quantico to New River, where he'd checked in with VMA-542, the Corp's squadron that flew the AV-8B Harrier. Both aircraft could lift up from no more than a helicopter pad, transition their engines to forward flight and then turn from lift to speed. But it took a special touch. And the touch was only acquired after tons of hours at the stick. He had flown a Harrier in his combat tour and was comfortable when in its seat; however, this jet still took getting used to. As a jet, it required more support than a small airfield would allow. So he flew to Westover Air Reserve Base. It could support the aircraft and was near Springfield, and with Springfield, he would be near Boston.

Merc drove her Toyota Land Cruiser to Springfield and the Hampton Inn, just off of the base. The Secret Service agents in their black SUV, her constant companions, checked into their own room. Mike had arrived first and obtained the room so that she didn't have to pass through the lobby. Using their best efforts, the Secret Service did not give away that someone special was staying in Room 204.

"I'm not sure about this school thing." Merc sipped a pinot from a plastic cup in the room. She only had one year left; however, the degree meant little to her. It was not as if the daughter of a past president needed to make cold calls with a résumé. Their relationship had changed over the last two years. She had become impatient with the career track of graduating and getting a job in some charity that would put her in a cubicle on the twentieth floor of a Manhattan sky scraper.

"Not that you need the paper." He didn't press her. Their relationship had changed. At first, she had been the college freshman infatuated with a Marine in his uniform. Somewhere along the way, she'd become the woman with different desires. And still, she respected him. Mike had treated her as his ward, protecting her, advising her, until the trip to Aspen when she had wanted more. Now, they had a relationship that required protecting.

"I want to do this ski thing."

"Okay." He paused. "It's a lot of hard work. Very hard work."

Winter had not come quite yet to New England, but it was approaching fast.

"This cell is only for you."

"Got it." He had the number in his directory.

She left the hotel well before he took a lift back to the air base and his jet. The weather helped the return to New River, and the hop back to Quantico in an Osprey got him back to Washington near dawn. Mike flew up the interstate to D.C. and raced into the White House, where he changed into his Charlies and beat it downstairs to the Kennedy Conference Room. The world knew it as the Situation Room. He tossed his cell in the lead box in the hallway and showed his identification pass to the sentry.

Mike slipped in just as the door was closing, but more importantly, before the new chief entered. His boss, an Air Force colonel, pointed to an empty chair next to him.

"Busy weekend?"

"Yes, sir, got my flight time in."

The colonel smiled.

"Sure. Probably to the northeast." His boss knew what was going on. "Keep your head down."

"Yes, sir." Mike knew the warning. There was a separation from the past administration to the present that was as wide and large as the Grand Canyon.

The President's chief of staff entered the room and everyone stood up.

"Sit down." He was a wiry, thin man with a face that looked like the skin had been pulled tightly over the boney structure underneath. The man had his master's in international relations from Harvard after graduating from the Air Force Academy. He had climbed the ranks before some had made it beyond captain.

"Threats?" He read from a list.

"We have a credible belief that there is a threat to the President." The man speaking was the director of the CIA. "This is classified need-to-know."

"Yeah." The chief seemed little concerned. Everyone in the room had top secret clearances, but need-to-know took it to another level. "We'll talk offline."

"We'll increase security on all. We'll add the past presidents and their families." The Secret Service was voicing what he thought was expected.

"Hold on." The chief held up his hand in a stopping motion. "How much will that cost?"

"Sir?"

"Let's talk off line."

Mike sat up in his chair. He had a vested interest in the news. Taking it offline would pull it into the shadows. It wasn't the classification that caught his attention. It was the attitude of how it was dismissed.

The meeting was, like the reputation of the chief of staff, short and to the point. Mike listened as his boss gave a quick update on the commitments of aircraft. The executive fleet had more than two 747 jumbo jets. There were also 757s and Gulfstreams, and demand was high.

"Is it Kerr with you?" The chief asked in a steely voice.

"Yes, sir."

Nothing else was said. Mike's heart jumped a beat. There could be only one reason that his name was singled out and spoken.

Mike looked across the room, trying to catch the eye of another Marine sitting against the wall. The woman wore the uniform of a well decorated colonel. He knew her by reputation. She had come over the river from the Pentagon. When the meeting ended, he worked his way towards the door so as to meet his fellow officer.

"Ma'am?"

"Hello, Skipper." It was a "do I know you?" type of hello.

"Mike Kerr. I work with the Presidential fleet."

"Yes?"

"Colonel Ritchie?"

Her face showed some hesitation regarding him knowing her name.

"I was wondering if I might come across for a visit?"

Colonel Ritchie looked around as the various staffers were leaving the meeting.

"Perhaps. How about a run?"

"Sure."

"I run the canal at five."

"Yes, ma'am."

"Start at the bridge across to the towpath off the parkway."

"I know right where that is." He had run the C&O Canal often. Its running path extended for miles.

She left the situation room without another word.

* * * *

"You can guess what's coming?" Kerr's boss was sitting behind his desk back in their cubicle of an office. The Air Force colonel had become a good friend in the short time that they'd worked together. He was a C-17 pilot who'd spent several combat tours flying the large cargo aircraft into Bagram.

"Yes, sir."

"Let me show you something." The colonel pulled up a photograph on his computer. It had some age to it as best told by the few that wore glasses. They were all in their Air Force uniforms. It appeared to be a class picture. Most were smiling, sending the message that they were among friends. One stood out, slightly separate from the others.

"I see."

"Not to be played with."

"I did like this job." Kerr said it with a smile. "But going back to some seat time wouldn't be bad." He, like all pilots, wanted to get back to a squadron.

"Don't be surprised where you go." The signal was clear. "I'll help you with the paper."

His boss was saying that there was a limit to how much he could help. Reassignment would take Kerr far from Washington, or Boston, or a fighter squadron. His boss would ensure that his fitness report reflected an officer who should be promoted to the next rank. It would take time for the dust to settle.

"How soon?"

"Nothing said yet. It's just in the air."

"Good. I have some things to do."

The morning run had suddenly become more important than expected.

* * * *

It was pitch black when he pulled his Volvo into the small turnoff at the canal. The parking lot had only a few spaces and most were taken. It was a common place for runners from Georgetown to get in their morning five miles. Mike locked the door to his black sports coupe. He had used his flight pay and combat duty pay to purchase the type of car that one might expect from a fighter pilot.

There was a lone figure standing under a light on the other side of the bridge. Even at this hour, the occasional runner or two would pass by.

"Let's go." Colonel Ritchie looked at her watch, confirming that he wasn't late but rather early. She had the frame of a woman who not only ran regularly and did the USMC physical fitness test in a first-class time, but did much more.

Kerr was ready for the challenge. She took off and he got on her shoulder like a team of fighter jets. They didn't speak for some time. Once above the rapids that paralleled the canal in the Potomac, she slowed to a quick walk.

"I know what you want." Ritchie started the conversation. They were well beyond any prying eyes. And the first light of dawn was rising in the east.

"Might need some help outside the system."

"You don't need to do that."

Kerr hesitated. His look reflected surprise at her reluctance.

"The Secret Service doesn't care who's the chief of staff."

Mike knew that she was right; however, he had learned early on in this tour that there were many ways to skin a cat in Washington.

"Her assigned agents said the word was that coverage would be cut down big time." Kerr recalled the conversation with the two at the hotel. He hadn't mentioned it to Merc. She was so strong headed that she would have heard the news with delight. "Besides, I feel a danger."

"There's a threat." Ritchie was privileged to the intelligence traffic that had been briefly mentioned in the situation room. "But her father is well protected."

"Okay."

Colonel Ritchie paused, turned around and started back toward Georgetown. "If you get caught between two administrations who hate each other and the shit hits the fan, there is one Marine that might be a help."

He was surprised at her bluntness. She, too, had gone through boot camp and sometimes the language of boot camp was the only way to express a thought clearly.

"If you need him, look for a cabin just south of Fort Benning. It overlooks the Chattahoochee River." said Ritchie.

Chapter 13

The Port of Guayaquil, Ecuador

Jamal knew exactly where to go.

Reet followed as the two walked past customs, briefly showing their paperwork of being two seamen just arriving in port. The security had seen too many seamen come and go for it to matter. They were looking for drugs, and even there, they were looking for more than the average drug dealer. And Ecuador was famous for not looking very hard at anyone. Even when shootings from Colombian military incursions crossing the border to the north caused the country to pause, it didn't pause for long.

"There's a cab." Jamal waved his hand. The first one passed as if he were only a ghost. Jamal stepped out into the street almost blocking the second one. It stopped. He handed the driver an American twenty-dollar bill and an address written on a piece of scrap paper.

"Let's go." He opened the door for Reet who climbed in. Neither was familiar with Spanish enough to try to communicate with the driver, so they sat in silence as the cab worked its way out of the center of the port city and into the suburbs. The heat was stifling. If the cab had air conditioning, it made no effort to use it.

Guayaquil's tall buildings stood out as they took the highway near the river. Palm trees and the occasional lush green park separated the green from the mostly white and clay colored structures. Soon they passed into the slums where the houses seemed stacked, one upon another, up the hill side. The buildings had alternate colorings of clay, sand, yellow, orange, blue and even the occasional aqua. It seemed that the owners used whatever they could to set their home apart; however, it all ended up in a hillside of bright, circus-like colorings. Rusty metal roofs were, however, the common denominator, as most, if not all, of the buildings were capped with the brown sheets of metal.

The cab stopped on a side street with the driver holding it in place on the steep hill while the two men jumped out. He pointed to the clay colored building up the alley.

Jamal didn't try to speak. He knew that any attempt would only show he and his friend were strangers. He opened the door, hopped out with his sack, followed by Reet, and waved to the man as the brake was released. The car fell back for a brief moment, and then accelerated away. The driver seemed to care little about his fare, which was no less preferred by Jamal.

The street went directly downhill, and up another hill heading towards a white lighthouse that stood on the perch of the hill mass. Jamal had heard the driver say the words, "Barrio Las Peñas." He paused, looking down the street towards the water and the city off to one side and then turned to look up the hill towards the lighthouse, a round structure capped with copper on top. Just below the lights were what appeared to be a walkway where he could see tourists standing and looking out over the city.

Not Yemen. He considered the thought for a moment, turned, looked at the address on the piece of paper, and headed up the alley. A smell of roasted meat filled the air.

"Goat!" Reet spoke as they walked down the alley.

It wasn't quite goat, but almost a stew made with goat.

"I'm hungry." Reet spoke up again.

Jamal gave him a glance. The time of movement was the most dangerous. One didn't stop, didn't talk if possible, and always looked down. They would have time for hunger when they were in a safe spot.

This was not a land of Islam either. Ecuador might not have cared about who came through their borders, nor who the Americans might worry about, but it wasn't because the country was full of Muslims. Their host was in it for the money.

A stairway led up to a door with a number painted in a darker blue than the color of the structure. Jamal glanced at the paper again, and then knocked.

A child came to the door. She spoke to them in Spanish, they both looked at her, and then a woman came from behind and signaled them to come in. Inside, they stood for some time while the woman was in the back on a cell phone, talking in a rapid Spanish voice. Soon, a man came to the door.

"You have the money?" He spoke the words in English. Both Jamal and Reet were far more comfortable with English than any other language in the country.

"Yes." Jamal pulled out of his sack a handful of fifty-dollar bills. They were crisp, new bills that still had the smell of new ink. In the humidity, they stuck together and he had to pull them apart so the man could see that the payment was legitimate.

Reet stared at him in amazement that this money had traveled with them all of this time and he had had no hint of it.

"You not stay long."

"No."

"Your papers?"

Jamal reluctantly handed him the passports of both himself and Reet. He then reached for the money and took out half.

"Two tickets to Montreal on Copa. Leaves at three tomorrow." Jamal knew what he was doing. Ironically, the flight had one stop in Panama City, however, the route was necessary. They would not go through customs in Panama, and more importantly, the airplane would arrive in Montreal at seven thirty in the morning. Canada was far greater on border security, but still a passable route for those heading to the United States. Jamal wanted to hit the airport security at the busiest hour. And Montreal had a far greater population of Muslims than many destinations. The two would blend in and then disappear.

The man left, speaking to the woman as he did. She signaled for them to come into the kitchen where she laid out two bowls of rice and then dished the goat stew on top. Both men were hungry at this point and consumed everything in the bowl. Reet acted as if he wanted more, but Jamal put his hand up to stop him. The child looked at the two for the entire time as if each were eating a meal for a king.

At dusk the man returned home with their passports and tickets.

"We leave early." It was clear that he didn't want them staying any longer than was necessary.

Chapter 14

El Arenal, Ecuador

She refilled her cup with the Cubanito.

I need to cut this out. Margarite Zorn looked at her image in the glass of one of her kitchen cabinets. Her teeth were being colored by the dark Ecuadorian coffee. She continued to stare at her face. The long hours in front of several computer screens, the late-night calls, the trips to the capital were all beginning to take their toll. Once she'd turned heads. Now, she noticed far fewer glances. There would be no children. Dates were non-existent. No one could be trusted.

The deep, tart smell of the Cubanito was addictive. She had given up cigarettes when it became too expensive to buy the American ones. A smell, such as that of the coffee, was a small benefit that helped ease into the day.

The main computer Margarite used was just off the French balcony doors that looked out over the Pacific. She had a direct link to the Ecuadorian customs system and particularly to the airport. In the last several days, she would scan the names of those coming in. It had caused her to feel cross-eyed. Langley had given her another asset. She was able to tie into the security cameras at the José Joaquín de Olmedo airport.

Margarite had narrowed the search down to flights to Mexico City and Montreal. One would not risk going to JFK or another venue in the United States where surveillance would be tighter. Those two cities offered a prime opportunity to cross the U.S. border. Names on the screen cropped up, one after another. She took another sip from her coffee. Once it had been double cream and double sugar, but now it was straight black. An acquired taste. Knowing that she'd be spending a day or two at a computer, she had on loose slacks, a pullover T-shirt with the red, yellow, and dark blue logo of the "BSC" football team, and a pair of gray Airbirds she had picked up the last time she'd visited her brother in the states.

"Wait!" She spoke the words as the name "Mahmoud" came through a ticket purchase. It had been made at the airport, hours ago, and for a flight the next day.

Mahmoud. Margarite recalled what little Arabic she had learned following her training at the farm in Virginia. Her first station was to be in the Middle East, but once she'd made the complaint that it didn't make sense with her contacts and knowledge to send her to anywhere but Ecuador, she had been moved. She switched to another, unclassified computer, and googled "Mahmoud." The definition came up as "praiseworthy," but in Yemen it had another meaning—"one who conceals the truth." She moved to the edge of her seat, her feet unconsciously coming up on her toes in the Airbirds.

"Can't be..." She was working the tradecraft in her mind as she stared at the screen. It made sense. Margarite pulled up another screen on the classified computer—the security cameras at the airport. The airline was based in Panama City. Copa had become one of the gateway airlines to Latin America. The camera just caught the ticket counter in an angled, sketchy, black-and-white view. She looked at the purchase time and cross-checked it over with the security tape history. Margarite stared at the line, seeing young mothers with children, an old man bent over with a cane, and others that didn't fit what she was looking for.

It would be smart. She wondered if they had used someone else, but it likewise would have caused suspicion if the purchaser didn't somewhat fit the ticket holder. The buyer had to be a man, probably in his thirties. Copa was known to allow one to purchase multiple tickets using identification for two.

A man showed up, looking around, scanning in both directions. She knew him.

"Pena!"

Margarite crossed checked Pena's name with some background info the agency had on him. He was a gun-for-hire who lived in the barrio.

She sent a flash message to the home office. It was clear what was going on, at least to her. And the flight left the next day. She requested an immediate call to the head of South America and hoped that it would quickly go up from there. Her message received the attention that she wanted.

In less than an hour her vIPer telephone rang.

"Zorn." She was expecting Olive, her immediate boss. Instead, she got the chief of staff to the CIA director. He asked one question.

"Are you sure?"

"Yes, sir." Margarite knew it was a gamble, but this one was a worthy career bet.

"Jamal?"

"It all makes sense." Margarite was absolute in her confidence that she'd spotted the killer.

"Why not on the other end?" It was a fair question. But there were risks and complications. The question was why not grab him when he lands, not when he takes off? Ecuador might complicate things.

"It changes in Mexico City, for one." It wasn't completely clear that he was going all the way to Canada. "And the best final solution would be here." Ecuador might help, but there were risks. They were the government that had offered sanctuary to Julian Assange. And a murder in Ecuador would hardly make a ripple. It was not a sure bet that the CIA's intervention in Ecuador could be pulled off. But just as risky was their not acting. If he got through and they had not tried, and an attack on American soil occurred, the investigation would be less forgiving.

"What do you need?"

Margarite paused for a moment. If it was who she thought it was, there would be bloodshed.

"We can't let the Ecuadorians know." She knew that only one would be safe.

"We have a MARSOC team next door."

Margarite had seen the name in several briefings. Next door translated to Colombia.

"Coveñas?" She asked the question, knowing that he wouldn't answer. It was also the headquarters in northern Colombia of the Colombian Marines. US Marines had been known to train with their compatriots since many of the cartels had been reduced to smaller outfits that were less of a risk to the government of the country. The Colombian Marines were gaining a reputation similar to the Mexican Corps. And it had become an opportunity for American Leathernecks to learn small raider tactics deep in a jungle environment. A Marine Raider team would be within short reach of Guayaquil.

"What do you suggest?" The chief was open to hearing from her.

Margarite instantly gained greater respect. They were willing to listen to the person on the ground. "My airport would be best."

"Okay. Stand by."

"If we don't get him on this end, it will be smoke."

"I understand." The chief of staff made one other comment. "I don't think this White House will be a problem."

She didn't fully understand the implication other than that this new administration wouldn't hesitate to go into another country, particularly Ecuador, if it meant getting the number one man on their list. And her guess was right. The decision for such an operation would be made by the "other chief," who would not be restrained nor even likely to visit the Oval Office to get approval on a matter with such a short fuse.

Sitting at her desk, Margarite knew that the proof was slim. She needed more. There was one other who could be brought into the game. She looked on her cell directory for a name that she hadn't called in some months. It was a risk to bring this outside of the agency, but this one was safe.

"Arthur?"

The agent for Mossad recognized the caller immediately. Ecuador was such a cross road for terrorists that even Israel had a presence in the country.

"Zorn."

"I need your help."

"Must be out of bounds for you to call me."

"We always cooperate."

"Depends."

"I need Pegasus." She was asking for something that was way out of bounds for her employer. The spyware would be so deep in a cell phone that only a few in the world could know it was there. Often it was discovered by working backwards. If a target had been killed and seemed to have no connection whatsoever to a terrorist cell, it then came to be assumed that the spyware had followed cell phone traffic. After a murder in Mexico of a prominent leader, the culprits were caught in a day. Only Pegasus could reach that deep.

"Who?"

"May have a lead on Jamal."

"We already have it."

Margarite leaned back in her chair with the news.

"What do you mean?"

"He is using burn phones and switching them every time, but we have someone he is calling."

"Does Langley know?"

"Not yet."

"Will you share?"

"As long as you get him."

"Where is he now?"

"Last call was here. Not sure exactly where, but here."

"The barrio?"

"Yes, the one near the lighthouse."

Another confirmation.

"I need to share this." She was asking for permission.

"I wouldn't have told you this if I didn't already have the green light."

It appeared to her that Mossad didn't mind the idea that an American team killing a terrorist in Ecuador was far better than a Mossad hit.

Margarite sent the word up the chain of command. It was confirmation that her idea had substance. With a Marine hunter-killer team en route, it was copied over to the intelligence cell at the Pentagon as well.

* * * *

Zorn had finished her fourth cup of coffee as the sun started to set on the ocean behind her home. Her computer's chime caught her attention while standing in the kitchen.

The message was clear.

"Be at Posorja. 2400. Have address."

The last comment made her more nervous than the others. She only had a few hours to come up with Pena's last known address. And she couldn't use any of her trusted sources except for one. And there was no time to fly to the capital. She selected a burn phone that she had never used before, with a chip from a source in the capital city.

"Pena's address?"

She hit send to José, hoping that he would text back quickly. Pena was well known to the military in the capital. The request was fraught with problems. She laid the cell down on the kitchen counter, waiting as silence followed for some time.

Just when she thought it a lost cause, the burn cell rang with a text.

"Callejon del Tesoro, blue no. 5 in alley just off main street to the light house."

Nothing else was said.

Zorn knew, however, the location. She had mined it for years for sources, particularly for the traffic of those coming in or going out on ships.

"Thank God." She considered what else was needed. A Yukon was kept at the airfield with the Pilatus. A plan formed in her mind as she glanced at the clock in her kitchen.

Chapter 15

"You're crazy!"

Elizabeth Jordan couldn't disagree. Her Harvard roommate called the past president's daughter, Liz. They shared a love of skiing. The two had been roommates for three years and were entering their senior year. It was meant to be a time of fun. Liz was slightly older than both her roommate and their friends, as she had held out a year before starting Harvard. They teased her as being the old woman.

"No, I've got this." She was part of a three-car caravan that had driven up from Boston when the snow had been reported. It was, however, still an early-season snowfall. The plan was renting a cottage in Vermont's Green Mountains outside of Ripton. The difficult part was her escaping her Secret Service detail. She and her friend had jointly devised a plan involving trading cars, with her roommate renting one in her own name and leaving Merc's vehicle at Logan Airport in Boston. She had also bought a cheap ticket home, which would also buy some time. The Service would think that she was blowing them off but heading home for a long weekend. She wouldn't, however, show up for the flight. Merc had forty-eight hours before the Secret Service would call her father. And even then, her father would only think that she was doing again, what she had done, albeit rarely, in the past.

"Don't you like the cabin?" Her roommate went by Jenny. She was from Colorado and had been raised in the snow. She was bright and had a sense of humor that admitted her to the group of friends instantly. She was a Catherine, but they'd nicknamed her Jen as she had the personality of the star of *Friends*. They called her Jenny and Jen interchangeably, and she was the energy of the party. She was a perfect fit to be the roommate of the president's daughter at Harvard. She had found the cabin deep in the woods, and being only a two bedroom, it was tight; however, the wine was ample. "It's not far from the Nordic Center."

"Yeah…uh…" Merc held back for a moment. "I'm not going back to Harvard this semester."

"Holy shit!" Jen didn't hold back.

"I've got a plan."

"Does Mike know?"

"He suspects, but not yet."

"Your father is going to go crazy."

"He can handle it." It wasn't her father that she worried about. It was her mother.

"Where are you going?"

"Just had a dump out west." She was talking about an early series of storms in the Rockies that provided plenty of snow for biathlon training. And it would be at altitude. The workouts would be brutal, but it could make her competitive. And she was planning on signing up for some of the races at Snow Mountain Ranch. Its Nordic center had miles of trails and the snow would be covering it soon. But she needed to go further into the Rockies. And it needed to be a place off the grid. "There isn't much snow yet here." The Nordic centers in the Green Mountains had had a decent layer, but were still short of good training trails.

"You didn't answer." Jenny pressed the point.

"You don't need to know." Knowledge could be deadly.

But then she made a mistake.

"Here." She showed a picture on her Instagram account from a year ago. "It's perfect. Pure Rocky."

"I bet I know who will join you."

"Not sure."

"Let's get a selfie." She called out to the others. "Okay, women I have some bad news." The roommate turned to the others.

"I'm still in for my share." Merc pulled out several hundred-dollar bills.

"If I wasn't a starving college student, I wouldn't take it." Her roommate stuffed the bills into her pocket. They lined up on the porch and shot a group selfie, which her roommate posted to Instagram.

"Okay." Merc didn't go for the starving part. Her father had helped coordinate the purchase of a major communications company by another. His home in Greenwich, Connecticut, was bigger than their last residence. "Let me get on the road."

She grabbed her bag, her boots, skis, and the case that held her rifle. Merc glanced at her Apple Watch, calculated the time and threw it all in her vehicle.

"If I can get south enough to avoid the snows, I can make some time. Going to drive straight through."

"More snow's coming, so get on out of here." The roommate and the other girls all gave her a hug.

"Thanks."

* * * *

Mercury's car made good time south on Highway 7 working her way down to Albany, and from there, turning west on the Interstate system. The freedom of the escape was something that she had never felt before. The trip was well-planned. She had destinations, bed and breakfast homes, and cash. The owners would think they recognized her; however, she would laugh it off and say, "I get that a lot." They would hardly take notice until several days later when the news hit the media. There, she knew the Service was on her side. It wasn't something that they would want to immediately broadcast, particularly since it all appeared as a foolish president's daughter on a lark. She drove to the point of near exhaustion and pulled off on the next exit that was near a B&B. The bed and breakfast also offered a meal with less people involved than any restaurant. Merc took a power nap and then got back on the road. It was a challenge to make the run as quickly as possible. And she loved the challenge.

"I'll be back in snow country by dawn." She said the words to herself as she passed by the sign that said "Overland Park." The radio predicted more snow in the Rockies.

Why isn't he answering? Merc tried Mike's number again. It reported his voicemail as being full. She texted him a brief message.

"On the road. Rocky 4." It was their inside joke about training since they'd first started to work out at Camp David. The boxing movie had become her motivation. Rocky had sought solitude when preparing for the fight of his life. She would do the same.

There was no response.

Odd, Merc thought, but imagined that with the new administration they were overwhelmed with requests.

I'll try on the other side of Denver.

Chapter 16

Mike tried her cell again. It went to voicemail, and then to the message that the voicemail box is full." His cell had been acting up as well. Calls were being dropped, many didn't go through.

Can't be. He had a random thought that the White House might have some new protective system that interfered with cell traffic. It would have been a crazy idea since everyone in the building lived by their cells.

He checked her Instagram, but it showed nothing new. And then he checked her roommate's account and saw the Instagram photo.

"Middle of nowhere." He wasn't happy with Mercury.

Mike stepped back into his office.

"Got the news." His boss had a sour look on his face. "You've got a week."

"Damn, this guy moves fast." Mike had expected the political retribution, but thought the system would slow it down some. The military sometimes moved quickly when a clear wish came down from the White House. It wasn't that the President was involved. This came from the chief of staff. But they were doing a cleaning of the house. Anyone remotely connected to the prior administration were given their notices. And he was more than casually connected to the prior administration. It actually came as a relief.

"Yeah, Guam."

"Guam?"

"The beautiful Pacific." The colonel tried to make some small joke of what was happening. It was clear that Kerr would be put somewhere far from the political high life and, as a consequence, far from the former president's daughter.

"No flying." Kerr sat in the chair comprehending the punishment laid out. It would be a non-flying billet.

"Did you hear the other news?"

"What?"

"Head of Secret Service was fired."

"The President did this?"

"He was called into the chief of staff's office."

"Oh." Mike hesitated as he absorbed the news. It had already been rumored that the service budget would be cut and the cuts would be aimed at the former presidents.

"I came by the chief of staff's office the other day as a man was leaving."

"So?" Mike had not seen his boss make a statement like that before. Hundreds came in and out of the White House.

"Visitor's pass."

Still it didn't register with Mike as being anything unusual.

"He had a L3 lapel pin and a high and tight."

It seemed from the description that the man was a past Marine aviator who was working for L3 Technologies which provided the electronics for the F-35 fighter.

"Probably hitting L3 up for some donations for the next cycle." Mike knew how the game was played.

"Yeah, probably. He looked like H.R. Haldeman. Too serious."

Mike vaguely recognized the name and his face showed it.

"Nixon's chief of staff." His boss was provided the context of his suspicions.

Mike hesitated.

"Watergate?" The boss gave him a look like shock that the younger officer didn't know his history.

"Colonel, might be that paranoia setting in." Mike laughed it off.

"They say that paranoia is the false sense that someone is coming after you. Here, it isn't false," said the man sitting behind the desk. Mike's boss was giving him some good advice.

This had been his boss's second tour in the White House. Like Mike, as a young Air Force officer and graduate of the academy, he had served in the White House Internship Program. Even in the back of the room in another administration, he had plied Mike with plenty of tales of power brokering in the White House mess.

But the Colonel had used that phrase before when describing the workings of the White House. It wasn't false if someone truly had his crosshairs on your back. There was something to that in the job they had. Many requests had to be turned down and, even with the government picking up first class tickets to Rome or London, it wasn't the same as the executive fleet. So some customers would scream and yell. It always seemed to be the multi-millionaires coming to the government for the wrong reasons who screamed the loudest.

"That's true."

"I may take up smoking again." The colonel clearly saw some rough waters ahead.

"You've got only six months till thirty?" Mike knew that, without a star, this would be a twilight tour for his boss. At thirty years, he would be vested in retirement for the rank. The colonel should have made the star; however, the politics were getting dangerous, particularly if he tried to protect Mike on the final fitness report.

"Yeah."

"Don't do anything foolish." Mike was saying. There was little need for his boss to protect him with a report that helped the young Marine's career. It was likely that Guam would be his last tour as well.

"Got farther than I ever expected. An ROTC boy from Idaho who loved to fly." The colonel expressed what many thought. "Got to say that bird on rotation got me every time." He was describing the feeling of being at the controls of a C-17 cargo aircraft as it hit VR. A pilot, like Mike who had heard this often, knew that VR was when the aircraft on takeoff reached that speed where Bernoulli's principle took over. The air rushing over the wing caused a vacuum that literally sucked the aircraft up, off the ground.

"You think I can get some flying in before getting out of here?" Mike knew that a call from a Marine at the White House always had a better chance of getting an aircraft than otherwise.

"Sure."

"Thanks."

* * * *

Mike returned to his office, got on the telephone, and called Marine Corps Air Station Beaufort. It seemed he'd have the chance to get more than a few days of seat time in the F-35B Lightning II.

"Is this the operations office of VMFAT-501?"

"Warlords." The squadron was formed in World War II and flew the F4U Corsair in the Pacific and the F4 Phantom in Vietnam. It had been shut down in the reductions of 1997, but brought back to life in 2010. And it had now become the home of the new bird, the F-35.

"I need to get some flight time."

"Yes, sir."

"Is the operations officer in?"

"He's in a meeting."

Mike gave him the specifics and particularly noted where the return call was being made to. The availability of the aircraft would not be a problem.

Mike pulled up Google Earth. He had a particular destination in mind.

Where did Ritchie say? He scanned the western part of Georgia and south of Columbus and Fort Benning. The army base had a ten-thousand-foot runway, but he was looking for something closer to where the man she wanted him to meet lived.

"She said a cabin overlooking a river." The jet didn't need much room, but he didn't want to make the evening news by putting it down in a grocery store parking lot.

"Perfect!" He had found his landing pad. A small runway in the deep woods near a cabin on top of a hill overlooking a river.

Chapter 17

Guayaquil, Ecuador

"So, everything?" Pena was sitting cross-legged on his floor across from Jamal and Reet. The only thing they shared was that they spoke English. The question was more along the lines of *have you gotten everything you needed?* As well as *when will I get paid?*

The wife had fed them like houseguests in Yemen. The guests ate first, and if there was not enough food, the hosts would not eat.

"Yes. Everything." Jamal looked at the man's daughter. She was older than Lala, but nevertheless reminded Jamal of what could have been. "Is she in school?"

"No." Pena, hardly out of his thirties, looked much older, and was a hard man whose life was reflected in his cold, steel blue eyes and leathery, wrinkled face spotted with those dark spots that someone in a rich country such as the United States would be worried indicated cancer. Here, he didn't have that luxury. His straight, coal-black hair covered his ears. His shirt, open at the top and extended down half way displayed a gold chain with an oversized gold cross.

"You'll be in Canada tomorrow."

"Yes." Jamal said no more than what Pena already knew.

"It'll be cold."

Jamal hadn't thought of that. He would have to worry about a coat for him and Reet when they got to the terminal.

"And America…"

Jamal wasn't going to insult him with a denial.

"Big money in America." Pena seemed reflective as he lit up a smoke. "I went to America years ago."

"And?"

"Worked there as a plumber helper. Good money."

"You came back?"

"Couldn't get my wife to leave here." He looked towards the kitchen where the sounds of pots, water, and clanking were heard. "Had a six-month visa. If I stayed, I would have had to stay away from the law."

Jamal thought of the journey they had taken so far. His travels had taken him west, crossing a continent, an ocean, a voyage south, and now a long flight to the north. He also thought of Pena. It was obvious that Pena knew Jamal had money. But Pena didn't rob Jamal. He would have, except that he didn't know what other money Jamal had or could have gotten. He was being well paid.

"What about a gun?" Jamal hadn't been this long without a weapon since his childhood.

"No need." Pena acted as if that was an inconvenience. It was as if he was saying that Jamal carrying a gun would either get Pena killed or put in prison for a long time. He didn't know the two men, other than that they were two transients who wanted to stay away from the law and get north. If he had some idea that he was harboring one of the most dangerous men in the world, a gun for each might have been a good idea. "You're safe."

Jamal didn't like the answer.

"You can sleep upstairs."

Jamal stood.

"The breeze comes up from the water." Pena led the way up a small, steep stairway to a dark room with shuttered windows. He pulled the shutters open and cool air hit Jamal on his face. It was cooler, but not cool. It reminded Jamal of Zinjinbar. A smell of saltwater, roasted meat, and the stench of a barrio came with the breeze.

"Sleep, my friends." Pena headed back down stairs.

A short while later Jamal heard a noise and looked out in the alleyway, seeing Pena walking towards the main street. He had smelled the whiff of alcohol when Pena had returned from the airport. Pena walked slowly, giving Jamal no alarm. His walk was steady, direct, and showed no sign of anything unusual. With this, however, Jamal walked to the back of the house to see if there was another way out of the building. There wasn't a stairway, or a ladder, or a series of ladders. However, the roofs went down, almost like a walkway to a small courtyard and another balcony of another home.

Jamal came back to find Reet in the corner, with his small bag as a pillow, snoring loudly. He looked out of the window to see the countless number of stars that came with the high elevation and being closer to the equator. Several airplanes were lit as they came down, slowly passing the hilltops and into the valley of Guayaquil.

"Tomorrow, Canada." He wadded up his small bag and lay in the corner closest to the back window. He stared at the ceiling for some time until sleep overcame his worry.

Chapter 18

The Farm in Stewart County, Georgia

Daylight was just beginning to break in the east as Will slipped downstairs with his gray Adidas runner's jacket, sweatpants, and New Balance running shoes. His two friends were asleep in a bunk room after a late night around the fire pit. Unlike Will, they had stayed up to well into the night. He had heard the laughter and sad, slow conversation as he'd drifted off to sleep. Stidham's name had been mentioned often and echoed through the cabin.

Will headed out to a run that would take him deep into the woods of the farm. The run was his therapy. Work with the chainsaw helped. Physical exhaustion took the mind off of the loss. He followed the road from his lodge, across the finger, down the hill and passed by the small steel hangar at the end of his air strip. A fluorescent light on a pole near the hangar started to flicker off as daylight activated the sensor. The glow of the blinking light passed through the few trees that separated the road to the lodge, and the cut-off to the airfield.

A frost caused a glisten on the grass as he passed the turn to the runway. Like the one in Alaska, his runway was paved, not very long compared to airport standards but enough to handle his HondaJet. It was well-made, a thick poured cement, scored for drainage and traction, so that the small jet could easily land in all types of weather. His warm breath projected out, the pace of the run increasing as he descended the hill. At the bottom Will turned onto the path that carried him around the farm and down, eventually, to the river. On the trail, he had to place each footstep with care, as a root catching a toe would cause a crash and burn. It required attention, which also took his mind off into another world. It was like a mission where one false step in even the slightest detail would bury one in pain.

Two deer stopped, frozen, staring at the sight of the other creature in their forest. As soon as he came within the focal point of their eyes so that they could take measure of a possible threat, they jumped up, turned, and ran into the woods, moving as if no gravity existed in their world. They floated over the brush and then disappeared into the pines.

Will crossed by the cemetery on his farm, which marked five miles from the cabin. From the cemetery the trail would take him back towards the river and through the open area where he and his team had cleared a path through the tornado-torn trees. He stopped on a ridge just before heading down into the trail surveying the damage. The sun had risen now to the point that its rays warmed everything and steam rose up from the field.

It was quiet, except for a pair of crows that seemed to be in a brawl over who owned the oak tree that they roosted on.

And then they, at the same instant, suddenly became silent.

Will turned to the east and saw movement just as the rumble came across the top of the pine tree line. He stared as the shape of the black and gray object moved slowly over his head. As the jet headed towards the airfield, he felt the heat from the engine when it transferred from forward flight to descending flight. The F-35 jet was coming in for a landing.

* * * *

Kevin Moncrief's truck sped for the airfield and arrived at the cut-off just as Will made it. The sound of the aircraft appeared to have woken up the two sleeping in the lodge. The Lightning jet was now still, its canopy open, and a man with his flight helmet off was standing next to its wing. He had on the flight suit with a USMC pilot wings patch on his chest.

"Lost?" Moncrief asked the question.

"Hope not." Captain Michael Kerr took off his flight gloves and extended his hand. "Can't be too many strips like this."

"Depends." Moncrief shook his hand.

"Looking for a Colonel William Parker."

"Oh, boy." Moncrief turned to Will and gave him a look saying *and you thought there'd be no more missions.*

"I'm Parker."

"Sir, Captain Mike Kerr." He put his helmet on the aircraft's wing. "I need your help. Colonel Ritchie sent me. You were the man that the instructors spoke of at Bridgeport."

It appeared that the captain had gone through a training cycle at the Mountain Warfare Training Center deep in the High Sierra of California. Will Parker had taught arctic and mountain survival there in the past. Ritchie had pointed Kerr in the right direction, but once the name was mentioned, Mike had known who she was talking about. The Marine Corps was small. The very few that reached a different level were known.

"Gail Ritchie?" said Will. The Captain did have an introduction that persuaded Will to hear him out.

"Yes, sir. You're the one from ANGLICO."

This hit more of a nerve. Will was also known for another reason.

The reference was to Will's mission in combat with his air naval gunfire team. More particularly, it pertained to his knocking an Army officer across the room after a command center had refused to allow an artillery-fire mission save a combat team in trouble.

The recon team had been caught in a well-set L-shaped ambush. They had gone into a deep valley where a village's buildings rose up on the hill side. Once they were deep inside the trap, gunfire had ripped through the team. Will had been within radio link as he and his team had heard the pleas of the remaining men for their help from another nearby valley. It appeared that the command center had been frozen by the idea that the artillery might hurt some civilians. All of the team were lost despite scores of bodies of dead Taliban surrounding them. A round or two of artillery could have saved them. The officers involved were ultimately reprimanded, which fell far short of the lives lost. Will's punch had broken the man's jaw.

Will looked past Kerr at the machine on his airfield. He walked the circumference of the jet, looking at the improvements made over the years to the aircraft.

"Nice ship."

"Yes, sir." Kerr smiled at the interest of another pilot.

"Let's go up to the lodge."

"Hop in." Moncrief climbed into his white extended cab GMC with Moncrief Paint Company on the side.

* * * *

"No need." Once inside the lodge, Will's answer was quick. He had heard Mike Kerr's pitch. The USMC aviator was impressive, but he sounded like an overly concerned lover. The change of administration didn't seem to be a great threat to a past president's daughter. A suspected conspiracy led by a devious chief of staff was not something new, and not something in need of Parker's involvement. He didn't see a need of a mission, or a random threat to either a past president or his daughter.

Kerr pressed the point.

"She's got a hard head. Just enough to get herself in trouble."

"The law would happy to step in." Will wasn't ready to take on something that wasn't necessary.

"Look at this." Kerr held up the photo from Instagram of Mercury's roommate. "A photo from Vermont, but after this, a text saying she wasn't going to be there."

"Okay?"

"I'll send them to you."

"Don't waste the effort." Will rarely used a cell and didn't see any reason to do so.

"She hasn't answered my calls. Full voicemail."

Kerr's voice sounded authentically worried. In fact, Will already knew this was more than a colleague worried about a past member of the First Family.

"Perhaps she's not worried about the relationship?" Will heard the words from his own mouth and thought they sounded like a counselor's.

"No, it's something else." Kerr gave him the story of the new chief of staff and his orders to Guam.

It did get Will Parker's attention that any Marine would be treated like that.

Nevertheless, it wasn't something that even came close to causing him to become involved.

"Sir, there's a threat out there, I feel it. And these people couldn't care less."

"I appreciate the airshow, but not me."

The Gunnery Sergeant looked on with dismay. His rank was special. It went back in the Corps to 1898. It spoke of a well-seasoned enlisted man who knew how get a mission done. And as a compliment, the men and women who served with one shortened the name to Gunny.

Will gave him a glance, but also understood the facial expression. Moncrief was tired of painting houses. He craved excitement.

"Not this time, Gunny."

They walked back to the truck. Will stopped at the edge of the driveway to the lodge as Moncrief drove Kerr back to the aircraft.

"Send those to me." Gunny stood at the end of his pick-up truck as he spoke to Kerr.

Kerr looked at Moncrief's cell, entered the number, and sent a series of pictures he had saved. They were of the young couple in several places. One was in front of a sign that said "Camp David." Another was in front of a cabin in the mountains. Another was of her in an evening dress and him in his dress blues. They had the smiles of people in it for the long run.

"He's wrong. She hasn't bailed." The Marine pilot had a relationship that was not in doubt. At least, not to Moncrief.

"Not that it'd help." Moncrief was not promising anything.

"Thanks, Gunny."

Moncrief pulled his truck back off the runway.

Mike began putting his gloves back on but stopped. He reached into his flight suit pocket and pulled out his cell.

Moncrief watched as the pilot spoke on the cell for some time. Kerr turned to the Gunny and gave him a thumbs up, then donned his gloves, helmet, and harness and climbed into the aircraft. Moncrief pulled his truck back watching the canopy close, the turbine spin up, and the energy build as the noise slowly increased to a defining roar. As it separated from the restraints of gravity, the aircraft rose, headed north, climbing out over the pine trees, and then converted to full forward flight. Its speed increased as it turned and did a circle around Parker's lodge, waggled its wings, and then turned to the north.

Will's truck could be heard as it came down the mountain from the cabin.

"Let's do some more." Moncrief signaled to Hernandez to climb aboard and follow Will in his truck. There were still a few downed trees, the chainsaws were oiled and refueled, and they headed back down the trail towards the river as the sound of the aircraft heading off echoed through the valley.

Chapter 19

Basalt, Colorado

"God, this feels good."

Elizabeth "Mercury" Jordan stood in the shower in the quasi-bed-and-breakfast rental just off the main street of the small village of Basalt for nearly an hour. The last part of the journey had been slow with her fighting traffic through the Eisenhower Tunnel. Another snowfall had descended upon the Rockies. Fortunately, the plows had stayed ahead of this one. She had driven through Denver in the early dawn darkness, tired, but determined to miss the traffic. Only stopping at the McDonald's drive-throughs, Merc had made the journey quickly but for the traffic delay in the mountains. This had been her first shower since Vermont.

Just after passing the Eisenhower tunnel in route to Aspen, she tried again on her cell.

"Hey." MK answered. "Where are you?"

"In Colorado."

"Serious?"

"Yes. I quit."

"Damn."

"It's okay. I told you I was going to do something different."

"Where in Colorado?"

"You know where."

"Okay, I'll be there in a couple of days."

His response surprised her.

"How?"

"Let's just say, I've got some free time. I'll give you the details when I see you."

"Great."

The owners, Mary and Virgil, were happy to receive the last-minute cash paying guest. It was between seasons, despite the snowfalls, and the downhill skiers had yet to descend on the valley. The mountains had just opened their lifts to the upper slopes. The owners had a spare bedroom that they rented, which helped put a dent in the mortgage. It was just off the highway in the quaint mountain town, and provided a breakfast of biscuits, eggs, and ham. She had warned them upon checking in that she would eat, shower, and then crash for some time.

Once awake, Merc went into the kitchen, grabbing a cup of coffee from the pot, adding her cream and sugar, and taking a sip. Mary was sitting at the small kitchen table and signaled her to the chair.

"In for some time?"

Elizabeth gave a nod. "Going up into the mountains."

"Really?"

"Heading to the huts." Merc was referencing what was called the 10th Mountain system of huts that were connected by more than three hundred miles of routes and trails.

"Wow."

"My boyfriend and I did one some time ago." The last time she and Kerr had gotten permission to go up into the mountains for an overnight. Two Secret Service men had served in the Army and were accomplished cross country skiers. The security hadn't impeded their little escape. Her memory of that trip was the reason, in part, for her return to Colorado.

"Really?"

"I'm trying to get some training in for this biathlon season." Merc was working the conversation in what she hoped to be a way that would bring as little suspicion as possible. She didn't need to worry.

"If you can make it to a cabin, that'd get you in shape," said Mary as she sipped on her own mug of coffee. "You doing it alone?"

"No, my boyfriend is joining me."

"Good."

"Think I might crash again."

"Take your time. The place is yours."

Merc understood why the rental received such good reviews. Better yet, it left no trail. She would pay with cash and be gone into the mountains.

* * * *

Merc took a good nap, repacked her backpack, checked her skis, boots, poles, and rifle, and prepared herself for the trek into the mountains. She said goodbye and then drove into town, stopping at City Market to gather up a week of basic supplies. She figured that seven days' worth would be more than enough to cover the time before MK arrived and resupplied them.

What the hell happened? She asked herself the question; however, it didn't take much to guess the answer. She wore a baseball hat pulled down, and sunglasses even though there was a dark cloud cover over the valley. She ducked her head as she passed the cameras in the parking lot. After getting what she needed, Merc headed back to the RFTA bus parking lot at Brush Creek and Highway 82. She knew that her vehicle could be parked there for some time without anyone caring or noticing. After parking, Merc climbed onto the bus with her skis, backpack, and rifle in its gun bag. Again, keeping her hat down over her eyes, she rode the bus back into the edge of Aspen, walked to the ski area's edge, looked at a map that she had gotten in the store, put some kicker skins on her skis to help climbing in the backcountry and headed out into the wilderness. Once she reached the hut and set out her training trail, she could return to waxing her skis and working on her speed.

A break in the weather had moved in. The bright sunlight glistened over the new snow. Merc's breath caused a cloud with every puff of air.

God, this is awesome. She felt the skis grab as she moved up the trail and headed around. The backpack didn't allow much speed in poling, but Merc felt her lungs burn as she worked her way around Aspen Mountain. There was one particular hut she had in mind.

Chapter 20

Guayaquil, Ecuador

"12." Margarite said the word as she looked at her cell. She was standing next to the hangar they kept the Pilatus in at the Posorja airfield.

As if on cue, Zorn saw a bright white light with a smaller red and green light on the tips of the wings. The aircraft landed with the runway's activated runway lights, and slowly taxied towards the pad before her hangar. It seemed quieter than most propeller-driven aircraft. She turned on the lights to the Yukon as it turned towards her. The smell of burnt kerosene filled the air as the turboprop blew a hot gas exhaust. The Cessna SkyCourier twin was painted gray, like its U-28 special operations cousin, with no markings that showed its owner. It was a new Cessna twin usually made for the FedEx market. This model was built for another customer—the U.S. military. Its six-thousand-pound cargo capacity, nine-hundred-mile range, and rugged landing gear made it perfect for a dirt runway deep in the jungles of South and Central America. It was made for special operations.

The door opened and she could see a man in the lights of her SUV descending the steps. He had a red-tinged beard and hair that extended over his ears, broad shoulders that tapered down to a small waist, and was dressed in blue jeans and a dark sports shirt that he wore outside of his pants. He was followed by several others who were dressed in similar civilian clothes. They looked like out of place American tourists not able to fully escape the image of a band of fraternity brothers or a traveling football team.

Once on the ground, five of the six men formed up a fire line and started handing down several brown bags through the door. Some were clearly the length and shape of gun bags and others looked like military flight bags. There worked in silence.

"Ms. Zorn?"

"Yes."

"This is my team." He knew her name but didn't offer his. He did offer a handshake. It was a solid grip that telegraphed his holding back on enough strength to break the bones in her small hand.

Margarite Zorn was not surprised of the lack of names. She knew some of the special operations hunter-killer team. Names would not be used, nor dog tags, nor identification of any kind. Tattoos were forbidden to maintain anonymity and security, in case of capture. The long hair and beards were encouraged.

"Let's go into the hangar." She pointed to the door that led to where her PC-12 was housed. A small table was at the rear of the aircraft.

"What are your thoughts?" He went straight to business. "We want to get out of here before first light."

The plan made sense. The aircraft would grab attention for several reasons. It was a military gray with few markings. The airfield was civilian with very few aircraft homed there, but it would still draw notice.

"Pena lives in the barrio. The two are with him." She was guessing that they were still there. They were still fifteen hours ahead of the Copa flight, so she figured even if they were heading to the airport early, they should still be in place.

"We need two taxis." The Marine had a plan. He put his Semper FiPad on the table. It looked like any other iPad until the password opened the machine. The cover was of a field of palm trees surrounded by a morning mist. It was meant to be art that gave no indication of its owner. He opened it up. A map of the city was displayed on the tablet. "Where?"

She moved the screen with her fingers, scanning in to the exact street and house of the target. Google Earth worked fine.

"Taxis?"

"The city airport is here." She pointed to the main airport.

"We'll grab two cabs and borrow them for a few hours."

She knew that the cab drivers would be outraged when they arrived at the small park near the waterfront, but would soon be calmed down when handed several thousands of dollars for the rental. The park was not far from the barrio.

"Let's go." He looked at his black, tactical watch. The team and Zorn crowded into the Yukon with their bags stuffed in the back.

The two taxis came from different ends of the airport while the Yukon went directly to the park. It was their rallying point. The team was fluent in Spanish and took the drivers aside, one by one, and spoke to them at the edge of the water. The only lighting was a street light that flickered, but it provided enough light that the drivers saw what was in their bags. Both men sat down on a bench near the water and lit cigarettes as if they were sobering up after a late night. They each held their bags close at hand, seemingly leery of the other and their circumstance. All they had to give up, as they were promised, were their cell phones.

The team used the back end of the Yukon to pull their Chinese QBZ-03 assault weapons out of their gun bags, load each, and suit up with headsets that allowed them to hear every word and movement. The assault rifles used a different round of ammunition. The automatic weapons used a 5.8 round instead of the NATO 5.6. The Chinese believed it to be superior. Here, the team wanted the spent cartridges left behind to give no indication that the Americans were involved. The team members also had Chinese military pistols, an updated Type 92, and one longer rifle, a QBU-10, with a large scope. Each was equipped with a suppressor. All were intended to confuse if lost or captured.

The team were all products of raider training and drilled by a past commandant as "combat hunters." The course had taught the Marines to turn the tables on an enemy who had the advantage of choosing the place and time of an attack. But here, the team was the hunter and not the hunted.

They climbed into the cabs and drove off toward the target.

Margarite Zorn was given a radio with ear buds as she listened to the radio traffic. There wasn't anything for some time. The suspense wore her out, so she reached for a cigarette and lit it up. Her Yukon was on the far end of the parking lot. She could see the two taxicab drivers on the other end. They didn't move an inch, as if scared that any movement would receive a bullet.

* * * *

The hunter-killer team reached the street that led into the alleyway. It was well into the morning, and the street was quiet. There was little movement. One man went to the rear of the taxi, pulled a small object out of a black bag, lifted it up above his head, and the small drone took off. He carefully sent it above the building. The team leader looked over his shoulder at the image, signaled the others to come to the vehicle, and pointed to several locations. With the precision of Rolex watchmakers, one worked his way up the stairs of an adjacent building and took his spot high over the alleyway. He carried his weapon, still in its gun bag, until he got in position on the adjacent roof. The sniper rifle with the thermal sight covered all of the alleyway and the target.

Another member moved to the rear of the building. All was set when the team leader gave the order to go.

* * * *

Margarite listened to what little traffic there was. The crack of the door could be heard in the background along with the shuffle of men.

"Get down." The team leader was quietly giving orders. A child's cry was in the background. But there were no sounds of gunfire. A woman cried out.

"They aren't here."

Margarite's stomach fell through the floor with the news.

* * * *

The taxis were returned to their owners who, realizing it had been a night of financial benefit that they would never see again, drove away from the park. There was no conversation as they headed back to Posorja.

"No one there?" Margarite asked the question.

The team leader was sitting in the front of the Yukon as they sped back towards the airport.

The black SUV pulled up near the hangar back at Posorja. While his team got out and began loading the aircraft as its turbines started to spin, the leader spoke to Margarite before getting in the plane.

"They were warned. Someone here is not your friend."

She turned off her vehicle and the lights as the plane started to taxi onto the runway. It only turned on its landing light when it increased its speed on takeoff. Once in the air, it turned to the north, extinguishing its landing light, and disappeared into some low clouds that had built up over the area.

"Yes, they were."

Chapter 21

The Northern Edge of Guayaquil

Jamal rubbed his eyes from the lack of sleep. His memory was foggy as he recalled reaching for the pistol that was not there when he'd felt a hand on his shoulder in the dark. Pena had bent over him and held his hand over Jamal's mouth. Jamal recalled the rough leather-like skin and the smell of stale liquor.

It had been several hours since they'd fled the house. The raid had barely missed the men.

Pena had taken them to an apartment on the far, northern end of the city. It had no furniture and Jamal and Reet again lay in the corner, trying to grab some sleep. The sun now shone through the window in a bright, brilliant light.

The back door opened and closed with a bang. Jamal rose up, again defenseless and unarmed, waiting as he heard the footsteps of one lone man come from the back towards the front of the apartment.

"Here." Pena came around the corner with a torn, oily, old green towel in his hands which he peeled away to show two automatic pistols. "This is all I could get."

Jamal pulled out several American fifty-dollar bills and handed them over. He handed one of the guns to Reet. The pistols seemed to be handmade, crafted from rough metal, with a dark greasy coating as if they had been stored away for the right time. Their stock handles were of a poor-quality wood. Jamal had paid much more than they were worth, but they were guns and he needed them.

"I'm going to the back." Reet headed towards the bathroom. Jamal heard the water running as he and Pena talked.

"The airport is out." Pena stated the obvious.

"Can you get us north?"

Pena gave him a look indicating that for the right price, everything was possible. "It'll be difficult."

"But can you?"

"I'll be back in an hour."

"Who was this?" Jamal thought their trail had been covered well. It was a dangerous lesson. Somewhere, their guard had been let down.

"Her name is Zorn. Margarite Zorn," said Pena.

Jamal didn't need to ask who she worked for. He already knew.

"I need to speak with the ELN." Jamal knew there was one group that might help.

"I don't do that." Pena hesitated when the idea was suggested. He knew that the ELN of Colombia was the new FARC. The Ejército de Liberación Nacional, or ELN, was as much a criminal gang as they were self-declared Marxist soldiers. They owned much of the territory of southern Colombia. And they were known to have terrorist gangs that reached as far as Guayaquil. Gangs were rarely seen in Ecuador since the government had taken a bold move to legalize them some years prior, but the few remaining gangs had seemingly become more brutal. The gangs came from neighboring or nearby countries such as Columbia and Venezuela and were known to bringing a new level of violence to the country. Shootings and knifings were common. And it often had to do with drug trafficking. The ships that left the port would have false walls and hidden holds. And, as in any endeavor involving drugs, fighting often broke out.

"Just get me to them. And I need to get to a computer."

"I'll see about a truck. It'll get you north."

"An internet café?"

Pena acted as if he had little idea about what Jamal was talking about. "It will be dangerous."

"I understand." It was essential for Jamal to get to the internet.

Pena turned to the door and passed Reet as he came back.

Jamal ejected the clip from the pistol and checked the 9mm rounds to ensure they were all there. He pulled the slide back, chambering one of the bullets, and then slowly let the hammer down.

"It's dawn," Reet reminded him.

"Let me wash and then we will pray." Neither Reet nor Jamal had a prayer rug or a rug of any kind. The apartment was bare, with old, dark-stained wooden floors, but they had the time to turn in the right direction and offer their prayers.

Jamal knew the stakes had become higher.

* * * *

"Come with me." Pena showed up a few hours later.
The two rose from the floor.
"No, only you."
Jamal followed him.
"I'll be back shortly."
Reet's face showed the doubt of being alone. He was not the warrior that Jamal was.

Pena's car had the paint job of a taxi that had been abandoned from its service and was now driven by a subsequent owner. It looked like a former police car sold at auction to someone in the public. As they drove into the center of the city, Jamal noticed that some on the sidewalk held up a hand as if to signal for a pickup.

"You better make it quick." Pena took the back streets through the city.

Jamal stayed low in the front seat, but watched as they passed a sign that said Martin Aviles. At the end of the street, they turned left onto an open boulevard and traveled a few blocks until Pena stopped briefly in front of a store with bright, colorful signs of computer games.

"I would like to use the internet." Jamal asked the clerk for a terminal. He was pointed to one in the back. There, he quickly went to an account that he had set up some time ago. It was a false Instagram account that showed him to be a student at Harvard. To give credibility, he followed several other students from the university.

He tried not to be obvious. The account painted a picture of a Harvard student who loved skiing. He himself had posted several false photos of a skier, presumably him, in the mountains of Vermont. The image allowed him to befriend several others who loved skiing. They all shared photos.

"Here it is." He saw the one picture he had been looking for. "Can I print a screen?"

The clerk agreed, especially when handed a new American fifty-dollar bill.

Chapter 22

Parker's Farm

"It looks good." Will surveyed the trail from the high point above its descent down into the dark hard woods, where much of the damage had been done by the tornado. With a thick canopy above, the path had been, in the past, several degrees below the temperature of the open fields. When Will ran into the darkness, the chill would hit even during the hot summer days. Now, the storm and his team of clearers had opened it up. Light struck the valley floor for the first time since the Creek Indians had camped in the ravine.

Will could now see the trail's descent into a deep cut through the hills. With the storm damage, it had opened the valley up to a view of the Chattahoochee River just beyond. The forest was on land that was never farmed due to its sharp topography of deep ravines, outcroppings of granite that formed steep nobs, and small open fields full of rocks. It was here, some time ago, on a cliff above the trail, that a hunter and fellow Marine had saved a life.

The sun began to set and with it, the temperature was dropping. A chill in the air took over. The sweat on their backs quickly turned cold.

"Time to go throw on some steaks." Moncrief led the charge as they put the chainsaws in the back of Will's truck. Hernandez threw an axe in the back and then climbed into the bed.

"Let's go." Hernandez hit the side of the truck with his hand.

Once at the cabin, the men put the tools away and headed towards the fire pit.

"I'll get the fire going." There was no shortage of split oak firewood for Moncrief to build a blaze.

"I know my job." Hernandez got the glasses, ice, and the last of the bottle of bourbon that they had saved from their final combat tour.

* * * *

Will came downstairs a few minutes later to see the two with chairs around the firepit, their boots on its edge, and Moncrief leaning backwards in an awkward stance. The sun's last light barely showed over the distant hills across the river to the west. Some of its rays still caught the water's surface, causing a glisten of reflective illumination.

"This helped." Kevin looked out over the open space as he took a long swallow from his glass.

Will didn't say anything. His muscles ached with the days of work moving the logs and holding the chainsaw out like a bowling ball with an outstretched arm, still feeling the burn in the tissue.

"You both need to get back." Will was expressing his appreciation for their coming, but they all knew that life needed to set back in to place.

"And you?" Moncrief already knew the answer.

"Probably head out for Alaska tomorrow."

"All the way back to your place?"

"No, winter's coming. Probably need to park the jet in Anchorage and then use my bush plane." Will was thinking of the logistics required. The HondaJet would stay in a heated hangar in Anchorage, while he would hop a ride up to his airfield and pull his bush plane out for trips north. Will knew that the outposts up near the Arctic Circle always needed resupply, and the oil companies paid much more than fuel for runs. He didn't need the funds, but the challenge of flying in the Arctic in an approaching winter would test all of his piloting skills. He had become friends with several of the families, some on the coast, and the mountain men who lived in the interior.

And Karen. He thought of her living in an outpost with others from the CDC. They lived separate lives, and this had become a good thing. She would always be in danger if he continued the missions. The past had proven it. The grant let her do what she was meant to do. And it kept her safe.

"I guess I can scare up a job or two." Moncrief didn't sound particularly excited about returning to the rat race of suburban Atlanta, where houses were being thrown up at an incredible pace. A good painter had plenty to do. "Let me go check my iPad to see what's up."

Will nodded as Moncrief headed into the lodge.

"And you?" he asked Hernandez.

"Back at the CDC." He had taken several days off from his security job at the facility.

"I appreciate your coming." It was an awkward comment as they all knew there had been no doubt of their coming.

"For the staff, not a problem." Hernandez was the closest in rank to Staff Sergeant Shane Stidham and, as a result, had shared more time with him than the other two. But the tours of combat had locked all of them in an unbreakable bond.

A howl came from behind them as they sat near the fire.

Moncrief was at the door, his face ashen white and even in the low light showing a man stunned.

"Colonel, you got to see this."

Kevin rarely used rank as a calling card. It could only mean devastating news.

Will and Hernandez sprang up and entered the large room of the lodge, as Moncrief pointed to the side office where Will kept his computer. They both headed over to the monitor to see it open to a CBS news channel. The announcer's voice was muted, but Will took a look at the still photo in the background. He stared at it in silence.

The image was of torn metal, burnt nearly beyond recognition but for a tail standing up with the markings of a military aircraft. It stood up like a tombstone over the other, nearly unrecognizable remains.

The VMA squadron F-35 Lightning had been on approach to the Air Station at Beaufort when it had gone into the ground. A burnt-out skeleton of the jet had crashed. The pilot had not survived. Will turned up the sound.

"The pilot, it appears, attempted to eject but was not able to. He was trapped inside the wreckage and lost his life." The newscaster's voice was somber and measured.

The three men watched in disbelief as the story continued. It was a particularly newsworthy story as the pilot's job was at the White House. Captain Kerr was described as a combat experienced jet pilot, but with little time in the Marine Corps' newest attack fighter jet.

The story went on to say that the crash was under investigation and it was not known yet what the cause was. It appeared that the jet had suffered a fire on board, and with a rapidly increasing emergency the pilot had attempted to land the aircraft in a field nearby that would have avoided his crashing into an elementary school.

A spokesman for the Marine Corps appeared onscreen, a lieutenant colonel in front of a set of microphones with the Marine Corps Air Station sign as a background.

"We have confidence in this aircraft; however, until such time as a cause is determined the jet will be grounded. The F-35 has not had an emergency such as this in its prior history."

"I don't like this." Will read something else between the lines. If the Pentagon had described Kerr as having "little time" in the aircraft this early, he knew the reason. The manufacturer would be relieved if the collision were written off to "pilot error." The eternal scapegoat of airplane crashes everywhere.

"I'm going to run up to Beaufort tomorrow."

"Count me in." Moncrief didn't hesitate.

"Enrico, no need for you to come."

"But…" Staff Sergeant Hernandez was willing.

"We'll let you know when we know more." Will understood that there were limits to what Hernandez could do. He had a job and a family. He and Moncrief, on the other hand, were independent of all ties.

"He didn't do anything wrong." Will had only met the Marine a few hours ago, but in the short time of the visit, he could tell the man knew how to fly. "Something else is going on."

Chapter 23

Aspen Mountain

The resort was in that in-between time of seasons that made the valley quiet. Although the snow had already turned the mountain white with a deep, thick dump and the lifts were starting to turn, the skiers had yet to descend.

Merc was behind the mountain, in the back country, where the drifts had already built up.

I like it cold, she thought. She had rarely been exposed to true cold growing up. Before the White House, she'd spent her early childhood in Arizona. And for the last eight years, she'd lived in the temperate climate of Washington, D.C.

The city had warmed over time, and snow came quickly and left quickly, if it came at all. It was on her trips with her father to meetings or vacations in the mountains that she'd fallen in love with the brisk chill in the air and the invigoration of cross-country skiing.

It was more than the sport. Other than competition, the biathlon athlete would spend hours alone, deep in the white snow-covered woods where the silence could be deafening. It was the silence that she loved the most. She took the criticisms of her father seriously. He had said on more than one occasion that it was foolish for her to think in such a way. But the crowds, even more so as she grew up, were a constant reminder. Many loved her father, but others felt otherwise.

It was April several years ago at her high school in Washington that suddenly, in the middle of English class, a throng of black-suited men had rushed into the room. She had literally been lifted up from her chair and taken out into the hall, passing the gasping eyes of her classmates and teachers, to a convoy of black SUVs. Some of her classmates had cried as she passed them by. A female agent had sat in the back with her as the cars sped away. She hadn't seen her father that day at all. Merc had spent the afternoon and evening with her mother, who'd sat in the quarters, in stone silence, watching the news. Shots had been fired, some had hit the window of the armored car known as "the Beast," and the shooter had been caught. It had caused little danger to her father, but it was a reminder—a stark reminder—of the cost of being either a president or a member of his family.

After that, the Secret Service agents seemed to be everywhere in her life. When the fear had passed, it had all quickly become more of a constant inconvenience. The scrutiny was always there. On more than one occasion, she wanted to scream. She would cry herself to sleep in the West Wing. She was a princess locked in a castle. The dates had been few. The boys she liked had been intimidated by it all. But after some time, she'd met the one man who didn't seem to care. He was older than her, but Merc wasn't dissuaded by the age difference.

Wonder when he'll get here. Merc had reached the top of the peak and was passing through the back-country gate heading down into the valley below. There were two men standing near a utility shed watching a small television in the metal building as she waved. They ignored her, as they seemed to be locked in following a story on one of the news channels.

Merc came up to the gate. A red sign with a skull and crossbones warned of danger and death. The bare outline of a road, marked on the map as 15G, descended down into the ravine. At the top of the road, she could see the valley that extended to the north. A breeze came over the mountain and slipped down her neck. She pulled up her wool cap, cutting off the chill.

Merc stopped at the gate, noting its warning signs of danger and possible death for those that entered, pulled off her backpack to check her cell one last time, and, seeing nothing, turned it off and stuffed it deep down inside.

Odd, she thought as she pulled the backpack up, pulled on her mittens, and grabbed her poles. Still no word from MK. Merc turned one last time toward the men on the sundeck. They had stopped sweeping the snow, looking back through the glass of the lodge at the large television set, seemingly transfixed by what was on the screen.

Merc turned back to the forest. She knew where she was going. She was familiar with the trail. What little there was of road 15G could be deciphered by the cut in the trees. At the bottom, she would pass through several short ravines, run into a stream or two, and then eventually connect with

Upper Hurricane Road. Eventually, she would find Richmond Hill Road, all buried in deep, fresh snow, and ski some flatlands for several miles.

When on Upper Hurricane Road, Merc ran into the tracks of other cross-country skiers. The trail was marked with the poling of two who had passed through on the same course. It gave her some comfort that there were others, like her, deep in the back country.

The light began to taper as she moved down the trail. She looked up to see clouds had quickly moved in as she had focused on the tracks and her pace. The air had warmed and she stopped to unzip her jacket. Steam came out from the burn.

"Snow!" The flakes were light at start. She pulled off her wrap-around sunglasses, wiped the melting flakes from them, and stuck out her tongue to feel the particles of ice.

"Not far." She was speaking to the person on her skis. In the far distance, on a rise above the snow-covered field she was in, Merc could see a column of smoke rising up. She gauged the distance knowing that it was in easy reach before the storm had any chance of setting in. It also meant that the tracks in the snow had arrived before her.

It would be near dark by the time she reached her destination. The hut was the closest to Aspen Mountain. The faint light of a lantern showed through the window. As she unbuckled her skis, climbed up on the porch, and knocked the snow from her boots, a man with a beard opened the door.

"Welcome!"

"Hello." Merc took in the view. He was standing at the door, and a young blonde woman, whose hair stuck out from under her sweater hat, stood behind him. They had stripped down to sweaters and loose pants.

"The wine is cold." He held up a clear plastic cup. "And the weed is mellow."

"Super."

"I'm Max and this is Dee." No last names seemed to be needed.

"I'm Liz but my friends call me Merc."

"Cool name." The woman spoke up as she took a sip from her wine cup.

"Some serious rosé." He offered her a cup of the pink liquid. It was cold, very cold, and it took every restraint in her body to not swallow it all in one gulp.

"I've plenty to share." Merc knew the rules of the road.

"Any wine?" Max posed the question.

Merc pulled her backpack off, stripped down to her sweater, pulled up a wooden bench and opened her pack. She pulled out a rosé as well.

"A Miraval!" Max grabbed the bottle. "This girl flies first class!" He handled the bottle as if it were his first newborn. "I've heard of this." He pointed to the label.

"It's good."

"Not good." Max opened the door to the porch. "Great."

He headed out the door in his wool socks and, without asking for permission, placed the bottle in a deep snow drift. The snow was a light, fluffy, powder that barely stuck to his socks. It shook off with the brush of his hand. Once he returned, he hesitated.

"I guess I needed to ask." Merc knew that the huts worked on limited space and reservations. She didn't have one. She didn't want one either. It might have meant a name, or a lie regarding a name. She thought it better to take the chance of some generous cabin mates. Those that went into the backcountry were usually a generous lot. The sharing of food, wine, and pot came with the spirit of those that spent time off the grid.

"It's fine."

Max held back for a moment.

"My guess is that you don't have a reservation?"

"I...uh..." She hesitated. Through much of her life, everything had been taken care of, but not this time. Intentionally or otherwise, she was depending on the generosity of strangers.

"No problem," Dee spoke up. "We had two friends that didn't make it. And they have the hut for a week."

"I can pay."

"Pay with food." Max was half joking. "Pay with your Miraval."

"Sounds fair."

* * * *

The couple had cooked a stew.

"You're in charge of the rice," Dee said. She handed Merc a small metal pot and a box of rice.

"Okay..."

Dee noticed the hesitation. "Have you cooked rice before?"

"Well."

"Oh, boy." Dee pulled out her pink water bottle, filled the small pot halfway up and turned to Merc standing near the kitchen shelf. "Hand me that box of salt."

Merc reached for the Morton's and watched as Dee poured some into the water.

"At this altitude, it takes time to get a boil."

Merc had learned another lesson.

Between the rosé, the weed, and the food, Merc could only lay her head against a bunk, laughing as they all told stories of stupid acts they did growing up. She carefully picked stories that left no trace of who she was, but the smell of the stew, the weed, and a lantern burning led quickly to their all agreeing it was time to climb into their bunks. Merc opened the door once, feeling the cold flakes strike her face, watching the wind blow up towards up the valley and the hut. The storm increased through the night, causing a drift of snow to form on the porch up to the rails.

* * * *

"I'm going to set out a training trail." Merc explained the purpose of her trip. The backcountry near this hut was well over nine thousand feet. The topography was perfect for a physical workout that would help get her in Olympic-level shape.

"I'll help." Max was the type that had, seemingly, an endless supply of energy.

They cut a trail that took them down the valley, to the east, and then back up below Star Peak.

Max stopped in an opening on the side of the mountain. "See that outcrop of rocks?" He pointed to an overhang just inside the tree line on the other side.

"Yeah."

"We'll take the trail down below this." He pointed to a path that would descend from where they were. "This opening is scary as shit."

Merc was surprised by his comment. He seemed more of the quiet mountain man type, and not apt to use profanity. It was the only time he had used it.

"You're wondering why?" He stopped and pointed up towards the peak. "The drifts are building. This is primed for an avalanche. I hate that you're doing this alone."

"My boyfriend should be here soon."

"Okay. Does he know what to do?"

"He's a Marine who has spent most of his life in the mountains."

"Ah..."

They forged a trail across the opening, below the outcrop, through a thick aspen grove, then circled back to the hut. The trail was made to test her. It climbed in certain sections and then dropped sharply. They would stop and trample the tracks down so as to help it stay established through a storm or two. The result was a clear parallel path of skis.

"Not as good as a training center, but this should get you in shape." Max seemed to know what he was talking about.

"Thanks."

"You going to be okay?" Max asked as they got back to the porch and were dusting off the light snow.

"Sure."

"We're trying to hit two more." Max started to pack up his gear. "Just got a week off. Made the reservation months ago. Planning to finish up with Goodwin-Greene before heading back." Max knew the hut system well. They seemed to have spent many a week in this back country.

"I understand."

"Wish you went with us on the next one. Got some hot springs."

She had the image in her mind of a quick dip in the warm waters of a steam vent while snow fell onto her head.

"Thanks, but he's expecting me here."

"Left you some food. Don't need it all."

"You guys are great."

"Well, you haven't seen the menu."

"I left some fresh fruit." Dee was the counter-balance to his humor. "And some cans of tuna. Plenty of rice."

"Like I said, thank you."

* * * *

At daylight the next morning, the pair packed up and headed out. Merc felt a touch of loneliness as she watched them disappear across the open field and into the next wood line. The silence returned. The snow began to fall again, and in a short period of time, the tracks of her new friends disappeared.

"Now, to get to work." She had set up a strict plan to train each day to the point of exhaustion, rest, and do it again. She was here for a purpose. Merc waxed her skis and set out on the course that covered most of three miles. The first run cut through the new snow. The second run increased her speed. It wasn't a groomed biathlon course, but for a workout course, it was all the better. The steam of her body heat rose up whenever she stopped. Merc timed the first run, stopped at the hut and marked it down on a tablet she was using to track the training. Again, on her second run, she stopped and looked at her Apple Watch. There was a slight improvement.

This time she strapped her rifle to her back. And again, she moved as fast as possible, working the climbs with her skis in a herringbone pattern where it was too deep to do otherwise.

On her break, she pulled out her thermos and drank the cold water. It had been melted the night before from the snow. She had several water jugs so she could stay hydrated. And she drank from one jug until it was drained.

Merc started another lap, keeping her head down as she focused on the trail. Her thighs burned when she started to climb the hills. It was the first time that she had seriously trained at such elevation. Merc sucked in the air as if it had barely any oxygen in it. It would take time, she knew, but it would make her lungs only stronger. The trail took her well above eleven thousand feet in some spots. She would descend into the valley and then climb again up the mountain. Finally, after several laps, she stopped at the hut and reached deep in her ski jacket for her cell phone. It showed no coverage from cell towers. She was off the net.

It was a good thing that she was beyond the communication of the world. At least, for now.

Chapter 24

The Colombian Border

The badly rutted road cut through a jungle so thick that they often stopped and all dismounted from the truck with machetes and cut a path. It was slow moving and hot, and they had exhausted the water the day before. The sun rarely made it through the thick triple canopy. Rain would come, a torrent of water that they would try to capture with their hands to help fend off the thirst. After the rain, a thick muggy air would descend on them, so thick that it felt like a wet fog. The air seemed to be draped over their shoulders and every breath was a labor.

They would take turns on cutting the path. When it was Jamal's turn to rest, he climbed into the back of the truck. He could barely get any rest on the metal floor, trying to lie on some empty cotton sacks for bedding. He would doze off and then the truck would hit another deep rut. Jamal would grab the pistol in a Pavlovian reaction. They had driven through the night avoiding the main roads. And as they got closer to the Ecuador-Colombia border they took the well rutted back road even deeper in the jungle. Deep puddles of water caused the truck to stall out on several occasions and the men had to push it out. Mud would come up to the hub caps of the wheels.

The terrain was a constant up-and-down of small hills and ravines. The lower areas would hold the wet, thick mud bogs. And again, when they came to a soaked hill, they had to work together so that it would not slip backwards. The wheels would spin and sprayed them all with the wet, gum-like orange mud that stuck like glue. Jamal worked to the point of exhaustion. They were thirsty and lost all hunger. The food was just as bad.

"Reet, remember the ship?" Jamal said. "The food?"

"Oh, yeah." Reet looked tired, his eyes a bloodshot red, as if he had not slept in days. "I thought that was bad."

"The stew the cook did?"

Reet laughed, a weak laugh built on his exhaustion. "I'd take that now… if I were hungry."

"Soon, we'll be having some of that fish stew from Togo."

"I didn't get any." Reet looked out at the jungle.

"Oh, right." Jamal and Reet were talking about food. Desperate men trying to keep their minds on something other than the jungle.

There were two who operated the truck. The truck drivers appeared familiar to this, as they would stop every day at the same exact time for a noon day meal and inhale it as if it were their last. The drivers' medicine was a tea sweetened with panela, a home cooked cane sugar which came in a dark brown brick, and they would stop at night, build a small fire and boil the water. Once hot, they would cut off a sliver of the panela and throw it in. The boiling killed the parasites and the sugar made the absence of tea not matter. But Jamal knew that any water that was not purified and in a sealed bottle was a danger.

"Maybe we should try it." Reet looked longingly at the two men as they drank the sugary drink. They smiled when they drank their cups of panela.

"No." Jamal acted as the older brother keeping a look out for the younger one. The risk was still great that the cup was not clean or parasites would somehow get into a drink.

The mosquitoes were just as deadly. And large flies buzzed constantly around their heads.

"Hey!" The driver slapped Jamal on the back when one fly landed on him. Jamal jumped.

The man took a butt of a well-used cigar from his pocket, lit it, and blew on it until there was a bright glow, then pulled Jamal's shirt down and stuck it directly into the red bite.

"What…?"

Jamal tried to grab his hand, but the burn came quickly. He shook with anger. He sprung back as if he had been stabbed in the back by a thief.

"Bad!" The man smiled and then drew a long draw from the cigar. He held a small white object in his fingers, no bigger than the small pearls Jamal had seen come out of the oceans.

"Oh." He tried to grab his back but it was just out of reach. The burn was stunningly painful for a moment.

The man handed him a small green leaf and pointed to his mouth as if Jamal should eat it.

The leaf was bitter, and then the pain went away.

"Coca."

Jamal knew enough that the driver was killing the worm egg planted under the skin.

And there was mud. The mud seemed to save them. After several rains, they were coated from head to toe in the orange and clay-colored mixture. It seemed to suppress the mosquitos and flies, but when it dried their clothes became stiff as if left out in sub-zero temperatures in the mountains. After days of being saturated, their hair took on the same coloring. Only their eyes stood out to prove they were human. Other men, less immune than Jamal and Reet, would not have survived even with the mud coating. But since birth, both men had lived in a world that was full of disease and harm.

"How far?" Jamal made little effort to speak to the two drivers, as they did not share languages. Again, he swatted the constant buzzing of another large fly that followed them everywhere. They had remained a constant since Jamal and Reet had entered into the jungle. Since the burn, he made more of a point of fighting them off.

"The fucking flies!" Jamal swung at one and hit it with his hand. It fell to the floor dead.

One less, he thought.

Jamal tried again to communicate with the driver. He repeated his question. His words weren't understood, but the message seemed to be.

"Camp," he spoke a word that Jamal understood.

The driver pointed with his hands at a rise not far off and smiled.

The trip was far from over.

Between them and the hill was a stream they attempted to cross. The banks were steep and muddy, but once in the stream, the bottom was rocky. The truck, an old Dodge, scraped its undercarriage on a series of rocks. A moment later, the truck's wheel became locked on one particular boulder. It seemed hopelessly stuck.

"This jungle!" Jamal hissed.

Reet looked at his frustrated friend.

"Will we ever get out of here?"

The men stared at the problems for some time until, almost magically, out of the dark, green wall of the jungle, several men appeared. Each had an AK-47 machine gun slung over his shoulder. Most used a simple cut of rope as their slings.

The drivers saluted their compatriots. One of the men went back into the jungle and came out with a pole, not perfectly straight, which he placed under the axle. The others pushed another boulder into place and they used the fulcrum to lift the back of the truck up. Once in the air the others pushed and the truck moved forward, coming down on its wheel. With the team of additional labor, the truck quickly crossed the creek and headed around one side of the hill. As they circled the rise, Jamal saw the smoke from several campfires. The men were dressed in an assortment of camouflaged jackets and blue jeans, and some had camouflaged pants and torn short-sleeved shirts. All were armed, and no man laid his down.

The driver pointed to a central hut and directed them to a spot where Jamal and Reet were to stand. The thirst was getting to both of them. Jamal stopped one man, no more than a teenager, and pointed to his mouth in a maneuver as if he were attempting to drink. The boy, at best thirteen or fourteen, and particularly short by virtue of his tribal heritage, seemed ready to please and ran away quickly, returning carrying two plastic water bottles.

Jamal inhaled the warm liquid. Soon he emptied the bottle, tilting it up so as to drain every last drop.

"You want to go north?" A taller man than the others, with a curly black beard and hair down below a black beret stood in front of them. He wore a military type jacket with cargo pockets, one stuffed with what appeared to be a map.

"Yes."

"How far?"

"America."

"Oh."

"We have the funds."

The commander of the ELN paused. He signaled two others with him to go.

"We have some better water." He pulled them aside. They had said the right thing to get the commander's attention. He yelled at another who quickly returned with more plastic water bottles.

"And your funds?" The commander pointed to several green plastic chairs around a campfire. The chairs seemed very much out of place in the jungle, probably brought in by one of the trucks coming up from the south.

"Yes."

"How can I be assured?"

Jamal laid out one of the packets of fifty-dollar bills that were wrapped in plastic.

"We can get you to the cartel in Mexico, but it will take more."

"Get me to a cell phone and you'll have your payment."

The commander, if he was worried, didn't seem to show it.

Jamal knew that the Mexicans would trade cash for the cocaine. Likewise, it was easy money for the Mexican cartel. Two passengers meant less of a load, but it would be cash. Likewise, if payment wasn't made, the Mexicans would have Jamal's head. Others who had failed to pay had fallen to the Mexicans' favorite way of execution—the use of a chainsaw at the neck.

"We'll get you to Mexico and from there they will get you to the border."

The plan for the jihad had begun.

* * * *

Jamal and Reet were taken to another camp some miles away in another valley. There, he bought from the commander another burner cell phone and called. The camp was on a small airfield. The strip was hardly a wide spot in the jungle and its surface was a clay-colored dirt road. The camp was, however, just over a ridge from a town. With proximity to the town, Jamal's call made it through.

The ELN had a friend in the capital of Colombia who, as a banker, didn't mind working with the rebels at the right price. He had provided Jamal with the routing numbers. The funds went from Yemen, to a friendly bank in Doha, to one in Italy, and from there to Bogotá. The charge was steep as it evaded all of the normal routes of transfer, but half a million dollars made it to the account.

"My friend, you were right." The commander offered Jamal a drink.

"Yes." Jamal understood quickly that these men of the jungle knew little about his faith but knew that a deal could be made between the criminals.

"The cartel will want more." The commander hadn't said anything that Jamal didn't anticipate.

"They will get more when we get across the American border." Jamal knew that this would be the safest money that both the ELN and the Mexican cartel had ever made.

A small twin-engine aircraft came in low over the jungle tops, turned, and did several circles before running its approach in for the landing. It was a non-descript white airplane with oval windows and what looked like pods at the ends of the wing tips for extra fuel. The men stood at the end of the runway as it taxied up. The strip was so tight that, once the engines were cut off, the men grabbed the airplane's wings and turned it in a circle so at to be aimed at the other end. Then they pushed it back as far as they could, with the tail touching the jungle growth. A white van pulled up and, just as it did, a very skinny, white, and badly freckled man climbed out of the airplane. His long red hair was matted down by sweat, or nerves, or just exhaustion. As soon as he stepped out of the way, the men began loading small, plastic-wrapped white cakes into the airplane. It was clear to Jamal that this was not the first trip for any of them.

The pilot talked to the ELN commander. He didn't seem pleased and, more than once, pointed his finger in the man's face. But soon, he calmed down. The pilot turned to Jamal, who was standing next to the wingtip of the twin turboprop Cessna. From afar, it seemed a clean, white aircraft, but when close, Jamal could see cracks in the edges of the wing, more cracks in the portal windows, and a long black streak of oil from the engine closest to him.

"How much do you weigh?" The pilot spoke English.

"Eighty-five kilograms."

"So about a hundred and ninety pounds." He wore a worn-out, off-white, short-sleeved shirt with missing shoulder boards as if he were a defrocked mainline carrier pilot. A pack of Marlboros stuck out of the shirt pocket. The man smelled of smoke, and when he showed a wiry smile, it revealed teeth tinted yellow. A close look at his eyes also showed a yellow tint from too much vodka. It had to be vodka, as all true alcoholics preferred the drink that disguised the habit best.

Jamal's temperature was rising.

"About one ninety."

"Your friend?"

"Less."

"How much?" The pilot stared at Reet as they spoke.

"Maybe one fifty."

"You got money?"

Jamal thought the bill had been paid, but he didn't belabor the point.

"$10,000 for each." Jamal made the offer.

"$20,000." The pilot seemed to be striking a deal separate from his bosses.

"Okay." Jamal pulled out of his sack another of the sealed packs of fifty dollar bills. The man ripped the plastic off, fingered the crisp funds, and jammed them all into his pocket.

"What about an offload?" said the commander. It wouldn't be of any help for the airplane to slam into the trees and jungle on the other end and burst up into flames.

"Burned up fuel getting here. Should be all right." Despite his looks and unfriendly attitude, the pilot had a level of confidence that helped. "Let's go."

"One other thing." Jamal pointed to the commander. They walked to the end of the aircraft and spoke briefly. "Another mission." Jamal pulled out of his bag something else he had not shown the commander before. The man nodded as Jamal gave him a specific order. He pulled out what looked like a wad of plastic debit cards and handed them over.

"The woman who was hunting us." Jamal knew she would remain on his trail if not stopped. "There is a hundred thousand dollars here." Jamal gave him a scoop of cards.

"It will be done."

They shook hands.

The pilot put Reet on a stack of cocaine and pointed to Jamal to take the seat up front. He then closed the door, latching it down as tight as possible. Reet's face showed plenty of fear.

"Let's do this." The pilot worked the throttles, turned several gauges, and then started the first engine. It cranked several times and then turned over. The second one was easier. He held his feet down on the pedals in a stiff brace holding the brakes on as he spun up the engines to a deafening roar. Jamal could feel the airplane lurch, waiting to be released. Suddenly, with a jerk, the Cessna sprung loose and headed towards the wall of jungle on the far end. At first, it seemed to barely move, making Jamal's palms sweat. It gained speed slowly, and then as it neared the wall, Jamal could feel the nose become lighter. It fought its way up into the air.

Finally, the Cessna took flight. Jamal looked down into the vegetation as it barely skated on top of it. He could see trails he had not seen before, and another camp near the landing strip. The engines strained under the load. The airplane struggled, eventually gaining some altitude, but then the pilot brought it down to tree level, turning the aircraft to the west, and after an hour or so it crossed over the shore and the water of the Pacific. After flying well away from the shore line, he then turned to the north, heading up just off the Pacific coast, keeping as near to the water's surface as he could take it.

They had left southern Colombia as the sun was beginning to set, and by the time they had reached the ocean it was dark. The airplane flew, without lights, into the darkness. Occasionally, the pilot would use a flashlight to check the compass, but then quickly turn it off. Once, in the darkness, Jamal saw a ship coming from what he assumed to be Panama. He and

Reet had now made a circle from their voyage on the ship to Guayaquil, but were finally heading north.

Just before daylight, the pilot turned towards the shoreline. In the low light Jamal could make out a small runway just off the beach. It was surrounded by mountains. The pilot flew the airplane as if he had made this run many times. He lined it up, slowed the aircraft down, extended the flaps, and, at the last minute, dropped the landing gear. There was not one light at the airfield. Once the wheels struck the pavement, he kept the speed up to a fast taxi as he pulled up between two metal Quonset hut buildings. Without any communication by radio or on the ground, he stopped the airplane and two men came out of the shadows with a pickup truck that had fifty-gallon barrels in the back. They backed up to the wings and started a refueling that took a matter of minutes.

"If you need a leak, do it now." The pilot went to the edge of the jungle and came back shortly. Both men followed his lead.

"We need a moment." Jamal stopped at the end of the wing.

"What?"

"Will be short." Jamal went to the tail of the aircraft with Reet, turned to the east, and knelt as they made their prayers. The prayer rugs were a thing of the past. And they still hadn't had the water to even wash off the caked mud on their arms. But they prayed and then headed back to the aircraft door.

"Let's get out of here." The pilot pointed to the sky. "They patrol this coast with drones."

"Yes." Jamal knew far better than the pilot the danger that the sky held. "Where are we?"

"El Salvador." The pilot smiled as if he were telling them a secret of the trade.

With the extra fuel, they went farther out over the Pacific. Still, they flew just above the waves. The pilot held the control yoke with both hands, not able, at the low altitude, to use the autopilot. Jamal watched as he handled the yoke as gently as one would hold a small bird.

* * * *

The sun followed them as they traveled north. As it began to set, Jamal saw the brilliant ball of light sink into the Pacific. As the light was fading, the pilot suddenly banked the aircraft in a ninety degree turn to the east. It was if there were a marker in the blue waters that told him to turn inland toward Mexico. As darkness fell again, the Cessna landed on another small strip in a northern Mexico valley. The men hadn't eaten or had anything to drink for the long trip from Colombia. The pilot didn't seem to care, as the most important thing was his unloading the airplane of the cocaine. A white van had met them at the end of the dirt runway along with a white Humvee. Jamal, Reet, and the pilot stood at the end of the wing watching as the men from the van moved quickly.

"Let's go, let's go!" the pilot shouted. He reached in and helped toss the blocks of plastic-wrapped drugs to the ground.

The others formed a fire line and tossed the drugs from one side of the airplane to the other, and to the one standing outside of the van. He would toss it into the vehicle.

When the last one had passed through the line, the men climbed into the van, slammed the door shut, and the driver spun his wheels as they took off into the jungle.

As the van left, a short Mexican walked over from the Humvee. He turned to the van and waved as they took off. With the sign, the driver of the van stuck out his hand and waved back.

Jamal looked up to a clear sky.

Even here... He thought of the drone from Yemen. And here, the drug men, likewise, worried about the sky. But this one didn't drop bombs. This one would follow the van and the men. It might also follow the airplane as it headed north.

He came up to the pilot with a small bag and handed it to him.

"You off for a week?" The Mexican spoke to the pilot in perfect English. He had a silver revolver with a pearl handle stuck in his pants. His front two teeth were capped in gold.

"*Si, senor.*" The pilot opened the bag and felt the cash. "Off to Vegas. Fly to Nogales, park this bird in a hangar, and burn some cash."

"You don't fly the gringos?"

"No, thanks." It was one thing to fly drugs, but another to fly Muslims who stopped to pray to the east.

"And you will pay?" The man had turned to Reet.

Jamal stepped forward.

"Across the border, half a million."

The Mexican smiled.

"We can do that." He didn't care who the men were or the reason that they wanted to head north.

Nor did he realize the danger the two caused to his own interests.

Chapter 25

Marine Corps Air Station, Beaufort, South Carolina

"Is your CO in?"

The Marine sergeant looked up from the counter to see a man standing in front of him dressed in civilian clothes. His choice of dress was that of a successful businessman, a blue shirt, starched and buttoned-down, and crisp khaki trousers. He had intense blue eyes.

"Sir?" The sergeant made the safe guess that this was an officer.

"I'm Colonel William Parker." Will never used his rank, but with the young sergeant it would get him directly into seeing the man he needed to see. The commanding officer would make the time for an officer. "Retired."

The sergeant did the next best thing to knocking on the commanding officer's door. He went straight to the senior enlisted man on the deck.

"Sir, we have a guy here that says he's a retired 0-6 and wants to talk to the commanding officer."

"Who?"

"A Colonel Parker?"

"Who?"

"William Parker."

"Shit." The master sergeant didn't hesitate. "Where's the CO?" He clearly knew of William Parker. The Marine Corps, on a good day, had a hundred and eighty thousand on active duty. A third were in training to either earn the right to wear the eagle, globe and anchor or learn a skill the Marine Corps needed. An aviation mechanic might be in school and training for well over a year. And another third were in staff jobs of some kind or another. Marines served in joint commands and at embassies. A third made up the fighting force. The Corps was small compared to the other service branches.

But some members of the Corps were well known. It had always been known that a fake Marine who claimed to be well decorated was likely to be found out. Marines knew of those few who had received the Medal of Honor, or the Navy Cross, or conducted operations that only were spoken of in whispers.

William Parker was known.

"I think he's coming back from a run."

"Go get him."

"Got it." The sergeant ran out of the room, past the front desk, and stopped briefly. "Sir, I will be right back."

* * * *

The duty Humvee stood outside the operations center. The running course at Beaufort was well known. The trail had been worn down by the daily workouts. After a short drive, the sergeant saw his boss heading away from the airfield.

"Sir, I was told to get you."

"What's up?"

"We got a visitor who has asked to speak with you. He is a retired colonel." The driver never left the Hummer, with the engine running as he spoke from behind the wheel.

"Name?"

"A William Parker."

The commanding officer didn't hesitate.

* * * *

"Colonel, it's a pleasure." Lieutenant Colonel T.G. Hill didn't salute, but he did extend a hand with a grip like a vice. His running shirt was not regulation. It had been printed just for him, as it had the wings of a Marine aviator on the chest, and below that the word "Highway." The one word was his call sign when he was flying F-35s. "I'm T.G. Hill."

"Thanks, Lieutenant Colonel. Pleasure."

"Please call me T.G. or Highway."

Marine pilots received their call sign early on in training. Often, these were not because of unusual acts of bravery. The squadron gave its new pilots a name.

"Highway?"

"Yes, sir." Hill smiled at a question he'd clearly been asked before. "Something about putting a trainer down on a highway when it ran out of gas. Let's go into my office."

Will followed him into a small space of an office with a window that looked out onto the airfield. The sounds of jet engines roared in the background as Will pulled up a metal-framed, government issued green leather chair. Like all squadron commanders, the desk and walls were filled with plaques from the various duties and commands he had held over the career of a combat experienced fighter pilot. One, hung on the wall, was for a Task Force whose mission had been Somalia.

"So, you did Somalia?" Will asked.

"Yes, sir, prior enlisted at the time." Many officers did tours as enlisted personnel and, after discovering their love for the Corps, used the G.I. Bill to go to college and eventually obtain a commission.

"What was your MOS?" It was common banter for Marines to ask what their military specialty was. Will knew that he was presently a flight officer, but his prior enlistment would have been for something else.

"6531."

"Ammo tech."

"Operation Restore Hope. That was 'eye mef.'" He meant I MEF or the One Marine Expeditionary Force. "The Somalis didn't mess with us much. Seemed a little backed off by a Marine unit, but the Army got wacked later after we left." Hill was stating what history had shown. "I was just a buck private. Wide eyed and scared to death."

"I understand."

"And you were in Somalia?" Hill asked. It seemed that the lieutenant colonel had heard of Will Parker's mission with the rescue of the doctors of Médecins Sans Frontières, or Doctors Without Borders.

"I didn't know it was public knowledge."

"Just Marine knowledge. So how can I help?"

"Michael Kerr came to visit me before his crash."

"Oh…"

"What happened?" Will wanted to hear it from a direct source.

"The aviation board's initial finding is pilot error."

Will showed his displeasure with the comment. The way to whitewash any crash was to tag it with pilot error. It was the catch-all that was used when the manufacturer didn't want the blame game to start. It also meant that the other branches that used the aircraft, whether Marines, Navy, or Air Force, didn't have to ground their fleet.

"Do you believe that?"

"Let's take a ride." Hill stood up and put on a baseball cap. He was only in his workout clothes, so the rules of the Marine Corps of not wearing a hat, or cover, indoors didn't apply. He led Parker out of his office and past the counter.

"I'm taking the duty Humvee."

"Sir, driver?"

"No, I've got this."

They drove across the airfield past the active flight line where both F-35's and the earlier Harriers were lined up. Will sat on the canvas covered seat, not built for pleasure riding, and bounced as they hit more than one speed bump. The vehicle drove to the far end of the flight line where a sole, almost lonesome-seeming hangar stood. A well-armed guard stood out front. The hangar doors were sealed shut, but a door on the side seemed to be the entrance point, where the guard stood with an M-4 automatic rifle.

"Let me show you something." Hill parked the vehicle in a spot marked "C.O."

Will climbed out of the vehicle and followed his driver to the door.

The guard snapped to attention, holding the rifle to his front in a salute. Hill, not in uniform, could not respond other than to say "Carry on."

The hangar was dimly lit with fluorescent lights on the ceiling, most of which were out. Will was struck by the aroma. It was sharp, and a combination of bitter smells of burnt tires, melted plastic, and something else he didn't recognize. He saw the shape of what could only be described as a pile of blackened and burnt shredded aluminum with the tail of an aircraft sticking up at the end. Everything was laid out, however, in a string and separated like players on a chess board.

"I flew with Mike Kerr in Afghanistan," Hill whispered. "It wasn't pilot error. Period."

"So, what happened?"

"A wire frayed, and started a fire. But that wasn't what killed him." Hill continued to whisper. "We found it on several others. You could say, as to that, he saved lives. We pulled the wiring on several and it was an easy fix."

Will folded his arms as he stared at the wreckage. It was the end of a man's life. And it was a man who only a few days earlier had asked him for his help.

"So, what killed him?"

"Let me show you." Hill went to a table near the wreckage. On it was a burnt-out seat with cords and wires. "It's a new one. With the F-35, we wear that high-speed helmet. Works great. Can see the world from it. But it's heavier."

"Okay."

"But that didn't kill him. It might break a pilot's neck, particularly if he is smaller, lighter than most. He was stuck in the bird."

"So, he never made it out?"

"The first step is an explosive charge that blows the canopy. It didn't blow."

"Shit." Will looked at the wreckage.

"The ejection seat. It doesn't work."

"What?"

"The ejection seat works on a laser that ignites the charge. The laser has to hit several reflectors and does it all in a nanosecond."

"So?"

"I heard that in other aircraft the mirrors have a problem." Hill was telling him rumors, but rumors that experienced pilots believed.

"Eighty-nine million a pop and they have bad ejection seats?"

"I didn't say it." Hill hesitated. "Let me say something else I never said."

Will turned to look directly at the man. They were of the same height and stood eye to eye. Everything was said in a whisper.

"Word is, it came down from the top that it would be pilot error."

"Top?" Will couldn't hold back the question.

"Pennsylvania Avenue. Someone didn't want the competitor's bid."

* * * *

Will headed through the front gate at Beaufort and turned south to the Hilton Head Island airfield. The thirty-mile journey didn't take long as it was early afternoon and the bases had not suffered the escape of traffic that goes with the end of the workday. The HondaJet was still in front of the Fixed Base Operation and Moncrief was sitting inside, with his feet up on a coffee table as he worked on a large bag of popcorn.

"Is it good?" Will asked as he came into the room.

"Not sure when you're going to feed me." Moncrief showed his typical lack of deference.

"We should be back in just over an hour." Will meant the flight time back to south Georgia. He went to the counter and asked for the gas ticket to sign. The aircraft had been fully fueled and was, like most private jets, ready for departure. "I need to file a flight plan."

The administrative work would take a few minutes. It would allow the regional air traffic control to monitor his flight, but also let him know of possible shortcuts and bad weather.

"There's a guy who's been waiting for you." Moncrief pointed to a man in a small conference room on the other side of a hallway.

"Any idea?"

"Nope."

"Okay, should be just a moment."

* * * *

Will knocked on the door, finding a man with black and gray curly hair, glasses like Buddy Holly, and a wrinkled, patterned short-sleeved shirt sitting at one end of a conference table. He was intently staring at his computer when the door opened and he looked up. As soon as he saw Will enter, he stood up and crossed over to the door.

"Sir, you must be William Parker?"

"Yeah."

"I'm Terrance Gill of the *Boston Globe*."

"A reporter?"

"Can I ask you a few questions about this crash?"

"Let me ask you some first."

The man nodded uncertainly.

"What do you know about me that you would want to ask?"

"Fair question," Gill said. "There are certain officers at the Pentagon who speak of your reputation."

"And?"

"You don't give a damn about saying anything but the truth."

"That might be a stretch."

"I heard of the incident. There was an official investigation." Gill played the card. "They killed some good men and you told them that."

He was speaking of the ANGLICO mission where a nearby fire team had been caught in a trap and needed artillery help to survive. An operations center had refused. Will didn't play the game of cover-up.

"Off the record?" Will wasn't prepared to wade into these deep waters without the complete disclaimer of statements being off the record. And he wasn't sure why the reporter thought he had any insight.

"Sure."

As a past district attorney, Will had dealt with the news media on several occasions and found a good relationship as long as one worked with them, but a conversation being "off the record" could only mean that. A reporter who violated that standard risked isolation and disrespect from his own industry.

"Flight trace had him at your farm?" asked Gill.

"Yes."

"Might I ask why?"

"He wanted my advice on how to handle a matter."

"Did he say anything about the White House?"

"Should he have?" Will parried with a question as if to ask *What've you got?*

Gill smiled at the technique. It was a fair point.

"Have the Marines said anything about a bad ejection seat in the F-35?"

The question hit a nerve with Will.

"Go on." Will wasn't ready to exchange chips.

"Someone in the administration has a lot invested in the company that makes the ejection seat. A grounding of a one hundred and fifty-billion-dollar program because of bad ejection seats would cost some serious money."

"Who?" Will asked the question.

"Can't say."

Gill wasn't ready to release the story even if it meant getting information. *Interesting.*

"That ejection seat is a good lead." Will gave him a bone. "Any word on who was informed of this loss?"

"I spoke with his parents." Gill seemed surprised, though it was an obvious question with, one would think, an obvious answer. The next of kin would be the first to know.

"How about his girlfriend?"

"Who was that? I wasn't aware of her."

"Yea, not sure much about her. Just that he spoke of her." Will didn't need to complicate things.

"No, no word on that whatsoever that I am aware of. Didn't know he had one."

"Thanks."

No one seemed to know if Merc had been told. It also meant that Will Parker was not going to turn down the young officer's last request. He would find Merc.

"Sir, here's my personal cell." Gill handed him a card. "Just in case. Sometimes some ink can kill better than a bullet."

* * * *

Parker went past Moncrief and straight to the flight desk.
"Change of plans."
The flight plan was filed for Washington, D.C.
"I need to make a call." Will headed out to the flight line and away from any ears. He dialed a number that he had rarely used.

Chapter 26

El Arenal, Ecuador

So embarrassing...

Margarite Zorn knew that the failure of the effort to find Jamal would be something Langley would not forget. Fortunately, no one was hurt, and the hunter-killer team had gotten out of the country with seemingly little attention. The light of dawn was starting to creep into the windows of her room overlooking the beach. She had the balcony doors open so that a constant breeze came through. It seemed a precursor of a storm as the weather increased. The little light of a dawn sun appeared suppressed and the wind blew into the room with enough energy that any papers that were not tied down with a weight were scattered.

Margarite drank from her well used coffee cup. The Ecuadorian black liquid was bitter and strong. She sat at her several computers, crossing from one to another trying to find any hint of a clue. Then she accessed the cell phone program.

"Fuck!" A cell call was traced to just beyond the border of Colombia. *At least I know where they're going.* It wasn't back to Yemen. She sent an email to Langley with the spreadsheet of addresses that she had used on the prior emails. It was well labeled "Top Secret" and highly confidential. She didn't note how she'd gotten the trace. Only that she had credible proof that Jamal was in Colombia and likely with the ELN. And if he was with the ELN, he had a credible chance of making it to the United States. She hit send and took another swallow of the chilled coffee.

A noise of shouting from the beach caused her to walk to the balcony.

She saw her guard, an amicable man with five children, stopped at the far end talking to a man. Soon, they were joined by four more strangers.

The guard turned to run and as he did she saw the flash from one of the men, saw him collapse to the ground, and then heard the sound as it traveled toward her.

Margarite Zorn turned to her computer bank. She had seconds to send an alert that her station was in jeopardy and then kill each of the machines. There were several and panic consumed her as she went from one to another. She turned to a filing cabinet marked "Top Secret" and turned the dial to the lock.

The commotion built below as two of her guards headed toward the beach. There were the sounds of fireworks. She glanced back towards the shoreline to see yellow flashes and a barrage of automatic gun fire. There was a safe room, but for some reason, she stood frozen staring at the conflict as if it were far from reality. One of the men moved up the beach following a wall of the compound. He had an object that looked like a long baseball bat with something fixed to its end.

"What the...?" Margarite uttered the words as she saw the flash of a bright yellow light come from the man. It was only in the milliseconds after the rocket propelled grenade left on its path that she realized it was aimed directly for the balcony door.

There was no place for protection.

The round struck the frame of the door, spreading both death and shards of glass into the room. Her lifeless body was thrown back to the wall. There was no cry. No time for screams. The fire leveled the hacienda rapidly, well before the rural firetruck even reached the front gate.

The fire was hot. A room, which Margarite had called the armory, had held weapons, ammunition, and some explosives for the rare chance of use. It had caused the villa to explode in a torrent of flames and heat. The fire truck had to pull back from the rapid conflagration as the blaze overwhelmed the men in their simple fire suits.

There was nothing left for Margarite Zorn's brother to bury. An urn of ash collected somewhere near where she was last believed to have been was placed in a grave.

The Agency would not take the loss lightly.

Chapter 27

The Mexican-American Border near Calexico

Jamal awoke from a deep sleep in the co-pilot's seat as the aircraft banked hard to its left. He tried to focus his eyes in the dim light. The pilot was intently working the airplane as it turned toward a landing. But the ground was dark. Jamal could barely make out the outline of what appeared to be a dirt road in a valley between several hills. As they approached, two vehicles turned on their headlights. Jamal sat on the edge of his seat and felt his legs tense up as he wondered if the plane would actually make it.

The aircraft slammed to the ground, bounced up and then settled down as it decelerated to a stop. The aircraft pulled up next to the first truck and as it did, a swarm of men in the shadows descended on it.

"This is your stop." The pilot smiled.

Reet looked lost in the back as the landing had woken him from his sleep.

The door swung open and a man said something to them in Spanish. He had a flashlight and shone it on the passengers and cargo of drugs.

The pilot had pulled the engines back to idle but kept them running. The first man climbed into the airplane and started to toss the kilos of drugs to another man at the door. They formed a line and passed the drugs on from one to another and into a waiting van.

"You need to speak to their boss." The pilot pointed to a man standing near another truck.

Jamal followed Reet out of the airplane as they climbed into the warm pre-dawn air. A cloud of dust hung over the aircraft.

"You come with me." The man near the truck said in perfect English. He led the way to a brand-new Ford pickup truck with the engine running. Jamal and Reet climbed in the back seat of the truck, with Jamal holding tightly to his backpack. As they pulled away, Jamal looked back to see the van take off in a different direction. As it did, the Cessna's engines spun up, the aircraft turned and was airborne before they left the valley. It all was a well-rehearsed exercise that had happened many times before.

After several miles the truck pulled onto a highway and continued to the north. They traveled in silence. The Mexican had turned on the radio and seemed unfazed by his passengers. He played his ranchera music full blast.

The lights of a city soon could be seen in the distance. They began to pass rows of small shacks along the side of the highway. The driver pulled out his cell and spoke in Spanish. Soon, a black truck with oversized tires, black tinted windows, and a large brush guard on its front fell in behind them.

"So, you go over the border?"

"Yea." Jamal hugged the backpack on his lap.

"Okay." The driver slowed the truck and as he did, he pointed up the highway to the lights beyond. "Mexicali," he said as he turned the truck onto a side road and pulled behind a small house on the outskirts of the city.

"Arriba, arriba. Hurry." The driver said as he swung his door open and pointed to the small shack. He led the way as the two followed through the back door and found an old woman sitting at a wooden table.

"You change!" The orders from the driver included pointing to a hose near the back door and some used jeans, shirts, and two pairs of cowboy boots.

The water was cold, but this was the first time that both Jamal and Reet had had the opportunity to wash off the remaining layers of mud that went back as far as the jungle. The house was on the very far end of the city. Jamal remembered the sign of a gas station that said Ejido el Choropo. The old woman had laid out two plastic dishes with a taco and frijoles. There were no towels, but they dressed as best as they could and finished the food. The boots were the wrong size, but fortunately they were too large, not too small. The driver gave them each a wide brim straw hat. One had traces of blood inside.

The drive from Ejido el Choropo had taken them through the crowded streets of Mexicali. Both Jamal and Reet had kept their heads down. Jamal had briefly looked out at the people when they came to one stop and noticed something different. The people on the street had looked away, as if they knew the trucks and wanted no part of what was in them.

Near the border, the trucks had quickly pulled inside the warehouse. A guard had opened the door just before they turned the street as if in concert with the effort. The Mexicans were, if anything, efficient in their trade. And there was honor among thieves. Jamal had the thought that a bullet in the back of their heads would have been easier than taking them across. There was, however, one thing on Jamal's side: the final payment would only be made when they were in the United States. He had made it clear that the money was not on him.

The doors shut with a bang that ricocheted through the building.

The driver didn't hesitate. He pointed to the back end of the warehouse. It was full of large wooden crates marked with Spanish words and pictures of agricultural tools. Well in the back there was a bathroom with a small shower and a toilet.

"What?" said Reet, intrigued but confused.

"Special one." The driver knew enough English to say those words.

A special bathroom? thought Jamal. A shower would be welcome but...

Their guide pulled the shower curtain back, grabbed the edge of the pan and pulled it up. The shower's floor swung upward on hinges, with a long flexible pipe attached to the drain that led downwards. He bent down, pulled up two wires, and attached them to a battery he had with him. Once attached, small light bulbs lit up a ladder and vertical tunnel that turned into the darkness.

"Andale!"

It was to be that simple.

Jamal led the way. As he climbed down into the dimly lit passage, it occurred to him that he had left the pistol in the airplane. The ladder creaked as he stepped down to the bottom. Reet followed him and they crowded together in the cramped tunnel below.

"Andale, andale!" The Mexican shoved Reet forward.

Reet's body was full of fear. Jamal didn't have to clearly see him in the dark to know that the close space was a torture to the small man.

Jamal pulled off his belt and handed one end to his companion.

"Hold on!"

And they began to crawl. The tunnel was wide enough that they could almost clamber next to each other. After struggling through the dimly lit tunnel, a reflection of bright daylight signaled the end. Reet was soaked from the crawl and initially refused to let go of the strap. Finally, they reached a spot where the two could stand up. The tunnel was open and a man stood at the base of a ladder.

Just as they saw the man, the lights went out. The Mexican guide had closed down his end of the tunnel.

Reet started to shake.

"Come on Reet." Jamal squeezed his arm. "Not far."

They slowly moved forward until they reached the other end.

"Come on, boys, let's get out of here." The voice was American. The man had a flashlight and was shining it in their faces. Jamal reached the end and was at eye level with the man's cowboy boots. They were black with white lace stiches of a bull and stood out from under long, well-worn blue jeans.

"Damn. You need a shower." It seemed that their escort was not happy with the hose shower that had been provided. He took their hats and tossed them to the side into another bathroom in what appeared to be a small craftsman-style home that could have been there since the fifties.

The home was sparsely furnished and he was the only occupant.

"Better clean up. Want to blend it." The cowboy gave his advice. "You've got a little time. Best wait until after dark."

* * * *

"Friend?" The American shook Jamal awake from a deep sleep. "Hello?" Jamal sat up.

"A car is in the garage. You can take it north." He pointed to a back door that led through a small alley to a garage separate from the house. "Here's map to the cabin."

Jamal understood.

"Don't get stopped."

They had changed clothes again. The cowboy had bought them some cheap white button down short-sleeved shirts and dark pants, with simple black shoes. The cowboy himself was now missing.

"And?" The Mexican who had left them in the tunnel had reappeared in the house on the American side of the border. While they slept, the driver had crossed over and joined them for one reason. He held out his hand.

"A phone?" Jamal likewise held out his hand. "And a bank?"

The Mexican seemed well experienced in this matter. He pulled out a cell for Jamal, and another one with notes. It was the wiring instructions to his bank of choice.

Jamal called and gave the information to Yemen.

They sat together for some time as it got darker, waiting for a phone call.

The Mexican's cell rang. It had a musical tone sounding like a mariachi band. He answered the call and then smiled.

"Go, my friends."

"Here." Jamal pulled out another of the small plastic packs of fifty-dollar bills. It had more than a thousand in each. He handed it to the Mexican and pointed to his pistol. The man smiled again; the gun was silver and flashy, and he clearly knew he could get another.

He handed the revolver to Jamal, who opened the cylinder to confirm there were bullets. It was a heavy piece of steel with a six-inch barrel. Jamal pulled out one round to see that it was a .357 Magnum with the stopping power of a tank.

Unusual for Calexico, the sky was dark and a high level of clouds blocked out any light from the sky. It was a new moon. Except for a streetlight on the far end of Dool Avenue, there was near complete darkness. A wall blocked off the end of the street, a stark reminder of two nations apart. The wall had a bright floodlight on top that pointed toward Mexico.

The Kia was dark and used with over a hundred thousand miles on it, and perfect for two men who wanted to look no different than others. Jamal pulled out of the garage and headed away from the wall, followed the signs and worked their way through Calexico, up north, past the Salton Sea and then on to Interstate 10. It was not the shortest route, but in Phoenix they took Interstate 17, north to Interstate 40 trying to move slowly away from the border.

At an exit, they traveled several miles before stopping briefly at a small gas station, where they bought baseball caps—one for the Dodgers, and another for the Giants—and sunglasses. The store was on a side street well off the exit. Jamal scanned the top of the buildings for cameras before stopping in the dark part of the parking lot. Inside, they grabbed a handful of drinks, and several bags of chips to stave off their growing hunger.

Once back outside, Jamal pulled the car up to a gas pump. He ran inside and gave the woman behind the counter another fifty.

"Fill up."

She didn't seem to care, as there was a television behind the counter and a local news show was on.

"I'll be back for the change."

She nodded.

The car's full tank cost twenty dollars. Reet stayed with the car in the passenger seat. Jamal had driven a car since he'd been old enough to reach the steering wheel, but Reet was from a village in Palestine and never had driven much.

Jamal went back in to retrieve the change. The woman was still watching the news.

The story caught Jamal's attention. He didn't react, but accepted the change and headed out the door.

"We must keep moving," Jamal whispered to Reet as he opened the driver's door. "I can't use them again."

"What?"

"The fifties." Jamal had to think of a way to turn the bills into something smaller.

Reet began eating the bag of chips.

"That's not our only problem." Jamal waited until they got back on the interstate.

"What?"

"The news." Jamal pulled in behind a Walmart tractor-trailer. He kept his distance behind the truck so as to attract little attention.

"A tunnel in Calexico was raided."

Reet sat up.

"How?"

Jamal racked his brain, thinking of what had gone wrong. The Mexicans could not have done anything wrong. It appeared that this had been a special tunnel not used often or before. The money had bought a secure crossing. Or at least, that was what Jamal had thought.

"I think I know what." Jamal realized two things. First, there had been a breach. Second, and perhaps more dangerous, the Mexican cartel would not take lightly the loss of a tunnel, the drugs in the warehouse, and the several who'd been killed in the raid.

"We need to change our plans."

* * * *

The two drove through the night. They left the interstate at the next exit and began working their way across the backroads, still heading away from the border. Safety lay in their being as far away from the border as possible. Originally, they had been heading to a remote cabin in the mountains north of Santa Fe. Red River had one cabin that was far from the others. Jamal had planned to stop, rest and adjust their plans there, but it was the Mexicans who had given them the name and location.

"They'll be waiting for us." Jamal spoke as they passed through Santa Fe and the exit to the north and the mountains. Whether to punish or rob them, he felt certain that he was right. They would be waiting at the cabin.

The sun's first light came up as they passed into Colorado. The two discussed what was needed from here.

Jamal pulled up the car to the Greyhound station just off of Arapahoe Street in Denver. He parked the car on a side street and left the rear window down with the keys in it.

They crossed over the street to a small store with a window full of "Mile High" sweatshirts, stickers, and hats. Jamal walked quickly through the aisles looking for several things. Reet followed like an obedient puppy. In the back they found several backpacks, some pink and some green, and brought two different-colored green backpacks to the counter. Again, he used two fifties.

"Would you mind making some change?"

The man behind the counter was reluctant.

"I'm from out of town and I'm having trouble with people taking these." Jamal put a wad of fifties on the counter. "My boss paid me with these. Got about a thousand here."

The man stood up from his stool. He had pitch-black hair, his dark skin indicative of South Asian ancestry, likely India. He wore gold-tinted glasses that had a crack in one lens.

"I don't mind getting five hundred back." Jamal played the risky card.

The man picked up one of the bills, marked a few with a pen, and held several up to the light. He studied the bills for what seemed a long time.

"Five hundred?" He asked. He seemed to be looking over Jamal's shoulder to see if anyone came in. No one did.

"It would be a big help." Jamal was standing on his toes. He had moved his hand to the big silver pistol in the back of his belt. It wasn't his intent to use it. They had come too far. But it might prove necessary.

"Just these?"

Jamal smiled.

They left the store with several wads of well-used bills in twenties, tens, and fives. It had started with a thousand, but the man had liked the deal. In the end, it totaled more than seven thousand dollars. The clerk had to go to the back of the store to get more of the money. And they bought hooded sweatshirts for backpacks, with stocking caps and gloves. Outside, Jamal went to an alley and opened Reet's backpack.

"Here is half the cash." He put several of the wads of bills inside a pocket. "And this."

Jamal had carried for some time what looked like a simple, hand-sewn money belt. Out of it, he pulled more debit cards.

"Each one is worth a hundred American dollars. Just in case."

Reet put the cards away and pulled the backpack up over his shoulder.

"This is where we part, my brother." Jamal hugged the little man whom he had not known until this journey had begun a short time ago.

"Allah be with you." Reet kissed him on the cheek.

"And with you." Jamal hugged him again as Reet headed across the street to the bus station. "Don't follow anything we had planned. The Mexicans will be waiting."

"Yes, I know."

Jamal watched as Reet headed into the bus station. Once he had disappeared, Jamal turned in the other direction and walked most of the day, heading as far as possible away from the station and anything that would connect him to what he'd left behind. He walked for several hours until he saw a sign. The Denver Zoo's entrance had a line of taxis and other vehicles. One had the black and white Uber sign in its front window.

"Can you take me to the airport?"

The man, no more than twenty-five years old, had a similar appearance to Jamal. They would have seemed cousins if viewed in a line-up.

"I've got cash."

The driver still hesitated.

"Here are three twenties. Would that do it?"

His attitude changed.

"It might be a little more. It's way out."

"Okay." Jamal just wanted transportation that left no trail. He would pay much more when they got there. Jamal sat in the back, trying to not say much. Fortunately, the driver didn't care about talking either.

Just before arriving at Denver International Airport, Jamal slid the revolver out of his pants and put it below the floor mat, well under the front seat. *With luck it will be several days before anyone finds it.* He knew the airport was no place to carry a weapon.

Jamal exited the small SUV and quickly headed into the terminal. He didn't like using air travel but time was running out. If the tunnel had been found, if the Mexicans were on his trail, and if there was no one he could trust or communicate with, speed was the only thing that could keep him alive.

The Frontier flight to Burlington had no stops. He looked up at the clock. Despite the long walk and the ride, he was still there in advance of the 8:00 a.m. departure. Jamal used a debit card to buy the $355 round-trip ticket. The second half would not be used. A round trip, however, caught little attention. He used his passport that he had carried from Yemen. The agent looked at it and then handed it back with no hesitation.

He ran to security and got in line. Jamal looked at the several TSA officers. One looked tired and nearing the end of her duty. He worked his way over to her line. Jamal held his head down, with the Dodgers cap pulled close. He could feel the sweat in his hands as he passed up to the TSA desk, and made a point of smiling. He laid his backpack down as he handed the security agent the passport and ticket. Jamal had picked the line that seemed both backed up and with the officer that seemed the most tired and distracted. The clerk looked like she was ready to go home. She circled the ticket and handed it back to him.

"Thank you." He smiled if she had just told him that he won the lottery.

The backpack had clothes and money, but the money was packed tightly in small packets. Some of it was tucked into his hoodie pocket. Somehow, it all passed through security.

This was as far as he wanted to go in risking the security system.

Jamal's seat was well back in the aircraft. He sat next to the window. A young mother with a child took the seats next to him. The child was only a few years older than his Lala. He tried not to stare, looking out the window as much as possible. The flight seemed to last an eternity. The child, however, reminded him of why he was there.

"Are you okay?" the mother pulled him from the trance he was in.

"Yes, yes, yes," he said. "Just had trouble getting to the airport. It's been a long day." Jamal turned back to the window and watched the land change below as they headed north. The earth below became whiter as snow blanketed the terrain. He glanced at the child again next to him. She was so well behaved that she barely moved.

Jamal's memory of his child's face seemed to be slipping away. And there was only one answer to how to bring it back. He would need to join his daughter, his wife, his family. The revenge of her death would set things right. Allah wanted the infidels to pay the price.

It would be the last place where sleep could be taken before blood was to be shed.

Chapter 28

Richmond Hill Road, Colorado

The snow kept on coming.

Merc's routine had become more difficult as she had to re-plow her training trail every day. She increased her water consumption as she burned more calories than ever before. The food held out. Between what her prior bunkmates had left and what she had planned for both her and Kerr, she was well stocked. But he was late. And between the daily workout and altitude, she was consuming calories at a fast rate.

She looked up valley toward Aspen Mountain as she held the thought: *He's late.*

Better not be because of that chief of staff. Merc had learned one thing living in the White House for eight years: there was no limit to political revenge. And it was known to some that she and Kerr had a special relationship. Normally, Merc never asked her father for anything. Often it would have been a waste of time. But the endless silence made her wonder. Could her father help?

Might need to call. She dreaded the thought. First, the lecture would be endless. And then he'd insist that a jet pick her up.

Plus, going back to town sucks. The trip back to Aspen would be a challenge in the new snow. And it would mean giving up. So, she dismissed the thought.

He should be here tomorrow. Next day at the latest.

She ran a propane tank to heat up snow for water. It had become a routine that she would boil water, clean out the plastic gallon containers, and then boil more water to fill them. She was too far away from anyone to risk getting sick. Then, just before dark set in, she would set them out on the porch. It took little time for the water to chill, nearly frozen, and she would carry them in and place them by the heater.

Another pot boiled the water for the rice. Merc would load up the rice with a can of meat. The workouts only increased her appetite. She scraped the bottom of her plastic bowl like that small poodle they'd had in the White House.

Doodle cleaned his bowl, and so will I.

She licked up the final scraps without hesitation. The workouts had done two things she had never experienced before. Food was meant to be eaten and she ate every bite. And sleep, deep sleep, came only a second or two after she pulled herself into the warm sleeping bag. Only her nose stuck out and she could feel the chill on what little skin was exposed.

The snow clouds held in the light and the blanket of white seemed to amplify what little light there was. As she lay in her sleeping bag, she would glance through the cabin's windows to see the dull light of the valley.

At first light, Merc prepared her equipment. Her skis were waxed with the choice of the day. Her boots were dried after a night near the propane heater and she had a change of clothes. It took three sets of clothes for any single pair to have the time to dry out.

She headed out on the trail when the light cleared the mountain.

The route took her up one small valley, turned towards the mountain, crossed just below it, and then went down to the valley.

Crack.

Merc stopped just beyond the crossover below the mountain. The sound came from above and behind her. The rush of wind hit her from her back side. It was a cold blast that almost knocked her down.

The crack was followed by a deep, frightening rumble. She could feel the ground shake.

"Shit!" Merc yelled as it knocked her off of her skis. She pulled up her arms and the poles to her chest and bent her knees up in a ball. A cloud of chilled, fog-like ice filled the air. The roar could be heard down the valley if any soul were there to hear it. But she was here alone. A scream would have done little good.

It stopped as quickly as it had started.

Merc lay there for several minutes trying to get a sense of things. Her goggles were iced over, and her bright red sweater and hat had been turned completely white. Finally, she used her poles to pull herself up. Once on her feet she stood and looked around, assessing the situation.

The avalanche was on the far end of the mountain. It had come within 100 yards of the trail, tearing out a path of trees, rocks, and bushes as if the hand of God had swiped the hillside.

Merc shook as she stared at the destruction. It was as if she were the only person on the planet and the planet had suffered a meteor strike from outer space.

She pulled herself together and headed back on her trail toward the cabin. Once there, she took off her ski equipment, sat on the bench that was built on the porch, shook, and cried.

"He'd better get here soon." She was not happy with Michael Kerr.

The snow came again that night. The mountains had not had snowfall like this in decades.

It brought quiet, but also danger. Danger came in so many forms.

Chapter 29

Will looked at his watch. It was near noon. He had followed his run from Key Bridge downriver toward the airport. The aircraft pattern also headed downriver towards Reagan. A low cloud cover caused the aircraft on approach to be particularly low. The smell of spent kerosene filled the air. A warm blast of the engines could be felt where the path passed directly below the approaching airplanes. As he passed the beginning of Arlington Cemetery, he saw a runner ahead. She was running alone at a slow pace.

"You don't have to slow down for me." Will joked as he pulled up alongside.

The woman had a touch of gray in her short hair, but had a tight body. More than one young lieutenant had made the mistake of trying to pass her on the physical fitness three-mile. She had ground them into the dirt. Gail Ritchie was made to be a Marine. A combat veteran, she had worked her way up with respect from her peers.

"Wasn't planning on it." She increased her pace as he pulled up alongside.

The two well-conditioned runners could handle a conversation while maintaining pace.

"What happened?" Will started the conversation. He knew that Gail had suggested Kerr contact him.

"A CIA officer in Ecuador had been tracking a person suspected to be Jamal."

"From the *Cole*?"

"Same."

"In Ecuador?"

"She thought so. Not sure anyone believed it at first." As one of the top intelligence officers at the Pentagon, Gail was in the loop on most sensitive communiqués.

"What's that got to do with Kerr?"

"Not sure if anything." Gail increased her pace as she started up a steep hill. "But his girlfriend is missing."

"So Secret Service should be all over it?"

"Except word is that the White House shut it down. The chief of staff over there reduced the security coverage for the children of his predecessor. Cut the funds and fired the head of the service."

"Where is she?"

"You might know better than us. Didn't Kerr visit you before the crash?"

"I told him no."

"One other thing. The officer in Ecuador had gone rogue. She'd used Mossad to put Pegasus on a cell." Pegasus could be placed deep inside a cell phone and allow a listener to follow every word, track every location, and read every text. It was such a hot software program that it even made the Pentagon nervous. Israel had killed more than one terrorist by Pegasus. But CIA field agents were not supposed to be using it. Certainly, not without Langley knowing of it.

"And?"

"She put it on a cell."

"Did it work?"

"The last word is that Jamal was in Calexico."

"California?"

"Went through a Mexican cartel tunnel. The information was shared with DEA and they torched it. Missed him."

"Not great."

"Exactly. He knows he's being traced."

"And the Mexicans can't be happy either."

"No. One of those killed in the warehouse was Nuñez's brother."

"The Sinaloa Cartel?"

"Yeah. Jamal had another person with him. No idea who he is."

"And now they are going deep."

"Oh, yeah."

"Kerr may have been killed." As Will said it, Gail stopped.

"A Marine?"

"Not sure."

"We've said enough." Gail turned around and resumed her run.

"I agree." Will continued on in the same direction. He was heading toward Reagan, where Coyote Six was parked at the FBO. Moncrief would be waiting.

Will Parker had fallen into a mission with several objectives, each likely to bring blood.

Chapter 30

Burlington, Vermont

Jamal sat up in his seat for the remainder of the trip. He never lowered it, refusing to relax one bit. As the jet taxied to the terminal, he stared out at the blanket of snow. It hurt his eyes. The mother next to him stood up and started to dress her child in a small pink parka. The child struggled with the sleeves.

"Come on Dottie," she said. "Have a safe day," to Jamal.

"Oh, yes." Jamal thought what an odd thing that was to say.

The child turned to him and handed him a colored piece of paper.

"Thank you, little sunshine." It was a saying he had often used with Lala.

Jamal had killed many in his life, but never children. This is what separated him from the evil of the president. And this is what drove him forward.

Jamal carried only his backpack away from the airplane. Leaving the terminal, he went straight to the taxi stand, stopping only to pull out the gray hooded sweatshirt from Denver. It was thicker than most, which not only worked well in the weather but also helped him not stand out.

"I'm looking for Carter's Cars." All of this had been planned. From as early as Jamal's use of the internet in Panama and Ecuador, he'd known what to do.

"Sure. Not far." The taxi driver was happy to get an easy fare.

Burlington had a chill and an overnight snowfall had left it a blinding white. Jamal pulled out of his pack the baseball hat and sunglasses.

"L.A.?" The driver asked.

"Sorry?"

"Dodgers?"

Jamal had forgotten the hat.

"Yeah. Good team."

"Not this year."

"In the past." Jamal tried not to engage in conversation.

At the dealership, he was looking for something specific. A used Hyundai SUV with four-wheel drive. One had well over a hundred thousand miles. They were asking just under $5000. Jamal came up with the story that he had a new job at a local lodge and couldn't pay more than $3500. The dealer balked until Jamal mentioned that he could pay cash. That made it easy.

Jamal had one of the driver's licenses that he had carried all the way from Yemen. The treasurer had supplied him with it and the other false documents. He hadn't noticed until now, but it was a New York state license. Jamal sat as still as possible in the chair with a smile, and the salesman scrutinized the license.

"Close to expiring."

"Really?" Jamal leaned over the desk to see it. "Thanks for telling me. I never would have caught it."

"It'll work."

* * * *

The car smelled of marijuana but it was clean and had a full tank of gas. He imagined the prior owner was a kid who lived for the mountains, probably a guide, and needed the money.

A temporary dealer tag was fixed on the back end. He would use it for a day or two until he got to a bigger city. His plan was simple. There, he would pull into the long-term parking lot at the airport and look for a car with another state's plate and covered in a foot of snow. He would choose a car far from any of the security cameras. The new plate would buy him more time. He was careful to put the dealer tag on the other car so as to not draw any more attention than necessary. He then tossed some of the snow onto it. The snow immediately froze to the plate, disguising enough of the numbers that even the car's owner would have to look closely to notice.

Jamal had another destination in mind.

The SUV traveled south and east to the Green Mountains. He had memorized the route. After some time, he passed over a bridge that marked the Barton River.

This is it.

He looked for another sign just beyond the bridge. The turn to the cabins was barely visible with the coating of snow, but the road had been freshly plowed. He followed the tracks made by some four-wheel vehicle that had snow chains. The SUV's four-wheel drive did well. He pulled up to the main office.

"Hello."

The clerk was a middle-aged woman with a well-worn red and yellow wool sweater and the tanned, wrinkled face of someone who had spent most of her life outdoors in the Vermont woods. She had a broad white smile and a heavy New England accent.

"Can I help?"

"I'd like to rent a cabin."

"Sure." The snow had brought an earlier crowd to the otherwise off season between the summer and winter cross country skiers. But the cabins were largely empty now.

"Do you have Hawk Haven?"

"You know about us." The woman took note of Jamal now.

"Only from the internet."

"First time?"

"Yeah."

"Well, happy to have you. We serve breakfast."

"Good." He didn't realize it as he glanced into the mirror to the side of the counter, but he was as tanned as she was. His already-dark complexion had only been darkened by the journey south of the border. But his face had small red bumps from the time in the jungle. Without thinking, he rubbed his forehead.

"Skier?" She had probably guessed the answer before asking the question.

"No, I always wanted to hunt black bear."

"Really?"

"Yes, I worked out of the country for several years and had this on my dream list."

"Good timing. Almost the end of the season." She had finally figured out the man. He was clearly someone who was in the military or had worked with the military. "Thanks for your service."

He didn't fully understand the comment and chose to act embarrassed, humble.

It was the reaction that she expected and it only reinforced her thought that he had done a tour on the other side of the world.

"I need a guide. Any suggestions?"

"Matter of fact…"

"Thanks."

"If you like, I'll make a call."

* * * *

Jamal lay down in the cabin. He had started a small fire in the fireplace. When he had opened the door, he could see his breath. But the heat of the fire quickly warmed it up. The room did not have a television. But it did have a telephone. As he relaxed on the soft pillows, the most comfortable he had felt since Yemen, the phone suddenly rang.

The sound caused him to jump up. He looked around to see the bright sunlight shining through the dark brown, rough-cut curtains on the windows.

"Yes?" As he said the word, he absentmindedly felt his waist for the pistol. Realizing it wasn't there, he felt a brief panic attack. In all of his years of life in Yemen, he was never without a weapon. Even as a child, he had carried a small Russian-made Makarov that carried eight .380 ACP cartridges. He always preferred the American-made bullets from Colt. They never caused a jam. But he'd left it in Yemen knowing that, at best, it would be either found or taken. Now, the lack of a weapon made him feel as if he were wearing his shoes without socks.

"Sir, this is Fred from Benson."

"Oh?" Jamal didn't immediately recognize the name of the next town to the south.

"They said you were looking for a guide. Perhaps a black bear hunt?"

"Yes, that would be great."

"I'm not far from you and am going out to see how my dog handles it."

"Oh, yes." Jamal didn't know much about the effort needed to kill a bear.

"Takes a tag and they are expensive." The guide quickly got down to the point. "In all, about $1500."

"Okay."

"It's the end of the season. Bears will be trying to fatten up as much as possible before they find a hole to climb into for winter. Have you shot a .338 Winchester Magnum?"

"Not really."

"Best not to mess with a wounded bear. How about in the morning we go shoot a few rounds?"

"Yes, that would be good."

Jamal lay back down on the bed and quickly went to sleep as the light outside became dim and the crackle of the fire made his eyelids feel weighed down with lead. He didn't even take off his clothes, except for the hoodie, and lay there, curled up, like a child. Exhaustion had trumped any hunger. Jamal slept for several hours, until the dream came back. He was standing there, always, looking into the hole from the bomb blast and seeing his daughter in its bottom, calling for him.

Jamal woke in a sweat. The fire had gone out. He made his way across the room in the dark, poked the embers and placed another cut log on it. Soon the wood began to crackle and there was light. He went to his backpack and pulled out a long-sleeved shirt bought in Denver, pulled it on and then fell back on the bed.

* * * *

The knock on the door came within a few minutes. Or so it seemed. At first, the knock was soft and barely audible. It came again, much louder. But it didn't seem to have an effect.

Again, there was a banging.

Jamal finally felt the vibration. He leaned up to realize that his good ear was buried deep in the pillow. Unconsciously, he felt the other one and, like it had been happening for some time, a small dab of fluid touched his finger.

Jamal rolled over to see the fire was out. He had slept for another several hours. It was before dawn. He walked over to the door, grabbed the iron poker from the fireplace, and stood to one side of the door as he pulled it open. He braced it with one foot on the inside in case there was a rush.

"Hey, I'm Fred." A man, large and burly with a dark, curly beard smiled. His beard, large black eyebrows, and small, fat, round nose were framed by a camouflaged wool cap. It was one of those with a brim and wool ear flaps. The flaps were folded up.

Jamal looked out to the plowed parking space directly in front of his cabin. The SUV was there with a light, thin coating of snow and to its side was an oversized Ford F-250 truck with its engine running.

"Hello."

"Thought we'd get an early start. Dog wants to run. Sorry if I woke you."

"Sure, no problem." Jamal grabbed his hoodie and pulled it over his head. He also grabbed the baseball hat, mainly for some warmth.

"Not done much hunting?"

"Some, but the airline lost my bag."

"Okay." Fred didn't seem surprised. It appeared that he had heard that before from people flying into Burlington. "Do you want to ride with me?"

Jamal thought for a moment.

"Perhaps I can follow you some of the way? I thought I might buy some hunting clothes afterwards." The plan made sense.

"Sure. Just thought we'd let you fire the gun and maybe run the dog."

The truck and the SUV drove past the main office as they left. It was dark. The owner appeared to not have been the early riser that the hunting party was.

They followed each other for several miles until the truck pulled over at a roadside park at the turnoff to another smaller road.

The driver jumped out and ran to Jamal's car.

"Best you leave yours here. Beyond this, without chains, we may not get you out."

"Good." Jamal followed him to the Ford.

The truck was warm. The guide's dog, a pit bull, sat calmly on the back bench. He stared at Jamal as if he had some sense of how authentic one was. He didn't growl but his eyes never left Jamal.

"Mutt's fine, but don't try to pet him."

Jamal glanced at the beast in the back.

"To hunt bear, you need a tough dog."

"He looks like it."

The hunter nodded. The truck had the smell of hot coffee. A YETI insulated cup had steam rising from it on the center dash.

"I brought you some." He pulled out a thermos. It was the old style with a screw-off metal cup and a stopper. "Sorry, just coffee, but it's hot."

"Thanks." Jamal poured a little, held it with both hands and slowly slipped the dark liquid. It warmed his body and soon he was actually too hot.

"We'll go out to a range and let you shoot this beast." The guide pointed to a rifle on the back-window rack.

Jamal took it all in. The man also carried a large-caliber pistol on his belt. "What's the pistol for?"

"In case you miss." The guide smiled. "It's a .44 Mag. It will stop anything."

"Oh."

"A wounded bear can come hard."

Jamal stuck his hands into the hoodie's pocket.

"Here are some extra gloves. You'll need them." The guide was generous. The gloves were well-used, leather, and soft from years of grease and sweat.

The sun came up as they drove the miles up the highway to a turnoff that headed deeper into the Green Mountains.

"I know this place." Jamal said it absentmindedly. He didn't want to give away anything, but the plan was working better than he thought.

"Really?"

"I think I was here years ago in the summer." Jamal raised a quick cover story. "There are cabins up this road."

"Several miles."

"Used by cross-country skiers."

"Yeah." The guide was impressed.

They turned on a snow-covered road. It was still early, so the snow chains were not needed for the depth, and the tires cut down to the gravel. They pulled up to another side road and went a short distance to a small ravine.

Jamal saw a mound of dirt on the other side of an opening and four wooden structures with a small plywood target on each. The shape of a bear had been painted on all of them.

"Not very fancy, but does the trick." The guide did a circle with the truck so that the tailgate would point toward the targets. He had to climb down from the cab as it had been lifted. A small black metal step allowed both him and Jamal to climb down.

The guide opened the back door and as soon as he did, the pit bull dog took off in a dart.

"Don't worry, she only goes after danger."

Jamal watched as the dog disappeared into the snow-covered woods.

"Let's see what you can do." He pulled the rifle out, checked the sight, and chambered a round. The cartridge was longer and thicker than anything Jamal had seen in years with his AK-47. "I'll shoot the first round."

The guide held the rifle to his shoulder and fired. The blast was deafening. Jamal reached for his ears too late. They rang with tinnitus. The target flopped backwards, struck by the force of the energy.

"You hit any central part of the bear and this will stop it." He handed the rifle to Jamal.

Jamal looked through the scope and saw the crosshairs. He pushed the weapon deep into his shoulder and leaned forward into the round. The energy would pass through all of his body and not just his shoulder. He slowly squeezed the trigger until the roar knocked him back on his heels. Another target fell.

"Good! Very good! You *have* shot something before."

"How many rounds does it hold?"

"I use three."

A box of bullets was sitting on the tail gate.

"They are 250 grains." The hunter was using a shell that was made for taking down a grizzly.

Jamal pulled out three rounds, opened the bolt, put one in the chamber, closed the bolt and then opened the hinged plate and put three more in.

"You do know your weapons." The guide turned to the targets. "Let me go straighten out those two."

Jamal watched as he headed towards the mound. He scanned the area. The range was remote. It was probably this guide's secret spot where he took customers and only customers. And it was a place that he could run his dog and likely know the dog would return to the same place. Otherwise, the forest was quiet, and the blanket of new snow hung off the limbs of the pine trees. The foliage was thick, except for the small open area, almost like it was an enclosed building.

Jamal lifted the rifle. He felt the butt of the stock fit into his shoulder.

The cross hairs were in the center of the guide's back when the blast lifted the man off of his feet. The magnum had so much force that a path of blood, coat, flesh, and life blew out over the untouched white before him. He fell forward like a pancake. A pool of blood quickly flooded the white snow that surrounded the body. The man struggled for a brief moment, reaching for the revolver on his side, but as Jamal watched, the gloved hand began to shake and then became still.

The sound was followed by a brief echo and then there was silence. Snow had started falling again.

Jamal quickly ran to the man, kicked him with his foot and then reached for the revolver.

He turned, running back toward the truck when he heard the sound.

The dog was on the far side of the opening just above the mound. He ran straight to his master, stopped, nudged the man with his nose and then turned to Jamal. By then, Jamal was at the back tailgate. The door, however, was as far as the moon. The dog would have been on him well before Jamal could have even placed his hand on the handle.

Jamal dropped the rifle and cocked the pistol. It was heavy, and took both hands to steady.

The dog charged him. It had clearly killed wounded bears. It was far more dangerous than any enemy that Jamal had ever faced.

The hammer of the gun was stiff. The butt was too large for his hand. He had but a moment to place the front sight on the shape. No time to do more.

Even with the glove on, the revolver's recoil stung his hand.

When the smoke settled, Jamal checked his arms and neck. He was shaking with fear.

A shape lay at his feet.

It didn't move.

The snow kept coming.

Jamal drove the guide's truck back onto the main road and turned right. The gun had served him well. And it would do so again, soon.

Chapter 31

"Any luck?" Moncrief was sitting in the Signature FBO lounge again, chowing down on a large bag of popcorn.

"Maybe. We may be in something up to our chest." Will stood next to him as he looked out on the flight line. Coyote Six was on the far end of a row of jets, all of which made the smaller aircraft look like the stepchild. But it had sleek lines that drew the attention of the men on the ground. He watched as he saw several pilots, with their white short-sleeved shirts and epaulets on their shoulders marking their level of experience, walk around the aircraft. The HondaJet was known to be fast and already had gained the reputation of being fun to fly.

Moncrief smiled. Trouble was what he lived for. He embraced something that Will refused to acknowledge: They both lived for the mission.

"Got a problem."

"What's that?"

"Kerr asked me to help, but I turned him down."

"So?"

"I have no idea how to find her."

Moncrief chuckled. He pulled out his phone to show the download from Kerr.

"Let's try Vermont."

Will smiled. It did take a team.

They studied what Kerr had given them. There was a cell phone number but it rang, rang, and then went to a blank voicemail. There was no identifier on the voicemail greeting. They could not be sure who was on the other end nor whether the message had been received.

As they sat there in the private terminal, CNN played in the background. A breaking-news report came on. The network was reporting that an attempt upon the president;s life had been discovered and stopped.

"What's this?" Moncrief looked up as the news coverage went to a reporter outside a hotel in Houston. They watched as the lips moved, but the sound was muted. A man in shackles was being shuffled out of a police station.

Will turned around to see that there were no other pilots in the lounge. He crossed over to the set and used the remote to turn up the volume.

"The man was apprehended after purchasing a rifle in a local gun store with a false driver's license." The woman's hair blew in the breeze as she gave her report.

"Who is he?" Will wondered.

As he did, she answered the question. "Authorities cannot say who he is; however he had a backpack with several thousand dollars in small bills and numerous debit cards."

The two sat forward in their chairs as the report continued.

"The president was here for a conference with former Secretary of State James Baker at Baker's institute at Rice University." The announcer spoke softly.

"Was it serious?" Will spoke the question out loud. It didn't seem well-planned enough to be a serious threat.

"Doesn't impress me." Kevin spoke with the authority of someone who was a member of that small club of people who could've pulled off the assassination of a president.

"Or something else?" Will looked at him.

* * * *

The filed flight plan took them to Burlington. It was a slow flight as the storm that moved into New England caused the airport to be closed for several hours while the visibility improved and the plows cleared the runway. Once on the ground, Will taxied to the FBO and shut the engines down. The sign of "Heritage Aviation" was emblazoned over the large doors to a hangar.

"Going to be here long?" asked the attendant.

"Might be, can you hangar it?"

"Happy to. First one of these on the field." The man smiled as he looked at the aircraft. "It looks dope!"

"What?" Moncrief asked.

"Sweet. Excellent?" The attendant, likely a student at the flight school working the line to make money for the hours needed to fly professionally, tried to translate his Gen Z term for the much older gunnery sergeant.

"That's what I thought." Moncrief slapped him on the back.

"We need to rent a vehicle. Four-wheel," Will told the lineman.

"No problem." He had a radio and microphone attached to his work suit. "Chains?"

"More snow coming?"

"Yes, sir, that's what they say."

"Okay, and we need to get some things out of the aircraft as well."

"No worries, just give me a moment."

"Are you thinking what I'm thinking?" Moncrief asked as the groundman attached a tractor to the aircraft and prepared it to be pulled into the hangar.

"Let's get it inside, unload, and then get a hotel." The sun had gone down and the temperature was dropping rapidly.

Once the aircraft was in the hangar and a black Yukon SUV was parked at the door, Kevin opened the jet's cargo door and pulled out several gun cases. Two were small, and two had long rifles. A plastic case was full of ammunition clips for both the Heckler & Koch VP40 semi-automatic pistols and a pair of MR556A1 5.56 semi-automatic rifles. The rifles were identical to the Special Forces' HK416, except that the 416 was automatic. Will and Kevin didn't want the 416. First, it would require explaining to any local trooper why several citizens had weapons that would make the news that night, and more importantly, they were both expert trained Marine marksmen. A spray of bullets was no substitute for one well-aimed shot. The jet also contained some Canada Goose winter parkas in white and black camouflage, along with pants, gloves, caps, and everything needed for a quick operation. No one was around as they moved the gear into the Yukon.

Both men hoped that the weapons would not be needed. It was, however, likely that they would be disappointed.

Chapter 32

Quito, Ecuador

A man with much to worry about will walk fast, especially when the sun starts to go down.

The colonel made a point of never walking alone after the sun started to set. At least not since what had happened on the coast. It had gotten out of hand. He had made a serious mistake. And he knew it.

The general had held a late staff meeting that went on too long. The colonel had fidgeted in the back of the room waiting for it to be over. Finally, the group's leader left, which allowed the others to follow suit.

The colonel's mistake had been the result of a rash decision made out of anger. It was a long-brewing hatred of the CIA's interference with his country that he despised. The discord had initially been softened by Zorn's offer to deposit funds to an account in Switzerland. But it hadn't gone down that way.

It had started innocently. Zorn's brother was a school friend. She'd stopped by as he had requested. They had gone out to dinner, and drank wine well into the evening. More importantly, the colonel's wife had fallen for Margarite. He couldn't warn his wife of what he'd heard about the woman. The trips had become more frequent and nothing was ever asked of him.

And then one day…

The colonel, at the time a major, had been responsible for the president's security on a trip to the northern border. The party would fly to Tulcán aboard eight Ecuadorian air force Bell 206 Jet Ranger helicopters. The week before the trip, all hell had broken loose.

"Sir, we only have three birds left and they just went down." The aircraft were temperamental and mechanical problems had often kept them on the ground. The other five were kept on the coast and had likewise been down. The air officer's report couldn't go up to higher authorities. The trip had been advertised for weeks. The president had been impatient and the cancellation of the trip would have been an embarrassment.

"What do we need?"

"I have a list of parts, but it will take weeks."

The young major had been heading home to get drunk when the telephone at headquarters had rung. He'd wanted to be drunk before he called the President's secretary. It would blunt the yelling that was coming. It would also have been the call that ended his career.

"I understand you have a problem."

He recognized her voice instantly.

"This can be fixed." Margarite Zorn had sounded like an accountant giving advice to a client.

It had been less of a surprise that Zorn could help than that she'd known of the problem at all. The conversations had all taken place in less than an hour from when he had left the office.

"How?"

"Trust me." Zorn had sounded like she knew what she was talking about. A small King Air transport, only white with no markings other than an unusual tail number, had landed at Mariscal Sucre Airport just after dawn. The airfield was less than eleven miles from the capital and was where the JetRangers were kept. The King Air had come with several mechanics.

An hour before the president's convoy had been set to leave Quito, the JetRangers had been brought back online. At the end of the day, the major had become a colonel.

Later, a simple request had been made. A young lieutenant had been up for promotion. Margarite Zorn had asked for help. It was then that she'd sent a thank-you note. It had an account number on a card and a telephone number as well. The number had an international code of 41 22. The colonel had googled the number to find that it was Geneva. He had called from a burner phone he'd bought in Guayaquil. The amount had shocked him. It was twice his pay for a year.

For days, he'd debated whether to return it, or stop it, or burn the number. But he'd put off the decision. His wife and daughter had wanted to travel to Disney World for Christmas. It was the gift that he had always wanted to give the child. The tickets had surprised both of them. Her smile had lit up the house for days. And then it could not be returned.

The colonel had tried to put it out of his mind as if it were a warning from a doctor about a spot on one's lung. Time had built resentment and regret. The price had come later when she'd asked for a copy of a report of what Ecuador was doing in its conflict with Peru. A report labeled "Top Secret." It had been far easier than he'd expected to make a copy. This effort had been made, however, for a reason. He'd been convinced that Ecuador needed the Americans' help in the situation and that it would save lives. Again, he'd gotten a thank-you letter with a card. And this time it was for a much larger sum.

When she'd called and asked for help on Jamal, he'd had enough.

He'd made a simple call to a man his intelligence officer knew. He hadn't needed to give a name. All he'd had to do was say, "Get her out."

What had happened to Zorn after had never been expected.

The colonel's wife and child were waiting on him for supper and he was late. It was the child's birthday and he had promised that he would not miss it.

He carried a small automatic, and as he headed down the street from where he'd left his compatriot, he patted the weapon in his pocket.

"Colonel?" The voice came out of a shadowy doorway.

"Who's there?"

A man stepped out.

"It's Fernando."

"Yes, Fernando. You startled me."

"Are you okay?" The neighbor had lived in the same house near him for most of a decade.

"Oh, yes."

"Good." He patted the colonel on the back of his shoulder as old friends do. "Let me walk you home."

"Yes, that would be good."

They walked the few blocks towards his house. As they approached, the colonel could hear his child playing on the other side of the wall and his wife singing the song that she often did. The trees were in early blossom as the sun had moved South America closer to its warmth. There was a sweet smell in the warm air.

Fernando didn't say anything.

The colonel felt comfortable with his neighbor. He loosened his grip on the pistol and turned to him, extending his hand to his friend when they reached the door.

"*Gracias,* my friend."

"You shouldn't have told them."

The colonel's face turned ash white in an instant as the blade cut deep into his stomach. It would have been easier for him if the blade had cut across the neck, but Margarite Zorn had been killed in a horrible way. The Agency would pay for the death of its officer in kind.

One last message was sent.

"Your accounts have all been emptied and the generals know of your betrayal to Pena. Your wife and child will receive nothing from the government." The man spoke the words in a whisper.

The neighbor had long lived in the same house with only one mission. He had remained a sleeper who had only one task, if it were ever needed.

The colonel fell to the ground holding onto the haft of the knife that had pierced his gut. The point of the blade extended through his back and caused the rear of his officer's jacket to stick out as if a pencil were pushing it outward. He sat on the steps of his home, hearing his child's laughter and his wife's singing. Soon the pain took over. He had no breath to cry out. And then the lights went out.

* * * *

Well to the north of Quito just inside the Colombian border, the ELN encampment was preparing for another raid. The commander had an old Nissan pickup truck hidden under a tarp. It was surrounded with several of the guerrillas who were pulling out the seats and packing the space with blocks of plastic explosives. Rojas, a man with several fingers missing from a past mishap with explosives, was directing the crew on how to rig the bomb.

"How much?"

"A hundred pounds." A small man, almost boy-like, was packing the charges. He stacked them up like bricks and then strapped them down with cord to hold them in place.

"More."

The man gave him a look.

"We have several more crates." Rojas pointed to the hut nearby. It had been recently resupplied by some funds that had come in unexpectedly to the commander and the ELN.

"How much more?"

"Another hundred." Rojas began inserting the blasting caps and running the wires to the steering wheel.

"They should all be there for formation." The commander held a map of the nearby city. He pointed to one spot on it that was marked *Policía*. "The academy starts a new class tomorrow morning."

"If this is to be my last, it will be a good one." Rojas smiled at the thought of the potential destruction.

"How is this?" The loader held the door open as the last of the explosives was put in place.

"Good." The commander looked at his cell phone.

"No calls!" Rojas stopped him. The cell had a remote chance of detonating the truck. The suicide bomber didn't want his mission to be ended there in the jungle by a simple mistake.

"Okay..."

"Let's eat a good meal." Rojas loved his aguardiente. The sugarcane and aniseed drink had a kick. With twenty-nine percent alcohol in his drink, Rojas would spend his last night in front of a fire mumbling about the adventures of his youth until first light.

The attack would cause countless deaths.

"What was that?" Rojas heard the faint sound of a jet high above the valley.

"There it is." The commander pointed to a silver object well above the clouds.

They stared at it as it moved across the sky. It was only at the last instant that Rojas saw the dark dot.

The explosion was not the first. It ignited the truck, and then the hut where the other plastic explosives were stacked in wooden crates.

For those that survived, there was no boom or clap.

Only a few on the far end of the camp crawled out of the destruction, their bodies bloody, some with limbs missing, their ears ringing as if they had been trapped in a bell tower for hours, only to see a crater.

Rojas was gone. The commander was gone. The cell phone from which Jamal had made the call was gone. The death of a Langley officer had been settled.

Except for one.

Chapter 33

A Cabin in the Green Mountains

"We need to lay off the rosé!" Merc's roommate Jenny was nursing a terrific headache. And with good reason. Their morning cross country run was the worst. They would climb out of their sleeping bags on the separate bunks, dress quickly, drink their cups of coffee, and eat a power bar. Then they would suit up, wax their skis, and climb out on the front porch of the cabin, where each would stretch, swing their arms to build up heat, slap their skis on, and head out on the trail.

"First one to the bend doesn't have to cook breakfast!" Jenny yelled back at the others. She only said that after she had captured the tracks and was moving out at a face pace.

"Bitch." The last one limped along. "That second bottle of rosé is killing me."

They all laughed, enjoying the first run and the friendship. The trail took them to the top of a low-lying ridge from which they could see across the valley. By then, the first light illuminated the white, snow-covered forest below.

"This is worth it." Jenny chimed in. "What's for breakfast?" She had easily won the race to the bend and beyond.

"Blueberry pancakes." Their other roommate shouted as she carried her skis to the porch.

"I love you, sister!" Jenny smiled. "Got to tell Merc what she's missing."

"That fool's probably eating power bars for all three meals." The other girl laughed at the comment.

"I think it's as much love as training." Jenny had hit a chord. After years of living in a fishbowl, Merc's training regimen would be competing with her golden opportunity to spend private time with the young pilot.

A boom echoed across the valley.

"What was that?"

The three looked at each other.

"Damn hunters. They are still hunting deer and bear this time of year."

"Great. Bear?" The last one in the race asked the question. "You let me be the last one with bears out there?"

"Oh yeah, been known to be seen," said Jenny.

Another boom echoed across the valley.

"What was that?"

"Probably a miss."

"Let's get back to the fire. I left my cell there." Jenny's breath let out a vapor.

"And I have to cook!" The third one was also the worst on skis. She had been raised in Texas and was new to this white world.

"Well, it was a good run."

"Mostly." Jen added. There were a few hills.

The Green Mountains where their cabin was were remote. The log structure sat on top of a lake, now lightly frozen, covered with a dust of snow. But there was nothing for miles. Not even the smoke from another chimney could be seen from the ridge. They were alone, just as the trip had been intended.

* * * *

In the cabin, Jenny pulled her chair in front of the fireplace.

"Where are those pancakes?" Jenny loved to harass their Texan friend in the kitchen.

"Working on it." A voice could be heard in the back along with the clanging of pots.

"It's getting colder." A third friend pulled her chair up to the fireplace as well. They were all brilliant and destined for everything an Ivy League education promised.

The rumble of a truck caused them to turn around.

"Who's that?"

They were joined by their Texan friend from the kitchen as they all walked out to the front porch.

A large green truck stopped in front of the cabin.

"Not Merc?" The Texan asked with her drawl.

"Not in that truck."

"Hello!" She waved at a man that was standing next to the door of the truck. He was blocking some of the writing on the cab's door, but between the shape of a deer head and the fragmented words of "HU..." she knew it was a guide.

The man waved but didn't say anything. He was tall, dark and had on a wool camouflage hat with the ears pulled down. He was also dressed in a thick dark-gray hoodie with the hood pulled back and he had on thick leather work gloves. He smiled a disarming smile at her.

"Are you Fred?" She spoke to him from the porch.

"You heard of me?" he carried an accent that seemed out of place for Vermont, but not oddly so

"The Murphys—we rented this cabin from them—said there was a hunting guide in the area named Fred."

"Yes."

"What was that sound?"

"The rifle shots?"

"Yeah, two."

As they stood there the others joined them and started taking off their skis. They first went to the truck, said hello, and then went to the porch to knock off the snow from their boots.

"I was wondering that as well. It's why I rode up here." The guide leaned away from the truck. As he did, she noticed that he had on cowboy boots, well worn, that seemed out of place for a man of the north woods.

"Let me get my cell." She started to head back in.

"Just you guys here?"

"Yeah." The question sent a chill down her back.

"Where is she?"

"I'm sorry?"

"His daughter."

The words sent an instant chill through Jenny. She had spent several years as a roommate to the daughter of the president. She and Merc had lived with the Secret Service for those years. One of the agents had given them a class one weekend. He had warned them repeatedly as to what to look out for.

Jenny turned toward the door. As she did the fear struck the others on the porch. There were screams, but no one heard, as the closest cabin was more than ten miles away and closed for the winter.

The .44 Magnum slug threw her against the front door, slicing through her clothes and splintering the wood as it passed into the cabin. Each woman ran in a different direction and was cut down. The young lady from Texas made it the farthest. She reached the edge of the lake before the blast threw her onto the thin ice. Her body cracked the surface, and she was halfway immersed, face down in the black water.

Jamal went to each body except the one in the lake, searching for their cell phones. He found all of them. He went through their pockets looking for something else. At each body, he scanned the lifeless face, taking a closer look to make sure it was not the target's. Not finding what he needed, Jamal went into the cabin looking for their backpacks and wallets. In one he found a wallet and what he was looking for.

The slip of paper, tucked deep inside the Gucci wallet, had a series of letters, some capitalized, along with numbers and figures.

* * * *

Jamal kept the guns.

It might have been a mistake in an ordinary crime, but it was less risky to keep the weapons than try to obtain new ones. He drove the truck to his SUV. There, Jamal went through the glove compartment and a sealed plastic case in the back seat. In each spot he retrieved more ammunition. The glove compartment had several boxes of the .44 Magnum shells and the ammo box was full of cartridges for the rifle. He quickly threw the guns and ammunition in the back seat and covered them up with a blanket he had pulled out of the truck.

He then drove the guide's vehicle up another side road and ran it deep into the trees. As he pulled through the pines, the limbs would break off and snow would fall onto the windshield. They each made a cracking noise as they hit the top of the truck and slapped back.

There was a ravine just behind the stand of pines. He pulled to the edge, climbed down, put the truck in gear and watched as it rolled forward. It slid down the hillside and settled at the bottom. The snow was still falling and the trail and truck tracks would soon disappear. The engine stopped running when it struck a boulder at the bottom of the ravine.

He walked back through the trees onto the plowed road and jogged the short distance back to the intersection where he had left his SUV. Fortunately, no other cars passed by.

Once in his SUV, Jamal headed south, passed the cabin he had rented for three days, and continued on. He was covered with sweat. His hands shook. Jamal calmed himself by focusing on Lala's face the last time he saw her. She had been in pain, badly dehydrated, but still managed a smile for her father. And then he thought of the man who had sent the bomb that took them all away.

The roads were not so snowed over that the plow trucks weren't well ahead of the conditions. The four-wheel vehicle's tires held the road well and he made good time. He soon was south of Benson, passing the guide's sign, and crossed over into New York shortly after.

Once on Interstate 87, the road became completely clear and he fell in behind a long-haul shipping truck that was running over 90 miles an hour. The truck seemed to be on the same path as Jamal as they quickly reached Albany. There, he looked for the sign to the airport, took the exit, pulled his hat down as he pulled into the long-term parking and found, far in the back, a similar SUV covered with stained, gray snow. As planned, he quickly jumped out, using a screwdriver from a small tool kit he had lifted from the guide's truck and changed license plates. Jamal was back on the road in less time than a security guard would have had the chance to scan any remote camera covering the far back side.

Jamal got back on the interstate, heading south to Newburgh, where he turned west.

As he passed into Pennsylvania, Jamal took an exit just beyond the state line, and took a side road heading towards High Point State Park. There, in a sheltered park area, he went to a picnic table and laid out the cell phones he'd taken from the women, plus the piece of paper. He'd gone far enough south to escape the early-winter snow line. He studied each, then began trying the code. The password worked on one. And with one, he could quickly connect with the others' Instagram accounts. They were in a chain, and each link provided him with insight as to his target.

There was an exchange of photos. The first, dated from just a few days before, showed them all standing in front of the cabin. Merc was in the center.

The next one was from Merc. Her account was private, but this cell had access. It showed her as she passed through a gate in a snow-covered country. Mountains were in the background. He used his fingers to enlarge the frame. Instagram made it easy. It had the name of the location on the photograph.

Yes.

Jamal went to another phone and searched the location on the maps app. *Got it.*

He pulled back on the interstate, heading west.

Just short of Pittsburgh, Jamal turned south, using back roads, went on to Morgantown and just south of there, he saw the turn to Parkersburg. After the turn, he saw what he was looking for. The sign said U.S. Highway 50. He turned west onto it just before midnight. Once in a while, he would break up the trip by taking what was signed as the "old" Highway 50. After he passed through one small town, Jamal saw what he had been looking for. Railroad tracks passed parallel to the highway and a coal train followed him at nearly the same pace. A short dirt road intersected with the highway and track. It was well past one in the morning. Jamal pulled up to the track, looked both ways, crossed it, drove a short distance, and then turned around. As he returned to the track, he could hear the wail of another train coming. Jamal jumped out, took the captured cell phones, ran down the track well into the shadows, and carefully placed each on the rail.

Jamal stopped at a McDonald's drive through just before it closed in West Virginia. He bought several hamburgers, fries, two milkshakes, and two cokes. On the other side of the small town, he pulled into a country gas station, filled up and used the bathroom. He washed his face with the cold water and dried with the paper towels. As he looked into the mirror, Jamal saw a man he barely recognized.

Who is this?

There was only the stubble of not shaving in twenty-four hours, and hair cut close. But he wasn't tired. The adrenaline had pushed him forward. He felt the .44 under his sweater and readjusted it.

"How much is that?" He asked the attendant the cost of a red ten-gallon plastic gas can.

"Five bucks."

"Good." He bought the can, filled it at the pump and put it in the back of the SUV. The rumble of returning to the road jostled the car. Jamal traveled on in the dark with only his headlights, and thought of how long it would take for his trail to be followed.

Time to find them and him missing. Jamal played a game in his mind of working backwards from the murders. He was thinking of the time it would take for someone to find the bodies of the three young women and the guide's corpse. The cabin was well back in the woods and no one would be expected. The guide spent from dawn to dusk in the forest, so he would not be deemed to be missing until at least supper. The calculations meant that he was safely able to travel the interstate system until late that night. They would look for the murderer in Vermont and possibly New York, but he was already beyond those two states. And he would travel, without stopping but for gas and food on side roads, to his target. The night before had given him the sleep he needed, and now the adrenaline passing through his veins kept him on edge.

Jamal passed through several small towns in the dark, with only the occasional fluorescent sign showing a gas station, most of which were closed.

"The gas can may help." He mumbled the words to the only man in the SUV. He liked his idea of an emergency source of fuel. He would drive straight through. No time would be lost.

The weather became a help. After leaving New England, the skies cleared across America. Only when he got back into the mountains of the Rockies would he see clouds. But as he listened to the radio, it described a storm predicted for the West.

Jamal was going to stop and steal another vehicle, but with the change in weather and his making good time, he decided to keep on moving.

"I'll make it in less than a day."

It was important that he got into the mountains before anyone was on his trail. There, he would be impossible to trace.

One sign at the intersection of U.S. Highway 50 and a state road said it all: "America's Loneliest Road."

It would provide safety to a killer.

Chapter 34

Federal Detention Center, Houston

"Face the back of the elevator!"

Reet stood with his nose pressed against the steel door. His orange jump suit was two sizes too big and he could barely keep the flip-flops on his feet. Most of his life, Reet had never worn shoes or socks. He'd received his first sandals when he was twelve. Prison, in some ways, was an improvement.

The elevator took him to the special unit on the seventh floor. He still had shackles on both ankles and his wrists. It was special security for a man charged with the highest crime in the country. The charge was a violation of the United States Code, more specifically, Chapter 18, Section 1751, and meant the death penalty.

Reet was not fazed by the charge. He'd anticipated it since leaving Yemen.

"All the media is outside." The one guard spoke to his compatriot.

"More?"

"Yeah, worse than when the guy wanted to have the federal judge killed."

"I remember that."

The door opened to a set of other guards waiting for the celebrity prisoner.

"They want him downstairs for interrogation in the morning."

The guard on the floor stopped Reet.

"Where's your ID?" He grabbed him by his arm and held him in place. The man was twice the size of Reet.

"He's got it."

The larger one searched the prisoner's shirt. It was tucked in the jumpsuit.

"Keep this out at all times!"

Reet understood half of what they were saying.

"An AR at Rice?" The guard was commenting on Reet's attempted shot with an assault rifle at the president while at a symposium at Rice University.

Reet's plan had fallen apart when he'd paid cash with a false driver's license for the weapon. The pawn shop dealer hadn't been thinking of a terrorist from Yemen when he'd called the police. He'd thought the man with broken English was a Latino with ties to a local gang.

Reet had gotten out of the store with the rifle. He'd tried to cover it up with a blanket he had carried with him from a sixty-nine-dollar motel room he had taken nearby. Reet had bought a newspaper in the dimly lit lobby of the motel. The front page lauded the visit of the president to the Rice campus. The local news shows had helped him to form his plan as well. Since as early as Panama, Reet had gone to the president's web site to see the posted schedule. The local television station and the newspaper had given him the other details he needed. Reet had walked the campus the day before. He'd had a good idea of when the guest would be arriving at the Baker Institute and where the cars would stop. It was a simple plan. He had purchased two banana clips for the automatic rifle with thirty cartridges each. The AR was well-used but functional, and had come with a laser sight. A man determined to die didn't need an extensive plan.

The plan had been to delay not one moment more than necessary after the purchase of the weapon. Moving to the target without hesitation had been his best chance at making the attack work.

"Didn't get away with it?" The guard was making fun of Reet's efforts.

Reet had made it two city blocks before a dozen police cars had him cornered. He'd fumbled with the blanket, trying to load a magazine into the rifle, but never made it. A Houston police officer had taken him out like an NFL linebacker who'd found a hole in the offensive line. Reet's head had bounced off of the concrete sidewalk. It bled profusely and still hurt.

"Put him in number six."

Reet stopped at the center counter facing forward as he was surrounded by no less than six guards.

"We got one in there."

"Everything else is full." The guard looked at a chart on the wall. "It's just for tonight."

"Have you had anything to eat?" There was one guard who seemed to have sympathy for his prisoner.

Reet stared at him with a sheepish look, only half understanding what was being said. He didn't reply.

"Don't think he has." The other guard answered the question.

"We need to get a tray up here."

"I'll call downstairs."

The guards stood there as if someone needed to decide.

"Let's get him in the cell and then we can get him fed."

The larger guard led Reet by his arm down the corridor of doors. Reet saw the cameras at every angle of the jail. The panel of televisions behind the counter seemed to cover every inch of the floor. He saw men pacing back and forth in the cells. One looked empty.

"Number six."

"Okay."

They walked him to a door marked with the number six.

"Open six." The door clicked and the guard swung it open.

They led Reet into the room and sat him down on a cold cement bunk with a thin mattress. The guard used his keys to unlock the cuffs and shackles. He put the chains over his shoulder like he was carrying a towel out of a gym.

As the guards backed out of the cell, Reet first noticed the man sitting in the corner of the room. He was much darker than Reet, his face was spotted by extensive sun exposure, perhaps the beginnings of skin cancer. He had bushy eyebrows and a Hispanic look. He shared the same orange jump suit and a name tag that announced what seemed like a Spanish surname.

"Food will be here shortly." A speaker's voice sounded in the room.

Reet sat on the bench, trying to think of his fate. He had failed his mission, but likewise, he had succeeded. His yells of *Allahu Akbar* as he was being arrested sent a message home to his people. When CNN International carried the story the next day in the Middle East, he would be praised. He made it to the United States and put fear into the hearts of the Americans. Reet would be a hero in his home village.

His cellmate stood up and came towards him.

The intercom yelled some words in English that Reet didn't catch.

"Garcia, sit down."

But Garcia was on a mission just like Reet was. He grabbed the little man and threw him into the cement bench. Garcia was serving several consecutive life sentences for several drug-related murders. He would never see anything other than the table with straps.

Garcia shoved Reet's skull into the edge of the bench until blood spurted out, covering much of both men's orange jump suits. Reet fought for a moment or two, but the attack had come as such a surprise that after the first blow to his skull, it was over. His skull fragments were thrown against the bench and the wall.

The guards rushed in and pulled Garcia off the body.

It took a medic some time to come up the elevator. The large guard put both of his knees on Garcia's back, almost choking out his breath. Soon the cell was full of guards, two medics, and then a doctor in a white coat.

"Oh, shit!" The senior guard knew the ramifications of his brief error. The breaking news would follow the first story.

And the glee of Reet's attempt on the American president would turn sour in his village when they learned of Reet's death. Soon, it would become an American conspiracy that had killed a hero.

Chapter 35

Burlington, Vermont

Will's black Yukon pulled out from Burlington heading south. It was another cold morning, and a light coating of ice had formed on the windshield. He used the wipers to clear the window.

"So, you know where this cabin is?" Will asked his navigator.

"Yep. Got it." Moncrief had been looking at the information Kerr had sent him. "Not too far, but out in the mountains."

"Be nice if we find a sorority party with her there with her friends." Will didn't expect the students to be anything more than a girls' lark on a long weekend, but hoped that the worst that could happen on this bad day was to tell Mercury the bad news about Kerr, if somehow she hadn't already heard. He didn't hold out much hope for that. The news of the crash should have traveled fast, both by national news and the interconnection of the women with their cell phones.

They followed the highway south from Burlington, and the area quickly turned into a rural world. The road was dotted with small farms tucked back in the trees. The occasional barn sat behind the home. They were all coated with a white layer of fresh snow. The trees started to droop as the snow's weight pulled the limbs down. They never saw a car or a truck. The beginnings of winter had started to slow Vermont down.

"Wonder if they need painters up here?" Kevin was looking at the homes, and barns which were mostly made of wood.

"You, in this cold?" Will threw it back at him.

"I handled Bridgeport."

They traveled on in silence for several miles.

"This should be the turnoff." Moncrief pointed to a side road. It headed east into the Green Mountains. After several miles, they came to another side road.

"I think this is it." Moncrief held up his cell phone looking at the details.

"Someone has been through here." The snow had dusted the roadway, but under the light covering, he could see the deep tracks of a truck. They passed a pull off area and then headed further up the road.

"Oh, shit!" Moncrief saw it first.

There, in the middle of the road, a large black dog was dragging itself towards them. He was leaving a bright trail of crimson behind.

Will hit the brakes.

The two got out, slowly approaching the wounded animal. It growled, showing its teeth as the strangers came close.

"Give me the cell." Will took it and hit 911.

They felt helpless watching the animal hold on for life. It seemed to take an eternity for the Vermont State Police unit to show up. Fortunately, Will had given a detailed description, so the officer was followed by a small black SUV well marked with an American flag and "Animal Control" on its side.

A woman with a blue polar fleece jacket got out, gave a glance towards the animal, and then returned to her SUV and pulled out her orange-colored medical kit that looked like a fishing lure box.

"Will he make it?" Kevin asked as he watched her carefully approach the animal and stick it with a dart she had tied to a long, straight stick. The animal, she knew, didn't know who was friend or foe. He would rip apart anyone who came close with his last breath. The drugs worked. The dog whimpered, and then went into a daze.

"He's a pit. Only a pit would make it through this." She pulled him over, and placed a heavy pressure bandage on the wound.

"What do you think?" the trooper asked as he stood nearby.

"Big bullet. Isn't it Fred's?" She seemed to know the pits in the area.

"Yep, he wouldn't let this happen." The trooper hit his microphone on his vest.

"We need some help up here."

* * * *

Will Parker showed the trooper his retired-military identification card. The rank on the card helped. The two were immediately beyond suspicion.

"There's a cabin around here we need to check out." Will's thoughts were already grim.

"Yeah, the Murphy cabin. They rent it out to cross country skiers." The trooper turned to his patrol car. The dog had been gently lifted up by his new caretaker and placed in the back of her SUV. With the dog out of the way, the trooper gave them the signal to follow him and the two vehicles headed up the road.

It wasn't far before they made the turn to the cabin.

Will got out and was struck by the absolute silence. He saw the shapes in the snow and immediately knew what had happened. They stayed for some time as nearly a dozen state troopers descended on the scene, with a crime lab truck and shortly thereafter, a van marked with the letters WCAX-TV and CBS. Will grabbed the trooper, gave him his contact information, and asked to be excused even before the newsmen got out of the van.

"We need to get out of here," he told Moncrief as they climbed back into the Yukon and headed north to the airport. "The man who did this is long gone."

* * * *

At the airport, Will and Kevin sat in the FBO as they drank a cup of coffee.

"I've got to file a flight plan." There was a sense of frustration in the air. It wasn't clear which way to go.

"Look at this." Moncrief showed him the pictures that Kerr had sent. One caught the eye of Parker. It was a place he had been to before.

"This burned down." Will pointed to the photo of the hut in the Rockies. "Lightning several years ago."

"No help."

Will studied the photos. None gave any insight other than the one cabin that had burned down some time ago.

"What did he say she wanted to do?" Will asked the question.

"Not sure that he said."

"Wanted to train. Train hard."

"That narrows it down to several states." Moncrief wasn't helping.

"If you really wanted to train for the biathlon, where would you go?" Will studied the photo again. "What's the snow doing in the Rockies now?"

He answered his own question by flipping Kevin's cell phone over to the search engine and putting in snow conditions for Aspen.

I've got an idea." Will got up and headed to the flight planning office.

"Good, I've got to make a call."

Kevin had been waiting for this for some time. He used his cell phone but went outside so that no one could hear. Especially his pilot. He wanted to have a conversation that Will Parker would not hear.

* * * *

"I've checked on the weather. We may be delayed." While driving back to the airport, a blanket of snow had come across the lake. The flight line was invisible.

"Where to?" Moncrief asked.

"Colorado."

"Won't we need a refuel stop?" Moncrief was ahead of his boss on this mission.

"Yeah." The jet easily topped twelve hundred nautical miles on one tank, but Colorado would be a push at eighteen hundred plus miles. And then there was the weather. One didn't fly into the Rockies pushing it close on fuel. "Best to do two. We can hit South Bend and then refuel at Centennial in Denver."

Moncrief had heard what he wanted to hear.

"Okay." He started texting on his cell.

"What's up?" Will thought Moncrief had been uncharacteristically quiet.

"We probably will need some arctic gear as well."

"We can get that in Leadville."

"I know that town. Something I heard about it. What was it?"

"Perhaps highest airport in the continental U.S.?"

"No, but I'll find out." Moncrief went back outside, under the awning and began texting again.

Sometime later that afternoon, a bright ray of sunlight broke through the dark sky. It took some time for the plows to clear the runway, and then they pulled out the jet. It had been hangared and was as clean as if it had been through a car wash. The white aircraft with its blue trim stood at the end of the flight line just in front of the FBO. The ground crew had an auxiliary power unit attached and steam was coming up from the diesel engine as it brought life to the aircraft.

"Here is the number." Will handed the woman behind the counter a plastic card. It wasn't a credit card or debit card. It had a number on it and a name. "Call that and everything will be taken care of."

She had a look of doubt on her face as she went to the back office to speak with her manager. Through the glass, Will saw him pick up the phone and call. He frowned and then smiled. He handed the card back to her.

"Thank you, sir." She handed the card back. It was clear that the call to the bank officer in Atlanta took care of all charges and convinced them that there would be no problem.

"Let's go." Will headed out the door with Moncrief in tow. The HondaJet was warm, the instruments all on line with their reds, yellows, blues, and greens. The engines spun up, Will spoke to control and in but a brief moment, the jet was well above Burlington and then passed through the clouds before turning west.

* * * *

"Look at this."

Moncrief sat in the co-pilot seat. The aircraft was on autopilot and cruising at over four hundred knots and at forty thousand feet. The winds had been favorable. The aircraft's ground speed was well over five hundred and fifty miles an hour. He had an iPad that was connected, through the aircraft, to the internet. It showed a sleek unmanned turboprop aircraft with the markings of PMA-247 and *Marine*.

"The MUX?" Will had heard of a new aircraft that flew like the osprey. It rose as a helicopter and then transitioned forward as a high-speed turboprop. The machine had, however, no pilot on board. The Bell airship was armed and moved like lightning.

"So?"

"Guess where it's undergoing altitude testing?" Moncrief stopped the video.

"This is what you thought you had heard about?"

"Yes. They have some MCCDC Marines at Leadville testing it now." Will looked at him.

"MCCDC? In Leadville?"

"Yes, sir."

"It's just on the other side of the mountain from the tenth mountain huts near Aspen."

"Yep."

The Marine Corps Combat Development Command was a Corps think tank concerned with technology and the future of the corps.

"And so, this is next?"

"Wonder what it can do…"

* * * *

Will's cell phone rang when they landed in South Bend for a refueling stop. The jet taxied up to another FBO with its name above its hangar— Corporate Wings. The lineman directed the aircraft to a holding spot where Will set the brakes. He missed the call while flying the jet inbound on the final approach to the landing. Once they were stopped and the door open, he and Kevin climbed out.

"Top her off."

The lineman gave the thumbs up and signaled the fuel truck to pull up to the airplane.

"Looks like the trooper." Will glanced at the number. It was from area code 802. "Let me take it in the office." Other jets were on the ramp and were taxiing both in and out. The warm blast of a passing Gulfstream would toss them back on their heels.

"Hello, Parker here."

"Sir, we have a lead." The trooper had promised to share any information he found.

"What's up?"

"Got a good picture of the suspect coming into Burlington Airport just before the killings."

"Just one guy?"

"Yes, the crime scene confirms that as well."

"Can you send it to me?"

"Where?"

"Hold on." Will turned to the counter. "I'm the HondaJet. Is there a computer that can receive an attachment of a photo?"

The young woman was dressed in a uniform like a pilot, with her named monogramed on the shirt as well as the Corporate Wings company name over her other breast. She had bright, long auburn hair that flowed over her shoulders and strikingly perfect features, a pure milk color complexion. But it was her strikingly green eyes that stood out. She smiled at the pilot standing in front of her.

"Yes, sir, whatever you need." She smiled again. "Is that your HondaJet?"

"Yes."

"Tell him to send it to parker12 at corporatewings.com."

"Thanks." He relayed the address to the trooper and shortly thereafter her computer terminal sounded an incoming message.

She opened it up, stopping for a second when she saw it came from the Vermont State Police. Her printer was a high-quality color one, and she brought back the photograph of a man standing at a counter. His head was partially disguised by a baseball hat. But Will could make out his features, and more importantly, his eyes.

"Someone bad?" she asked.

"You see that?" He pointed to a television behind the counter that was on CNN. A newsbreak was showing pictures of a cabin in the snow-packed mountains and there was yellow police tape from tree to tree. The caption said *Multiple Murders—Three Female Harvard Students.*

"Shit," she breathed.

Will went back on his cell. He turned away from the woman and cupped his hand over his phone's mouthpiece. "There may have been a fourth he missed."

"Any idea?" The trooper wanted to know.

"Not sure yet. May have been." Will knew that if he mentioned the involvement of the past president's daughter's, things would get out of control quickly. As much as it might spur the Secret Service to action, if the present White House would let it, the word would also quickly get out to the killer. And if he was right, and Elizabeth Jordan was holing up in a remote cabin in the Rockies, she would have no warning until it was too late.

"Officer, anything missing from the cabin?" Will had a suspicion that he already knew the answer.

"Yea, no cell phones."

"Thanks." The man had a leg up on them.

Chapter 36

Glenwood Springs, Colorado

Jamal was standing at the locked front door as the lights came on.

"Hey, can I help you?" The man unlocking the door had a gray goatee that extended down below his shirt collar. His matching gray hair, which extended over the back of the same shirt collar, and a well-tanned wrinkled face gave him the credentials of someone who owned the Factory Outdoor Outlet store in Glenwood Springs. He wore a well-worn wool plaid red-and-black shirt that seemed like the uniform of those who lived in these mountains.

"I'm going camping with a friend and need some gear." Jamal still had his Dodgers hat on. His clothes looked like he had driven through a carwash, minus the water. The drive across the country, with few stops, had left him looking worn out.

"You came to the right place." Jamal could tell that the store manager usually didn't get a customer waiting at the door when it was first unlocked.

"Yeah."

"Where are you going?"

"Deep into the mountains."

"Anywhere in particular?"

"A hut."

"One of the 10th Mountain ones?"

"Yeah."

"I've got a map for that." He walked behind the counter and pulled out a laminated, waterproof map marked with several spots well back in the mountains.

Jamal had a specific name in mind, but didn't dare disclose it.

"I'll take the map."

"What else?"

"Ah…" Jamal didn't want to show his lack of knowledge as to what he needed.

"Hiking in?"

"Yeah."

"Got it. We can set you up."

An hour later, Jamal had what he needed. He tossed a backpack in the rear of the Hyundai SUV. The truck was covered in dirt, the grime of spent snow, and the wear of crossing the country in a day and a half. He threw a red sleeping bag in the back over the rifle and placed a pair of snow shoes on the floor board.

Jamal next stopped at a gas station and bought a full tank of gas with several twenty-dollar bills, along with some sandwiches from the cooler.

"Where is that?" he asked the clerk behind the counter. The man's face looked like well-worn leather, his Caucasian skin permanently tanned by living outside at this altitude.

"What?"

"That." He pointed to a picture labeled Maroon Lake. Something in the picture had caught his eye.

"Up ten miles. Turn towards the Highlands."

Jamal acted like he knew what was being said.

"I need a map of the roads."

The clerk pointed to a shelf on the other side of the store.

As they were standing there, a man came in and stood behind Jamal. At first he didn't notice him. When he turned around, the deputy sheriff stared at him. Jamal looked at the uniform, but only saw the Glock in its holster.

What? He unconsciously reached to his hip only to feel it empty. The .44 was still in the truck. After driving for twenty-four hours with it poking in his side, Jamal had placed the revolver down between the seats. He glanced over the sheriff's shoulder to see his Hyundai on the far end of the pumps.

"You okay, feller?"

Jamal didn't move. He had unconsciously turned to the side of the officer.

"You okay?"

Jamal saw his lips move. He realized that his damaged ear was pointed directly towards the policeman.

"Oh, sorry!" He pointed to his deaf ear. The blast had also frayed and scarred it enough to make it obvious to a bystander.

"Oh." The sheriff seemed apologetic. "Got that overseas?"

"Yeah."

"Thanks for your service."

"Yes." Jamal picked up the sandwiches and headed for the door.

* * * *

Twenty miles later Jamal drove past the turn to Maroon Creek, then turned on to Castle Creek Road, up Highway 15, and headed into the mountains. The road was well plowed. After traveling the winding road, he saw what he was looking for. The snow was piled up on the side, but a small wide space in the road extended into the woods and had also been well plowed. It was as if the plow truck had used this as a place to turn around.

At the turnaround there was a trace of another highway that turned towards the mountain. A sign, slightly covered and crusted in snow, showed the turn to Highway 15G. This road provided a path across the range and connected in the next valley with Highway 15E. Jamal stopped the car in the middle of the road, got out, and looked both ways. It was dead quiet. He then backed up the Hyundai into the side road, pushing it as far as it could go, slipped out of the vehicle, and tossed snow onto the hood, front window, and roof. Jamal grabbed some green boughs from a pine tree and covered the remainder of the car. When he finished, it was nearly dark. He climbed through the driver's seat, into the back, pulled down the bench, got out the sleeping bag and climbed in. Jamal placed the revolver next to his head, ate one of the sandwiches, and then fell asleep.

Before first light, Jamal changed into his winter gear, tearing off the new tags and stickers, checked his back pack, with the sleeping bag tightly lashed to a small, light frame, put on the new snowshoes, pulled out the map, and turned to the mountain. He had two jugs of water that he clipped to the pack.

Jamal checked on the most important items last. The big rifle was slung over his shoulder and he slipped the .44 into his front pocket. He loaded a box of extra shells for both the .338 Magnum rifle and .44 pistol, plus extra cartridges in his two side pockets.

A visit from the trooper would not end well.

Jamal had spent many a night in the mountains of Yemen. The capital of Sanaa alone rose over 7,000 feet. Jabal An-Nabi Shu'ayb, a peak nearby, reached 12,000 feet, and during a life of fighting Jamal had often used those mountains as a place to hide and from which to strike. In the mountains of Yemen, Jamal had needed less gear. They would hike the rocky ground with sandals and carry one blanket that doubled for a coat and a sleeping cover. Caves protected them from the Saudi drones and fighter jets. Every day, Jamal and his men would move, changing caves and sleeping under overhangs of rocks, always aware that they were targets. These mountains were easier. Except for one problem.

"Damn snow!" Jamal hadn't worn boots in the mountains of Yemen, and had never worn snowshoes. He had learned quickly that one followed the faint outline of the road, as once he'd wandered off it and fallen into a smothering blanket of soft, dry snow. It had taken him most of an hour to climb out, using the rifle as a support, and work his way back onto the road. He was now soaked in sweat, and stopped and drained one of the water bottles before again heading out. The trip took most of a day. Well before dark, at the intersection where the highway split again and pointed up the valley, Jamal set out his small tent, pulled his sleeping bag in, and used a small propane heater to boil some of the fresh snow.

"My Lala." He spoke the words as the sun set, on his knees in the tent, turned to the east. He used some of the water sparingly and washed, then said his prayers. "Tomorrow may bring what I have come for."

The odd thought he had was that he barely knew what she looked like. He had only seen a few pictures on the news, and he knew the pictures rarely told the story. He had abandoned all of the cell phones long ago, knowing that they were a tracking danger.

On my own. Jamal knew he was well beyond any help. There would not be a friendly face within ten thousand miles.

At least all are targets. Any man or woman who approached was apt to be a danger. Therefore, any who approached would soon be dead.

Jamal was well trained for the final part of his mission.

* * * *

"Hello?" A voice woke Jamal from his tent. He reached for the .44, felt its cold steel on his bare hand, and slowly unzipped the tent. There was more sunlight than he had expected. Perhaps the chill of the air or the warmth of the sleeping bag had brought on a deep sleep. It seemed well into the morning.

"Hello?" The voice repeated the call.

"Yes!" Jamal stuck his head into the cold air. There was still a cover of clouds and a light snow was falling.

"We saw your tent. Are you okay?" A man with a woman stood on their cross-country skis, resting their hands on their poles.

"Yes, thank you."

"Need anything?" Those that came through the mountains were like the men and women he knew in the mountains of Yemen. It was the word of Allah that travelers shared.

"No, I'm fine, thank you." Jamal pressed the revolver to his side.

"Not many travel alone in these mountains." The man leaned forward on his poles.

"Yes, I'm meeting someone."

"Oh, right..." The man seemed to think he know what Jamal meant

"She's expecting you." The woman chimed in from behind the man.

"Oh, great." Jamal forced a broad smile.

"Lindley's closed, but she's in Barnard."

From his study of the map, Jamal knew that hut was the closest to the back side of Aspen Mountain and near Star Peak.

"Oh, thank you so much." Jamal smiled. "How far to Barnard, would you say?"

"Snow's deep, but shouldn't be more than a day."

"You're a help."

"We're heading back. Been up here for several days." The woman had a broad smile as if to confirm that it was the ending of a vacation to be remembered. "We left some extra food with her so you should be okay."

"I can't thank you enough!" Jamal hesitated. "Seen anyone else up here?"

"Not a soul."

"Okay." He'd learned what he needed to know.

The couple turned back towards the trail that led back down the mountain. By now, Jamal had hastily pulled on his jacket and boots and come fully outside the tent. As the skiers started to leave, the man looked back at Jamal. His gaze lingered. It was then that Jamal realized that he had left the revolver at the edge of the tent, within sight. They shared a look and then the man started to ski away, hard.

Jamal scooped up the gun, reached into the tent, grabbed the sleeping bag, and pulled it out. He wrapped the pistol with the bag, aimed and squeezed the trigger. The sound was somewhat muffled and the bag's stuffing flew everywhere, but the man struck the snow as if he had been hit in the center of the back by a sledgehammer. His girlfriend screamed out. She stopped, reaching for the slumped over body, but the hesitation in escaping made her an easy target. Jamal lined up the shot and fired again with the bag as a makeshift silencer. The slug hit her in the head, just below her wool ski cap. A spray of bright red blood covered the snowdrifts beyond the bodies.

Jamal approached the two with his revolver trained on the targets. He kicked the lifeless bodies and then looked around, out of habit, to see if there were any witnesses. There were none. He dragged the bodies, one at a time, to place them below a small-growth pine. As he worked, Jamal sank in the snow, struggling to pull the dead weight as his legs went down in the soft banks. The work, particularly at the altitude, caused him to pant, reaching for any breath. When the woman's body was under the pine, he stopped, seeing a small backpack she was wearing. It had a pink water bottle clipped onto it. He took the bottle, drank some of the cold water, kicked some of the loose snow over the two, and went back to the tent.

Need to move. Jamal quickly packed the tent, finished dressing, put on his snow shoes, and headed out towards Star Peak. He put on his backpack, wadded up the punctured sleeping bag, and quickly buried it under another small pine. The snow was now falling in earnest and would quickly cover up the scene of the crime. Soon, he hoped to find the last road, and thereafter, Barnard. The storm continued to build and a wind caused the sheets of snow to come down at an angle. He pulled his hood down as low as he could and held on to the sunglasses. They were not needed for any blinding light, but rather, to stop the icy flakes from burning his eyes. The clouds coming in from the west were black and angry.

Ka-boom...

A clap of thunder caused him to fall back over his snow shoes.

A winter thunderstorm was coming across the range. The storm made the mountains especially dangerous.

Chapter 37

"Boss, try that one." Kevin pointed to a large hangar marked with the words "TAC Air" at the executive airport just south of the larger one of Denver. The HondaJet had just taxied off of the active runway and the tower was asking which ramp the jet wanted.

"Okay…" Will looked at his co-pilot with a thin smile. He soon understood why Moncrief had made the request.

Near the TAC hangar, two figures stood just off the flight line, next to several brown duffel bags and a black box the size of a Marine foot locker. Will didn't recognize the two until the jet taxied close enough to see the shape of the person. He turned to Moncrief, but this time he didn't smile.

"Figured we needed a doctor on this one." Kevin clearly knew he was in trouble, but no one would be turning around and going home.

The jet pulled up to its mark and stopped.

"Hello, Dr. Stidham." Will's greeting was chilly. "Are you sure about this? And Hernandez, you a part of this scheme as well?"

"Since I shot my first rifle." Kaili Stidham didn't hesitate.

Hernandez did. He looked like a kid caught in a candy shop.

"I'm not so sure of that." Will looked her directly in the eyes. "We're hunting down a killer."

"I know. Three college students who didn't do anything wrong." Kaili looked him in the eye. "I can imagine their last moments."

"But can you kill a mad dog?"

"I've seen as much death as you. And I can get mad too." Kaili was already dressed in 5.11 Tactical gear from head to toe, all black, a tactical XPRT rapid shirt, cargo pants, storm boots, and a black cap with her short hair extending from underneath. Staff Sergeant Hernandez was likewise in his combat gear, but his was desert brown.

"Probably more." Moncrief added.

Will gave him a look that would have meant a demotion if the two had been on active duty.

"They brought some important gear," said Moncrief.

"We can take a look at it in Leadville." Will gave his orders, and with them, his reluctant approval.

"I've brought my M-17 bag." She held up a large rectangular brown bag. "Not only the medic-issued gear, but also some other items that might be needed."

"Okay." It was an argument Will couldn't refute. Every Marine mission had a medic.

The jet was refueled, the FBO called the bank's number for payment, and the aircraft was almost ready.

"We have this." Moncrief tossed the duffel bags into the aft baggage compartment of the aircraft. They were sealed with red plastic Velcro straps marked with the letters DARPA. "Should be some help."

"The weather doesn't look good." Will had a printout of the weather map from the FBO. The chart had tight millibar lines that covered the mountains. Some were close together in a pattern that showed a wave followed by another wave. "We may not make it in."

* * * *

The HondaJet rose quickly to altitude, but as it started to cross the first peaks of the front range west of Denver, the aircraft jumped and dropped. The clouds were dark and ominous, and even at their altitude, sheets of snow blanketed the airplane. The trip to Leadville was short, but the weather was relentless. They were flying blind, being buffeted by the storm, until Will descended into the high valley near the small town. The aircraft fell down, like a roller coaster out of control, in visibility so poor that Moncrief could not see the nose of the jet. He held his hand on a handle just to the side of the co-pilot's seat, bracing for the next bump. Will noticed that Moncrief's hand was turning white as the tension squeezed off his circulation.

"Hold on." Will focused on his instruments, unfazed by the whiteout.

The airplane continued to descend and then suddenly, like someone coming out from behind a curtain, came into sunlight. The small town of Leadville seemed to be sitting in a gap in the storm. The snow-covered valley below was a blinding white. Will banked the aircraft in a sharp turn, followed by another, using the radio and lined up with a small single strip of asphalt. Even as he banked to his final approach, the aircraft bounced wildly. It sank, slowly, crossing the threshold, with its wheels and landing gear down and fixed, hitting the runway with a quick squeal of rubber on the pavement. The runway had a well plowed strip down the center.

"Did you see what's next to that last hangar?" Moncrief spoke through his headphones.

Will leaned up, looking over his panel, seeing several large shelters being used for hangar bays. In one of them was something he had never seen before.

"So, that's it?" Will studied the craft beneath the makeshift bay.

The nose of a strange, sleek air machine stuck out at one end. It was an odd sight, as there were no windows for the pilot. Nevertheless, it had an aerodynamic shape: The wings were tilted up, and large, black blades pointed to the top of the shelter. The airplane, particularly with the blades, barely fit in the small hangar.

Otherwise, the remainder of the encampment was much smaller. The rows of tents looked like the early days of Camp Bastion airfield in Afghanistan. There were also two gray, sleek Bell UH-1Y Super Huey helicopters on that end of the flight line. The word "Marines" in a dull black shone on the Venoms' tail booms.

A Marine in a thick brown parka watched as the HondaJet taxied to a location just to one side of the flight operations building. He was wearing the "happy suit." whose official name was the extreme cold weather parka, with matching pants. He saluted as the jet came to a stop.

The crew climbed out into the sub-zero cold. The clear air over Leadville had also brought a brutal drop in the temperature. Their breath set out clouds of fog as they were met by the Marine.

"Sir, Gunny Wilbur Works." He shook Will's hand.

Will was surprised by the greeting until Works turned to Moncrief.

"You son-of-a-bitch, still short!" Works extended his hand to his fellow gunnery sergeant.

"Still tall enough to kick you in the…" Moncrief stopped when he realized that Kaili Stidham was standing behind him.

"And you must be Shane's daughter?"

"Yeah," she said quietly.

"Served two tours with him. I am very sorry for your loss."

"Thank you."

It felt like a gathering of a family.

"So, got you a tent, some of our happy suit gear, over whites, warming layers, MSRs if you need them…and what else?"

"Thanks, Gunny." Will followed as Works headed towards one of the tents. It had several large flexible air ducts that were attached to the tent and a humming noise. The tent bulged like a hot air balloon being inflated.

"So, how is it going?" Moncrief opened the question.

"This bird will be a game changer." Works showed them a tent of bunks, already equipped with cots and sleeping bags.

"No cockpit windows," Will said.

"No need. This V-247 is tilt-rotor just like the Osprey. You know what the identification means?" Works didn't wait for a response. "Missions twenty-four hours, seven days, no stopping it."

"How's it doing on altitude?" Will asked.

"That's why we're here." Works stopped. "Doing great. Want some coffee?" He led them into a small mess tent. "Guess I need to ask why you're here."

"We're trying to help out a Marine." Will didn't get into Mike Kerr's request, their mission, or even the possibility of danger out there.

Works nodded and sneaked a glance at Kaili. "Whatever you need."

* * * *

Will and Kevin tried the cell phone number that Mike had given Moncrief again. There was still no answer. They tried to locate the phone, but the mountainous terrain would not let anything through.

The mess had a small television that they watched as they sat at a table with a map in front of them. Will looked up at the news. A man in Houston, arrested in a failed attempt on the former president's life, had been murdered while in custody. The media had already identified him as a known terrorist from Palestine. The broadcaster noted that authorities believed that the man was not alone, that he'd come across the Mexican border through a tunnel of the cartel, and that his death might have been a result of that tunnel being discovered. It went on to describe the gunfight in Calexico resulting in the death of several members of the cartel, and another gunfight at a house just inside the American border.

"Related?" Will posed the question to the group.

"One to get the former president, another to get his daughter?"

"Maybe. They sure came a long way to try."

"Any chance he'd get into these mountains?" Moncrief swiped his hand over the range of mountains on the map before him.

"Yea. He had the others' cells and knew where to go. And he could drive straight through. He would be ahead of us." Will worked the math in his mind. If the man had driven through the night, he would be in Colorado by now. Only a madman on a mission of revenge could keep going without sleep. But the more Will learned of this, the more he believed that it was possible.

"An underestimation can get someone killed."

"Yeah, Team D in Afghanistan." Moncrief spoke of the Marine ANGLICO team assigned to help the Georgians defend an airbase. They'd tried to take out a missile launch site in the hills above the base, but it had been a trap. Every Marine that had made it through infantry training knew that the most effective killing field was the shape of an L. The cross-fire would mow down anything standing in its way.

"I think I know where she might be. If we go in with an attack force, if he's there, she would never make it." Will studied the map. "Plus, she doesn't know about Mike. She won't know who to trust. I need to go in on foot."

"Okay."

"Let's see if that Venom can drop me off at Independence Pass tomorrow before first light."

"More weather is coming in." Wilbur Works brought the news into the tent.

"How bad?"

"Bad, and closing in fast. Got the chopper pilots to commit, but only if we get it going now."

"How about the cavalry, Colonel?" Works was speaking to the fact that the window was closing on the weather, and if there would be other help, it needed to be called in now.

"And if this is a waste? If she isn't there or is having a glass of wine with her friends?" Will had more to lose by calling in help. "And if they show up at the wrong time? While she has a gun to her head? Can a bird get me up to the Pass?"

"It can," said Works. "But only if you leave in the next hour."

Chapter 38

Barnard Cabin

"What?" Merc heard the odd, muffled sound beyond the ridge. She knew what it was. The blast echoed across the valley. It was followed by another close at hand.

"Blowing an avalanche risk on the slope at Highlands," she told herself. "Or Aspen."

The snowfall had seemed unstoppable during the last week, causing the risk at the ski resorts to increase daily. Between the storms, the sun broke through and warmed the slopes. Then, at nightfall, the temperatures dropped to well below freezing. One night, it had fallen to below zero. It had become the perfect deadly condition for danger on the mountains—a layer of ice covered by a pile of fresh snow. Tons of weight hung in the balance, ready to be triggered at the slightest provocation.

The ski patrol had its remedy. In the mornings, they would climb up to the overhangs, plant charges, and cause a controlled avalanche. If an avalanche could ever be called *controlled*...Another muffled sound followed shortly after the first. It didn't alarm her except for one thought.

Odd. In the days she had been there, Merc had heard several of the same sounds. But they had come earlier in the morning, usually well before the slopes opened. These were different.

The visibility continued to decrease as the snow continued to fall.

Pow...

"God!" She breathed the word as the flash of light was followed by the boom. The bolt of lightning sent a surge of fear through her body. But the odd sound after a brief flash of light seemed muffled for a thunderclap. It caused her to step back from the porch and take shelter in the hut. Unlike the previous two blasts, this one had come from the heavens.

In the nanosecond of the strike, she followed the bolt down towards the valley just beyond a ridge. It seemed to leave a vapor trail as the charged electrons passed through the cold air full of water molecules.

Oh, great. She thought about how much metal she carried with her on her training runs. Starting with her rifle.

A lightning rod on my back.

Her poles didn't help.

Merc glanced at her Apple Watch. Normally, by this time she was starting her first run. She had developed a well-disciplined routine. Before first light, she would exercise, do yoga for stretching, and eat her power breakfast. The oatmeal was starting to run low. And still, she had not heard from Mike. She checked her cell, but it showed no connection with the outside world.

Guess it's time to head in. There was a race at Snow Mountain Ranch in two weeks, but she was not ready yet. She had taken a flyer that was hung on a nail in the cabin wall. It noted that this was the first race of the season and there was a women's 15 kilometer. But it required her taking the rifle-safety course. Without it, she couldn't use her .22 caliber rifle. Moreover, she generally lacked confidence. Mike was her source of strength. He was the one who'd told her that she could actually do this.

"I need you," she said to the person missing from the conversation.

Merc looked outside again. The storm had made the visibility drop further; now she could barely see the pines down the valley.

"Guess I'll pack. But probably won't get out today." Merc knew that if she attempted it, she would probably only make it several hundred yards before needing to turn around. If she didn't, the hut would disappear behind her. And the way to Aspen would be cloaked by the storm.

"I'm going to kill him when I see him."

Chapter 39

Leadville Airport

The wind howled as the tent's sides flapped. The sunlight had left the valley and it became increasingly dark.

A fluorescent light lit up the table.

Moncrief came in with one of the brown duffel bags. It had the red tag that showed the letters DARPA above the smaller letters that said Secret. He put the bag on a camp-type chair and pulled off the tag.

"A couple of gifts from my friend in Virginia." Kevin had worked with the gunnery sergeant assigned to the Marine liaison officer at DARPA. "We're officially conducting a field test." He was addressing the fact that much of what he had in his surprise bag was not yet ready to leave the laboratory. This kind of "field testing" broke every parameter used for actual gear. If the gear helped this mission, it would be used. It was only testing in the sense that there would be no control except whether the gear worked. But that didn't matter.

"What's that?" Will was handed a small, clear case with a pill inside of it no bigger than a large Tylenol.

"This provides an automatic password. No need to remember numbers or letters, and it gets you into this Semper FiPad." Moncrief handed him the combat-tested iPad and another water bottle. "Best to drink plenty of water anyway."

Will studied the pill and then took it with the entire bottle. He knew that forcing all the water he could in the next few hours would buy him time before dehydration started to set in.

"Drink all you can hold." Kaili Stidham came through the tent opening as he was chugging down the water.

"And you know these." Kevin held two skin-colored patches.

"What's that?" Kaili held out her hand. She examined the packages. "Modafinil?"

"Yea. Only if needed." Moncrief gave the warning.

"A eugeroic." Kaili handed the patches back to Will. The drugs were apt to create a warrior on overdrive. "My guess is this will seriously hype you up. No naps with this."

"He said to use only if pushed to the limit." Moncrief shared the warning that the DARPA Marine had given him.

"If the guy you think is out there, he may be on Captagon," Kaili added.

"What ISIL uses?" Will asked. "They don't stop no matter how much lead is in them."

"Exactly."

"They were on that in Fallujah. Pretty much requires a head shot." Will had on a set of over-whites that covered his winter clothing. He put the patches in a pocket underneath his outer layer.

'You may need this as well." Kaili handed him a small canvas bag that easily fit into his backpack.

"What's this?"

"Blood clot, something for shock, and some fentanyl." Dr. Stidham's emergency medical kit had all of the big stuff. "Haven't used these in some time, but we have some lollipops."

"The fentanyl?"

"Yeah, don't bite on them." The narcotic had been formed into a lollipop so that a severely injured man could slowly absorb the drug. "The blood clot kit is what the IDF uses."

Will was impressed. "Israel Defense Force? How did you get this?"

"Got my sources." Kaili Stidham smiled with the pleasure of knowing that she had surprised the Marine.

"Got the sweater on?" Moncrief was referring to the other item that had been provided by his friend at DARPA.

"Yeah." Will had used it before. The sweater was made from spider threads that had been chemically infused in such a way that the strands were essentially as strong as Kevlar. A bullet would bruise but not penetrate.

Will had the other gear on the table before him. He picked up his semi-automatic pistol.

"Will that stop someone?" Moncrief asked. The Heckler & Koch USP Compact 9mm fit snugly in Will's hand. It was smaller than what they'd used in missions before.

"With these it will." He handed Moncrief one of the magazines for the pistol.

"What's this?" Moncrief studied the bullets. They were shaped in a different way than what he had seen before.

"PolyCase Inceptors." Will pushed one of the rounds out from the clip and handed it to Kevin. "Penetrate up to sixteen inches. Even with this." He handed Moncrief a short black tube.

"Crux?"

"Yep. Axe 9." The small tube was officially known as a suppressor, but most laypeople would call it a silencer.

"What about the AR?"

"If she's alone, don't need it. If he's there already, he'll know as soon as he sees it who I am."

Will's plan was to use his over-whites until he got close, and then shed them if there were two at the hut. Underneath, he had dressed in a gray camo parka with snow pants. The Canada Goose gear would be upscale and civilian. His backpack was also civilian, but he wore a black pair of gloves that looked slightly different. The gloves had a special feature: he could work the FiPad with them on.

"All the shit you need to be a deadly warrior," Moncrief said.

Will smiled.

"Are you scared?" Kaili asked.

It was followed by silence and a look from Moncrief that said *Why did I bring you here?*

Moncrief answered for Will. "If he's scared, the other guy better take his game to a new level."

"Hope all we're doing is letting a woman know that someone is not coming for her." Will said.

The wind gusted into the tent as Wilbur Works came inside.

"We best get going if we're going at all." Gunny Works had his hood pulled over his head from the "happy suit" with gloves, pants, and white arctic-styled boots.

The flight line had two Venom-series Hueys spinning up, causing a gust of cold air and a blinding ground snow. The helicopter's crew chief was standing on one of the runners with his headset attached to a cable that ran into the aircraft. He was giving a frantic wave to the three.

"Where's Hernandez?" Will asked in a shout over the sound of the helicopter to Moncrief.

"He's helping out with the MUX in its control room. You have maps on the FiPad and can see what the MUX sees when it's on station," Moncrief shouted. "I'm going with you to the drop-off. She's staying here."

Will gave him a look that said *Really?*.

"Says she's afraid of helicopters flying in snowstorms."

"And who asked if we're afraid?" Will got in the dig.

"I've got faith in her, Colonel." Moncrief always reserved the rank for only those special points that he wanted to make.

They climbed on board, and the Venoms' turbines spun up to a louder level of sound. The small cabin had Will's cross-country skis, poles, and backpack. Soon they headed up the valley, with the two flying in formation. The aircraft was frequently blinded by a wave of snow, followed by a short break. In the breaks, Will looked down to see a two-lane road with no cars or trucks, fences and cattle bunched together braced for the storm.

The Venom seemed to climb, then suddenly descend, in a roller coaster run of ups and downs. He felt the bird turn, and heard what sounded like the jet engine straining as the helicopter tried to gain altitude. Will's last glance of the ground was an iced-over lake, with an even smaller two-lane road, winding in turns and curves into a white, snow-covered forest of trees. A small group of buildings were on both sides of the road like the final gas station stop before entering into the mountains.

A single man stood on the front porch of one of the buildings looking up at the strange sight of two gray helicopters just above his head, plunging into the wall of white. His building had a chimney that was producing smoke from a fire inside.

The crew chief slid over to the two men on one knee and shouted, "Hold on! If we can make it, this will be the worst." He stayed on one knee. "Lucky this is a Yankee." The Venom had an advantage that prior Hueys didn't. "Yankee" indicated the designation Y. In military language, it meant that this had two brand-new General Electric engines that provided more power than any Huey before.

"Got new FLIR as well." He was speaking of the forward-looking infrared system that gave the pilot a view of the mountains through the snow and absent visibility. "But we got to worry about droop."

Even with Will's time as a pilot and his many missions flown on helicopters, he hesitated. "What?"

"If you get high enough, the blades can lose their lift."

In these mountains and with this storm, there would be no gentle landing.

Will felt the nose point upward; the aircraft banked left and moved slowly up the ridgeline.

"Where's the other one?" Moncrief shouted to the chief.

"He's not as crazy."

* * * *

The Venom continued to climb. Will felt the sensation of being on a rollercoaster just before it topped the peak. They were pushed back in their seats. The aircraft continued to bank and turn and climb.

The crew chief hit his switch to reply to the pilot. He gave his passengers a thumbs-up and slid the door open. The fridge gust of air came into the cabin as the helicopter seemed to stop mid-air and hold its position until a gust caused it to rise, and then fall.

"This is as close as we can get. You aren't going to be on the ground," the crew chief shouted.

Will slid to the door. It seemed to be nothing but a fog of white.

"He says you're about ten feet up."

The FLIR gave the pilot the view that his passengers didn't have. He also was wearing a "heads-up" helmet. Through its visor, he saw an overlay of terrain and data that the others could not. Still, with the lack of depth in the snow-covered terrain, much of it was flying with skill and feel.

"Okay." Will put his feet on the skids, and then slowly worked his feet to the edge.

"One final weapon if you need it!" Moncrief shouted. "The DARPA box! It's Nimbus!"

Will was aware of the project.

"Only if you need it. He wasn't sure of the strike zone."

"If I need it, you'll know!" Will gave him a knuckle bump.

"Semper Fi!" Moncrief shouted to Will as he jumped, falling to the snow bank below. It was a safe bet since the snow cover was several feet thick—as long he didn't hit an out-of-place boulder.

He hit the snow, bending his knees as in the many parachute drops he'd made, and rolled deeper into a snow drift. Will quickly stood up, moving away from the aircraft as his skis, poles, and pack followed him to the ground. He saw Moncrief smile and give him a thumbs-up. Will returned the message.

The Venom turned to the west and then dropped over the side of the mountain like a car being pulled off of a cliff. Soon, the whine of the engines disappeared into the wall of snow. It became almost instantly quiet.

Will surveyed his gear, put skins on his skis, mounted them, checked the FiPad, and took a bearing. He stuck his hand into his parka below the over-whites and felt the semi-automatic in his shoulder holster. He then started out over a ridge line that would connect him to the valley beyond Aspen.

A sign, covered in ice and snow, had some words visible.

"Independence Pass." And below "12,095 feet," the words "Continental Divide" were mostly obscured.

The journey would be dangerous. Will knew this from his days at Bridgeport. Like the Mountain Warfare Training Center, this back country held deep ravines and mountain creeks that could drop off in an instant.

Will's Fi-Pad was loaded with maps of the areas, and he had placed the coordinates of two huts in the system. It was their best guess as to where Merc would be. They were the closest to the back side of Aspen Mountain. Since she was there for isolated training, she would pick a hut near a valley and, with her being alone and waiting for Kerr, not too deep into the backcountry.

The most dangerous path was a descent down to Grizzly Creek where he could follow it to a small lake by the same name. At the end of the ridgeline from the Pass, he would need to climb down, following the drop of the creek to the valley below.

Will made it to the edge of the drop rapidly, cutting his skis through the fresh snow.

The storm seemed to be increasing in intensity.

Will stopped to drink some water from a bottle in his backpack, and as he did, he realized he was only a few feet away from dropping off a precipice. The tips of his skis were nearly at the edge.

Shit. He thought of how close the danger had come. A fall of more than a thousand feet would end it all. With the FiPad on him, his compatriots would hunt for his body and, with luck, find it before the snow melted in the spring.

Will perched on the edge of the cliff, looking at the FiPad, studying the descent.

As he stood there on his skis, the silence was broken by the fall of water nearby as it dropped over the rocks.

"There we go." He pulled back with his skis, slowly and carefully away from the edge, following the tracks he had left, to a safe point where he turned and followed the sound of the creek. At the creek, he dismounted and tied the skis and poles to his backpack, which he dragged behind him as he slowly worked his way through the rocks and down the drop in the terrain.

When he reached the valley, Will stopped, took off his over white jacket and his parka, and rested on a rock below the cover of a tall pine, sitting there as the steam from his body heat caused its own fog. He studied the FiPad as he cooled off, plotting his course to the first hut.

"Goodwin-Greene should be in the next valley." Will had taught his Marine mountain students to not fight the terrain. Sometimes it was better to go several miles out of the way than climb a mountain, particularly where the mountains held deadly drops.

"It's going to be dark soon." He judged the fading light. "Won't make it to the first hut in the dark." Will looked at a past satellite photo of the valley he was in and saw near Grizzly Reservoir what he needed. He'd wanted to move fast; for that reason, he didn't carry a tent. The plan was making it to a hut for shelter, and then moving from hut to hut, but the storm didn't make it easy. He needed protection from the wind, and the campground had the chance of providing him with what he needed.

Once on the valley floor, he found the trace of a gravel road heading towards the small lake and followed it quickly. As he put his skis back on, the sweat had turned to a chill, and now the movement brought back heat to his body.

Darkness had fallen over the valley well before sunset as the blizzard continued relentlessly. Will had a small light but didn't want to use it, as it would only reflect back on him with the sheets of snow and might give away his position to anyone out there. He sensed the portal area, even in the darkness, as it was a clearing at the edge of the frozen lake.

Got it!

Will had found what he was looking for.

He lacked a proper hut, but the campground's wooden-planked picnic table with cement legs would provide the shelter he needed for the night. Will used his over-white pants as bedding, and the jacket as a makeshift tent that blocked out the snow.

Tomorrow, he thought, *we find the young woman and get her out of here.*

Chapter 40

The Valley below Richmond Hill

Jamal was thrown back on his ass, his bad ear ringing, the heat from the metal bindings in his snowshoes having passed through his boots to the bottoms of his feet. He was under the limbs at the edge of an aspen grove. Across from where he sat, there was a burnt ring in the snow, a puddle of water, and a smoldering piece of metal and fractured wood.

He had laid the rifle against a snow-covered boulder for a moment when the bolt of lightning had struck. A moment before, Jamal had had the weapon slung over his back. The electricity would have blown through his body. His journey would have ended there.

Allah wants me to finish this.

Jamal took the near miss as a message from above that he would finish this mission. It was meant to be that he would end the life of another, as Lala's life had been ended.

Jamal sat in place as the snow continued to drop onto his face. It struck his face like small hot irons pecking the skin.

I miss home. Yemen was torn in shreds from one end to another, but his war was to save it for other Lalas. To save his religion. His beliefs didn't hesitate.

I miss Bushra's khubz tawwa.

His mother's bread had always been warm and crisp. The taste lingered in his memory as if it were yesterday. The thought reminded him of Bushra's death. A Saudi bomb from one of its fighter jets. The hate had begun with the loss of his mother. He had just celebrated his tenth birthday.

The thought of his mother's bread brought back the memory of a fight he'd had several years later as a teenager. A boy in his village had yelled out Bushra's name. Jamal picked up a rock the size of a golf ball and threw it at his head with all the force he could muster. The Americans wouldn't understand that you never spoke the name of someone's mother. Nor mention a sister. It was as low as another could stoop.

"Must go." He was talking to himself. Jamal could feel his heart pounding in his chest. The near-miss made him feel as if the organ were coming out of his chest. "Must go."

Jamal slowly picked himself up from the base of the tree that he had used as a backstop. He shook the snow from his coat, refastened his boots to the snow shoes, adjusted his backpack and pulled the revolver out from his pocket. The cylinder had several spent cartridges in it, which he ejected and reloaded. Jamal pulled out the water bottle he had stolen and took a long draw. The water was cold and worked on his thirst.

Thirst...

Water would be needed soon. He had lived in a desert for much of his life, but this was a different type of thirst. The altitude made his mouth dry even after drinking.

Jamal had to make it to the hut before dark set in again.

Your map. He was a good map reader. It was an important skill he had learned in the combat he'd endured for the past decade. A soldier that was lost was a dead one. And even with the snow, Jamal knew the mountains. He'd always had a good sense of locale. Even when fishing with his father on the sea, he could have been out of sight of land and known which way to head home. The sky could have blocked out the sun and he would know which way to go.

That way. He pointed his pole toward a gap in the mountains and in a direction to the west. Jamal couldn't see the hills ahead, nor the gap between the peaks that he would have to cross over to the other valley, but he knew he was right. Beyond the finger, he would follow the bare outline of the road that was marked on the map. It would head up the valley. All of this he did with a combination of map memory and his built-in radar.

Thinking of his mother's bread reminded him of the fact that he hadn't eaten in some time. When he took the woman's water bottle, he had looked through her backpack and found several power bars. He still had them in his pocket.

Jamal pulled out one of the bars and ripped through its wrapper. It was a frozen chunk of chocolate chips and oats.

"How do they eat these things?" It was like his eating a bar of soap. He forced himself to consume the entire protein bar, then washed it down with the remaining water in her bottle.

"It's better than the jungle" he told himself. The words brought back his memory of how far he had come. From one extreme climate to another.

Hot to cold. The bottom of the world to the top.

The extreme opposites reminded him again of why he'd come.

Lala.

Jamal didn't even have a photograph of the child. He only had the memory of her wearing her small sandals. But the memory was fading. His picture of her small face and curly hair was slipping away. As were those of his wife and his lieutenant.

"Nothing to bury." It was as if the three never existed.

Jamal stood up and began the journey.

What after?

He thought as he put one foot in front of another. He would never return to Yemen. He would die in this strange land. His body would not receive the burial it was due, but in his village they would praise his name. He would be remembered until the child of the child of the child of the youngest member in his village had become an old man.

They will remember that I was the one.

It meant much to him.

Chapter 41

The Airfield at Leadville

"What's up?" Moncrief stepped into the dome tent next to the makeshift hangar that sheltered the large drone aircraft.

"Just getting ready to make the run." A Marine corporal sat at the table with three large computer terminals. A thick cushion raised him up in the camp chair. To his side was Hernandez.

"Is it loaded?" Kevin asked Hernandez.

"Yep, on and ready." He was talking about the silver cylinder that hung under one of the drone's wings. Hernandez had some ammo-tech experience from serving with a Cobra attack helicopter squadron. Even though he didn't have the military designation, or MOS as the corps called it, he had on-the-job training aplenty. If Will had been there, he would have been the second one present with an ammo-tech background.

"Any problems?" Moncrief asked.

"No, came with directions."

"Good. Just in case."

Moncrief saw on one of the computer screens a security-camera-type view of the airfield from an angle that showed several Marines using a tug to pull the MUX drone out from its cover. The snow continued to drop, but they pulled the aircraft down a ramp and onto the center of the main runway.

As they stood there, the screens before the corporal drone operator came alive. He had a joystick in the center and the throttle controls of a jet pilot.

"How long have you done this?" Hernandez asked.

"You mean can I fly this fifty-million-dollar machine?" The young Marine had the attitude that made them Teufelhundens. "I'm Group 5 trained."

"Okay?"

"You must be old corps." The Marine threw back a barb.

"Old *gunny.*" Moncrief gave him the reminder of exactly who he was. It translated into the universal truth that one did not mess with a Marine gunnery sergeant, whether active or retired.

"Group 5 is the big drones like the Air Force use. I spent a year with them flying missions with the Reaper. High-altitude stuff."

Moncrief and Hernandez stood in silence, watching the drone pilot. He had the gentle touch of someone who knew that it only took the slightest movements to turn, lift, or drop the aircraft.

"Just like holding a tube of toothpaste in your hand. Don't squeeze too hard." The operator was giving them a lesson in drone flight.

The ground crew chief gave a thumbs-up from the runway; at the same time, the pilot heard it over his headphones. The turbines started to spin up, one at a time, and then in unison, the large, black blades started to spin. Moncrief watched as the flight line crew turned their backs to the aircraft and went down on their knees as the blast of spinning air stirred up everything in sight. It was as if a tornado had descended on the airfield. The surveillance camera was barely able to show a picture.

At the same time, the MUX's FLIR and sensors came on line. The center screen had a picture with several dials and flight instruments showing below.

"Like the HondaJet," Moncrief noted.

The bird started to rise, going straight up, and as it did, one of the displays showed the airfield and tents below. As it rose, the tent was buffeted by the blast of air. There was a smell of kerosene. The air itself became warmer. The blast of the jet engines was like a heater blasting the campsite.

They watched as the pilot transferred to forward movement. The aircraft flew quickly out of sight, but Moncrief could hear it in the distance.

"Okay, what do you want to check out?" the pilot asked.

"Let's start with our man."

* * * *

The aircraft passed over Grizzly Reservoir well above the clouds. The sensor showed the heat of a man, but it was blocked by some object. Only a portion of the figure showed on the thermal detector.

"Is he okay?" Kevin leaned over the chair of the operator.

"Yeah, see the movement?"

"Wow, this thing is a beast," Hernandez praised the MUX.

"How about the huts?"

"Just the ones in this area?" The operator pointed to the screen as he pulled the picture out to cover a larger area.

"Yeah."

The next valley over showed the plume of heat rising from the chimney of a hut. There was no movement, but the sensor didn't penetrate the walls of the cabin.

"Someone in that one," the operator commented.

"Which one is that?" Moncrief asked.

"Barnard." Hernandez had the map.

"Okay. I'll send it to him." Kevin sent a message to Will's Fi-Pad.

"What's this?" Hernandez pointed to something on the side of the screen.

The pilot panned over to the valley to the north. A heat image of a figure appeared on the screen. It seemed stationary. Then, it moved.

"Look at that." Moncrief pointed to the other side of the figure.

Two shapes lay side by side. The heat from the figures was more of a blue than the red projected by the others on the screen.

Moncrief stood and leaned over the chair. "Is that what I think it is?"

"Gotta make a call." Kevin stepped away from the control center. This had become more than a military mission. "Anyone got the number for the sheriff of Pitkin County?"

Another Marine in the tent was online and called the phone number out.

"This is going to take some explaining." Moncrief didn't relish the job.

Chapter 42

Grizzly Reservoir

A dull light broke through the makeshift tent that Will had fashioned over the table. The snow had continued to build up in the valley and had drifted around the small structure.

The cold had seeped through Will's body, particularly where it contacted the ground. His hip and arms felt frozen. Will sat up in the small space, rubbing the body parts that were the coldest. He climbed out from the small shelter, putting the over-whites back on and shaking off the snow from his backpack and skis.

I thought Korea was cold.

But the cold of Korea, along with his time in the Arctic Circle and at Bridgeport, reminded him of the worst cold ever.

Twenty-Nine Palms. The desert training command had begun Will's military career. As an artillery officer who became attached to his first ANGLICO unit, he would call artillery missions for Marine artillery of the 11th out of Camp Pendleton. The worst had come when a sudden sand storm would strike the high desert. They would sleep in their gas masks, but the fine powder would collect in their ears and on the back of their necks.

The cold, however, derived from the wide swing of temperatures. It might have been blisteringly hot in the afternoon, but once the sun fell beyond the mountains, the thermometer could drop twenty degrees. Their utilities, soaked with sweat from the day, would turn into a chilling wet blanket on the skin.

Focus, Will.

Head to the end of this valley. He pulled the FiPad out of the backpack and pulled up the map. A pin showed his location. Will spread out the map to a larger scale. He had loaded it up with the coordinates of the several huts to this side of Highway 82. The tablet had direct access to the military GPS, which took it to a higher level of precision than what civilian GPS could provide.

It works. Will's thought was directed to the fact that the small computer opened up with a screen, showing a scan for where others would have a password, and then opening. The password pill opened the door. And it was a door that no one else could open with this particular FiPad. Only by the pill in his gut was he able to directly access it.

The skis were cold. He stretched the cross-country ski skins out over them. The skins would let him slide downhill, but provide grip when he climbed. Both the skis and skins would warm up with the motion as he headed out. Just below the lake, a flat path marked what would be, on a sunny day in August, the gravel road that served as a roadway up here. He pulled out the semi-automatic, more for assurance that it was there. Its suppressor extended it only an extra six inches, which allowed it to fit well into the shoulder holster under his parka. Will drank from a water bottle he carried attached to his pack.

Let's do it. He moved quickly over the snow, occasionally running into a drift that caused his skis to disappear under the surface. His body heat quickly increased. Soon, the chill from the night had passed.

The snowstorm continued with the same force. He had brought a pair of goggles; they worked well but caused him to stop frequently to wipe the ice and snow that had obscured the visibility. Will's breath came out in puffs causing a wisp of vapor to blow out. He concentrated on his motion, keeping his movement in sync with his breath and arm movement. Will followed the path of the creek and the outline of the road until he reached the end of the valley. There, he passed the end of the mountain that separated this valley from the next. He turned back into the next valley, moving forward. He stopped where a stream crossed his path and took off his skis. He crossed the rocks, stepping over the flow of water, and climbed up on the other side. Will traveled this path for some time. The wind cut through the space between his parka and his wool hat. He stopped again.

"This may be wrong." Will could barely see the trees ahead. It was impossible to see the mountain that formed the valley. He stopped, pulled out the Fi-Pad, covering it with his arms as he bent over it.

The hut should be here.

The first cabin was somewhere near the apex of this valley.

Come on, come on. Where's Goodwin-Greene?

Will looked at the marker he had set on the map with the cabin's coordinates.

"I'll be damned." He was standing next to its porch.

* * * *

The hut was empty. And it was not the structure Will had seen in the photo from Kerr's phone. It was the wrong hut.

"It must be Barnard."

Will shook the snow from his clothes and backpack. He used the cabin's propane heater to dry his clothes.

The FiPad had a message.

See this. Moncrief had forwarded a news article from Houston with a bold headline: *Assassination Attempt Foiled. Terrorist Entered From Mexico.*

It concerned the capture of a Palestinian who had attempted to kill the president. The story tracked the man from his border crossing in California through a tunnel that was destroyed shortly after. The story continued to describe what had happened to the would-be assassin while in federal custody.

"So, why the daughter?" Will asked himself as he read on.

There was one thing clear from the article. The cartel whose tunnel was ruined would be looking for the other man as avidly as the authorities.

"He won't want them to find him."

It also meant something else to Will. Being a past prosecutor, he'd known plenty of murderers who had nothing to lose. A prison sentence for several life terms in consecutive order meant that a killer would never see the light of day. And some faced with that fact would kill just to get a sentence of the death penalty. Some wanted to die. A terrorist that believed in both revenge and Allah was in that same category.

The safest place on the planet right now for the assassin would be these mountains.

Will also knew that the man, if he were on the trail of the past president's daughter, would not allow himself to be captured.

Another message came across from Moncrief. It was several hours old. The message apparently hadn't linked up with the tablet when first sent.

He's on the way to her. She's at Barnard. Two bodies to the west of Barnard hut! Kevin's message confirmed what they'd suspected. The blizzard, however, didn't help. The hut was unreachable except by skis.

"The MUX thermogear must have picked up the bodies." Will looked at the FiPad.

He sent back a reply.

Call Vermont and tell them where their killer is. Will had promised the trooper that if he learned anything, he would share it. The killer would not make it out of these mountains, whether due to Will Parker or the law. He thought about his message for a moment and sent another. *Call Aspen as well. Tell them they have another Ted Bundy, but this one will kill before being captured. Don't tell them about her.* Will was still unsure that the cavalry would be of help in saving her life. The storm bought him time. Time to find out if he and the killer were both on the right trail. And he had one advantage—he knew about Mike Kerr. It would give him the chance to plead for her trust. But it all had to do with time.

It was a calculated risk. If the man had already arrived and was in the hut, or reached it before others could come, it would be a certain death sentence for her if the authorities suddenly descended on the hut. She may have been already dead, lying in a puddle of her own blood.

Will pulled on his parka, over-whites, gloves, and goggles. He checked his H&K pistol, pulled out the magazine to see the Inceptor bullets, and chambered one. He tightened the suppressor on the barrel and then slipped it back into the holster. Will unbuttoned the top buttons of his over-whites and parka so that his hand could easily slip to the pistol.

The storm remained relentless. Will stepped out of the hut and into the cold air, pulled his backpack on, and stepped into his skis. The alpine binding tightly fit around his boots. He had taken a bearing from the FiPad. There was a small ridgeline that he had to cross; it would put him just above Barnard hut.

The movement was brutal. The storm didn't relent. The faint outline of the road went through stands of pine trees. Their branches were weighed down with the accumulation of snow.

This is what I needed. The weather provided Will with the cover that would conceal him until he wanted to be revealed. He would not be seen until he wanted to be seen. The killer would have no idea that his hunter had the upper hand—and the element of surprise.

Will reached the top of the ridgeline just before dark.

There was a small break in the weather as he hid behind several aspens at the edge of an aspen grove. He watched the hut from his position. There was a light in the cabin and heat rose from the chimney. He saw a figure moving inside. It wasn't clear whether the figure was alone.

But at least they were alive.

For now.

Chapter 43

Barnard Hut

Elizabeth Jordan was beginning to feel that something was terribly wrong.

This isn't right.

"He would not be late," she said to herself. "Not him." Her stomach made a turn. If there was one thing she knew, the jet pilot did not show up late for anything. In fact, it was the opposite.

"Maybe he's tried to get word to me?" she asked herself. The cell phone had been useless since she had gotten to the hut. And the storm, particularly with its thunder, would have closed out most aircraft.

"He used to call me a late developer." She smiled at the thought. But he was right. Even with the help of one of the most exclusive staffs in the world at the White House, she was known as sometimes needing the use of the blue light with the Secret Service for her run to St. Albans. Her father had taken no favor when he learned of this and ordered the staff to wake her an extra hour early every day.

"A late developer."

Plus, she was getting bored. Cabin fever. No cell service, no internet, and most importantly, no ability to train on the skis.

If I go out in this, I'll be lost in a couple of hundred yards. She felt the cold glass on her hand as she touched it. The cabin held just enough heat that the windows would frost over. There was a map on the wall that showed the valley and peaks that surrounded Barnard.

She walked over to it, studying the highs and lows. With her finger, she followed what she had used for her training trail. The overhang of rocks was closer than she had thought. It was just to the west of the cabin towards the peak.

She heard a sizzling noise. The pot of coffee she had made on the small stove was boiling over.

"Out of coffee, out of sugar..." She counted off the shortage of goods. "The bananas were gone a day ago. It's time to go." Her voice fell to deaf ears. The roof of the hut had several feet of snow on it, and between that and the mounds that surrounded the cabin, it provided an insulator to sound. Only the porch, the windows, and the door gave any shape to the structure.

"In this weather, you could pass this place and never know it was here." Again, Merc found herself talking to the four walls. And it was this that scared her.

Can I make it?

Without Mike and some luck, her journey back over the mountain to Aspen might not end well. And once committed, her ability to return to the hut would quickly vanish.

Doubt? What did he say about doubt? She pondered the thought as she turned back to the storm at the window.

"Our doubts are *traitors*!" She shouted out the words but didn't feel an instant confidence boost.

"If he doesn't show up, as soon as this lets up, I'm gone."

Her emotions were wrapped in both anger and fear.

I'll head out in this storm, first thing! The answer was in her not staying at the cabin. *But not tonight!* She thought as she sipped her coffee, in a chair, next to the window.

"Too dangerous to head out in this storm." She spoke the words to her coffee cup, wrapped up in her sleeping bag, sitting in the chair and listening to the window creak as the wind blew snow and ice at it.

She didn't know that it was less dangerous to brave the worst of the storm than to stay at Barnard.

Chapter 44

The Pass through the Mountains near Barnard Hut

I'm lost.

The storm caused all direction to be turned around. He pulled his goggles off, cleaned them with the back of his hand, and let the cold air enter the space between them and his face. His snow shoes were deep into the snow and, at times, the drifts caused him to sink into it up to his knees.

"I can't be lost." He carried on a conversation with himself as he tried to study the terrain. "It's to the east."

But east wasn't easily found in the storm. He didn't carry a compass and he didn't dare turn on a cell phone.

Need to get rid of all of them. He thought of the two he had left. Jamal stopped, opened his pack, pulled out the cells and their chips, cracked the chips, and tossed them into the deep snow.

Jamal pulled out the map and, seeing the outline of Richmond Hill Road, continued the hike in what he thought was the proper direction, when suddenly the world fell out from underneath him.

"Oh!" He tumbled down what seemed to be a wall flipping end over end. Snow flew up in the air as he rolled, bounding off of boulders. He covered his head with his hands and pulled his knees up into his chest.

Finally, he stopped.

Jamal was on the edge of a creek. He sat in the snow, first extending his arms and legs to see if any were broken. They were not. The bank of deep powdery snow had protected him. The same fall in the summer would have been deadly.

"Allah, please protect me." He whispered the words that he should have never said out loud.

"We're not pacifists. We never doubted warfare. It is a calling of our faith." Jamal recalled the teachings he had learned as a child. "And the death of those that kill our faithful is a must."

He realized he was cheering himself on as he sat on a rock at the bottom of the ravine.

"What is more of an enemy than the ones who kill us?" he shouted into the storm.

The fall had shaken him.

She will have protection.

The operative in him anticipated that there could be men with machine guns protecting the young woman. He found it hard to believe that she would or could have abandoned the Secret Service to be alone in these mountains.

Jamal looked at the map. The road had turned and he'd missed the turn. He'd fallen down a drop ending up at the bottom of Woody Creek. It was, however, very fortunate. This fall was harmless. A few yards back and it would have been over the side of a cliff.

It also meant that he could follow the stream up several hundred yards back to the valley and find his target. The stream would work as a guiding path straight to Barnard, which stood on a small hill where the stream connected back with the road.

"I must be ready."

He checked the backpack, which had stayed on him, water bottle attached, and removed the snowshoes. Jamal hooked them onto the backpack and slowly headed up the partially ice-covered creek. At the top, near the road, he would put the snowshoes back on.

Jamal pulled his glove off and reached into this parka, feeling for the most important item.

The cold steel of the revolver felt like a relief. It was there. He pulled it out to examine it and ensure that the killing tool was ready and fully loaded.

He felt something else in the backpack he had forgotten about. There, folded into the remaining wad of fifty-dollar bills was a small plastic pack. He pulled it open, finding one of several small white tablets.

"It is time." Jamal had judged that the cabin was close, very close. And it would be guarded with men ready to kill. He took the last of the water from the water bottle and swallowed the Captagon pill. For a limited time, it would make him nearly invincible.

The creek and the ravine also provided cover from the winds of the storm. It was silent in the ravine apart from the gurgle of the water as it passed over the rocks.

"Again, He has saved me."

Jamal decided that the creek and even his fall, particularly at the point when he'd fallen into the ravine, were directions, not warnings.

I will show no mercy.

Chapter 45

Barnard Hut

"What's that?" Elizabeth Jordan's heart jumped a foot.

A shape seemed to appear, and then disappear, in the storm.

"Mike!" Merc screamed. "Mike!"

The shape materialized, then disappeared again.

Merc ran and grabbed her boots. They were tight after more than a day of disuse due to the storm. The chill of the room had hardened the plastic.

"Get on! Get on!" she yelled as she tugged them on. Her foot slipped into the boot as her heel sank down into it. She followed with the other boot, again struggling to put it on. She stood up, using her body weight to settle down into them. Merc grabbed her parka, gloves, and wool hat, and headed for the door. The skis were the last items.

"Where did he go?"

The shape was nowhere to be seen in the driving snowstorm.

God, he could miss the cabin altogether.

Only the windows of Barnard could be seen—and only if he looked closely at the white terrain. The porch had drifted into a mound of snow. Ideally, MK's eyes would catch the unusual shape of a man-made object against the pines. But with the wind and white conditions, he could walk past the cabin within feet and never see it.

"Coming!" Merc cried and pushed the snow on the porch out of the way, struggling to find the steps. The snow was so thick and drifted that she could ski down them.

Still can't see him.

Merc got down on level ground and took a bearing on where she last saw him.

Can't be far. She tried to orient herself.

"I'll count the steps." It was a rough plan that would help her judge the distance in the near whiteout conditions.

"One, two, three." Merc counted only with her left foot. The snow covered her skis. She felt it pull, slightly, against her knees.

"God, this is deep."

Merc continued on her path.

"He's here somewhere."

She looked back to the hut and only made out its outline by looking back at her tracks, which led back in that direction. The tracks looked small and insignificant.

The cold had started to sweep into the openings between her neck and parka, her gloves and wrists. It seemed the temperature was dropping.

"The storm must be clearing." Merc knew that the blanket of clouds that came with a snowstorm had one upside: they held the temperature at a warmer point. A clearing of the storm also meant that the temperature could drop quickly—or rise if the sun came out. For now, it seemed to be dropping.

A bolt of lightning illuminated the snowy air, followed quickly by a massive thunderclap.

"God, the thunder!" she said.

My poles. She realized that they were metal. The skis and the bindings too made potential lightning rods. The lightning had struck the ground with such violent force that she heard the cabin shake. The windows rattled in their frames. Snow fell off the roof.

It doesn't matter. The risk had to be taken.

Her greatest fear was that MK was lost and had passed the cabin. It wasn't guaranteed that this storm was over. A lull would help, but a second wave could come behind this one. She had to find him and do it now.

Where is he?

"MK…MK…MK…!" Merc yelled into the wind. There was no response.

"Mike?" She shouted as loud as she could. It felt like she was screaming into a wet blanket.

"Mike!" The scream seemed to leave her mouth and drop off into the wall of snow.

Merc felt icy tears roll down her cheeks. She used the back of her glove to wipe them away.

Wait. There he is! A shape had appeared during a short break in the wind, only a few steps away.

"Michael!" She screamed out the words.

The shape didn't move. It showed no reaction.

Merc took several steps toward it.

"Goddamn it!" she shouted as she realized it wasn't him.

The wind had pulled the snow from a stump. An old, large pine had been logged or cut down for some other reason, well in the past, leaving a dark shape the size of a man.

She fell to her knees, sobbing, as she touched the cold wood.

"Not him, not him." With this crushing realization, she understood that Mike was more than her caretaker, her mentor, her cheerleader. He was the man she loved.

Chapter 46

The Hut

"Must be near." Jamal stopped, looked around and aimed again for the edge of the tree line. He had concluded that, once he left the creek bed, if he followed the edge of the trees it would take him directly to the cabin. The snowshoes sank deeper into the thick, white mounds. It had become a struggle to pull his legs out with each step.

What? He heard a sound. It wasn't from the direction he expected. Nor was it a sound he expected. *From the left?*

It seemed like a wail—short, anguished, and then silent. It happened again. Neither lasted long enough for him to get much of a bearing. But it did give him hope that he was near the hut.

Jamal followed the trees, stepping heavily again and again, the snow coming up to his knees. The deep powder floated up in the air as his steps disturbed the surface. His thirst was increasing.

"I need a drink. Water!" He tried to speak the words but his tongue didn't allow him to form what was being said.

Sana'a, he thought.

Once in the battle of Sana'a, they'd gone without water for several days. It, too, was at altitude. The capital was one of the highest in the Middle East. He'd had to keep his men from drinking out of a puddle of chocolate-colored liquid teeming with flies. The dysentery would have killed as quickly as the bullets of the soldiers. He'd held a gun to their chests ordering them to obey him. At the same time, Jamal had looked at the puddle, wanting himself to dip his face into it. He felt the same now, except here he was surrounded by water that he could not drink. He put a small ball of snow in his mouth and felt the chill. It bought some time, but did little to stop his body from shaking with the need.

Jamal took another step and his snowshoe hit something solid.

"What?" He pulled off his goggles and stared at the shape in front of him. It was a shape that did not fit in nature. Mounds of snow camouflaged the small structure, but it was manmade. It was Barnard.

Jamal's first thought was that of a soldier.

Her protection detail.

He reached into his parka and pulled out the revolver. There was no assurance of what he would find. He worked his way around the porch and found an opening in the railing that must have been where there were steps. He noticed two parallel tracks that came down from the porch and went into the storm.

Jamal slowly climbed up onto the porch, reaching the door and waiting for a sound. He slipped off his snowshoes and put them to one side.

Her guards must be inside. He held the revolver at the ready, cocking the hammer and pushing the door with his other hand. It swung open. He listened for a sound, but there was none.

Empty. He looked around the tiny cabin, expecting someone to jump out at any moment. A sleeping bag hung over a chair and a cup was out, half full of coffee.

Jamal went to the stove. A tin coffee pot, still warm, was full of water. It had been used to melt snow. He couldn't stop himself. He drank from it with large gulps, stopping only for a quick breath.

Someone had recently been here, but the place was now empty.

The anger swelled through his body.

Where is *she?*

Jamal turned back to the door, staring at the white, trying to decide what next to do. If she had been alerted, he could not get close. With the murders, he couldn't get off this mountain alive. All would be lost.

"Where?"

The sounds he'd heard had come from the same direction that the ski tracks led, across the porch, down the stairs, and out into the storm.

They were important for another reason.

There were only two parallel ski tracks. Although a good skier might follow another in the same track, it could not happen in this snow.

She was alone.

Jamal put on his snowshoes and slowly uncocked his pistol, trying to contain the sudden burst of energy surging through him. The woman was alone and without a weapon. He was close, very close to his prey.

Jamal felt like the marathon runner who had crossed the twenty-five-mile mark and realized he still had the energy to make it to the end that was in sight. Despite the exhaustion, the adrenaline coursed through his bloodstream. From Yemen, to Africa, to Central America, to South America, Mexico, and here, Jamal had been brought to this moment and place.

He worked his snowshoes down the drop from the porch and started to follow the tracks in the snow. Jamal moved one foot at a time, in a hopping-like movement, lifting the shoes up in the air so that they could be moved forward. After several yards, he saw a figure. It was heading toward him. It seemed smaller than Jamal, moving its skis quickly, gliding over the snow. He stood and watched as his prey came to him.

She stopped, mid-stride, and stared at him. At first, she seemed overjoyed, excited, and moved forward again. And then, like someone who had witnessed a pedestrian struck in a crosswalk, she stopped. He clearly was not who she was looking for. Nevertheless, she came forward, deliberately, toward him.

"Hello!" Jamal yelled out.

"Hey!" The former President's daughter shouted back.

He didn't care if she was alarmed, but he hadn't come this far for a simple kill. He wanted to let her know why.

"I'm lost." He spoke the words with an accent he could not disguise.

* * * *

"Oh..." Merc seemed hesitant. She had lived in the bubble for so long that she was far from trusting a stranger in the wilderness. Living with the Secret Service had given her a sense of what to be wary of. But the choices in such moments were few. She had been instructed to flee. It would have done no good here. Or hide. There was no place to hide. Or look for a place of protection. The only place of protection was behind the stranger.

"I can help." Merc's answer was not naïve. It was the only choice.

"Thank you."

"I'll show you the way." Merc went past him back to the hut. "You've been to the hut?"

"Yes, I found that. But no one was there. Is it just you?"

His question made her instantly uncomfortable.

"Well, my boyfriend should be here any minute."

"Oh?"

The two made their way back to Barnard, her skiing, him shuffling. The second wave of the storm was starting to roll in. And with the second storm, the temperature was rising.

"I'm short on food," Merc said.

"I understand. I hope I won't be here long."

"What are you doing out here?" She turned her head as she spoke the words back to him.

"I was supposed to meet a friend."

"At this hut?"

Jamal had to think quickly. He remembered another hut nearby.

"No, at Goodwin."

His words seemed to help.

"Goodwin-Greene?"

"Yes."

"You *are* lost." His words gave Merc some comfort. A stranger in the mountains that had a destination she recognized was not likely to be a danger. "A couple who came by here a few days ago were going there."

"Oh, really?"

They were approaching the hut, now visible through the blizzard. Neither Merc nor Jamal had any sense that another set of eyes followed every step.

Chapter 47

The Aspen Grove

Will made no movement whatsoever.

As both a trained Marine sniper and deer hunter, he would not give any hint of his presence with the flick of a finger or by lifting his head. The over-whites had served him well. The storm's reduction of visibility would have made it difficult at best for him to be seen, but he would not take the chance. He could stay motionless for hours if the need presented itself.

The two seemed to be comfortable with each other. They traveled in line, one on skis and one on snowshoes, heading back to the hut. They were in open country, but if Will had made one mistake, it was that he carried his semi-automatic and not the .556 caliber rifle.

The shot would have worked, he thought as he trailed the two with his eyes. They reached Barnard, each taking off their skis and snowshoes and going inside the cabin. He continued to study them to see any hint of danger on her part.

Mercury stomped off the snow and shook off it from her parka. The larger figure did the same and started to head through the door.

As he did, Will detected a hesitation. Mercury stopped, almost freezing, as the man walked in and took off his backpack.

She seemed spooked.

Will reviewed his options.

I've got to get inside, he thought as he lay in the snow. Inside, out of sight, Mercury could be dead in a moment. There was no option but to play the card.

Will slid back below the bank. He scanned the aspen grove and saw, just beyond, the outcrop of a rock overhang. He made his way to the rocky ledge and cleared out a space below. The ledge was near a clearing with several aspen trees sheared off on each side as if a massive force had plowed through the woods. He used the rock cover to strip off the over-whites. They were the one clear clue that he was military. He surveyed his clothing, looking for anything else that said military. As per the plan, he was dressed in a Canada Goose grey camo parka. It had a style like the military, but was far from it. The parka was more that of an upscale back-country skier, someone stylish who might have come over the mountain from Aspen or the Highlands. The Goose pants were black, the skis were Rossignols, and the boots were Fischer Backcountry—all the prototypical gear of a civilian.

The skis had snow frozen to their bottoms from lying in the drift the whole time he had been there. Will used his gloves to scrape the icy snow from them and put his foot into the first binding.

A sound issued from his backpack. It was a small alert, barely audible. The FiPad showed a message.

"Ready?"

"Going in." Will typed the words back to Moncrief. He buried the Fi-Pad deep in the backpack. It was a danger, but it was a risk that had to be taken. The device was the only way to communicate with the outside world. Or to be traced, in case worst came to worst.

Will slipped the backpack on, turned his skis towards the hut and slid out of the aspen grove.

He was her only hope...if it wasn't already too late.

Chapter 48

The Confrontation

Darkness would be descending on the mountains soon.

Will could see his breath as he moved toward the hut. He needed not to set off any alarm. Somehow, he had to get inside without exciting the pair.

As he neared the porch, Will saw the two figures lit by a lamp. They were standing together, talking, and neither seemed alarmed. One was a woman and the other a man.

"Hello!" Will shouted. He yelled again in his best command voice. "Hello!"

He waited for a response.

On the third yell, he saw a reaction. It seemed that the woman turned to the door while the man stepped back. His hand reached to the inside of his parka, but he didn't move it.

Will took off his skis, stuck his poles in the snow, loosened his boots, and clunked up the stairs to the porch.

"Hello!" he yelled again. It was important to alert them so they could comprehend what was going on without causing any more alarm than a stranger coming to seek shelter. The rule of the backcountry was to provide warmth and food to a stranger. Oddly similar, in fact, to a common tenet of Jamal's faith. A religion that had grown up in the desert had rules inherited from the desert. One rule was to render help to a traveler.

The stranger's hesitation may have been due to this rule. He didn't reach for his revolver.

Merc opened the door.

She had a scared look on her face and red eyes, as if she'd been crying. It was as if she held a terrible secret that could not be shared.

"Hello," Merc greeted him.

"Hey, I'm Will Parker. I'm sorry if I shocked you two," he said with a smile on his face. "I was heading in and the storm put me back a day. Just in from Grizzly Reservoir where I was camping out."

"Sure, come in." Merc seemed happy to have a third person in the cabin.

"I have a can of tuna I can donate if it helps." Will pulled his parka off and hung it on a hook. He had taken his semi-automatic out of its holster, left the shoulder holster in the aspen grove, and put the gun in the back of his snow pants, pulling his sweater down over the weapon.

"That would be great. We don't have much, and if this storm stops tonight, I'm heading in at first light."

Interesting. She seemed to be trying to extract herself. *So, he hasn't made a move yet.* Will went over to the man and extended his hand.

"Will Parker."

The man froze for a second.

Will studied the man. He was as tall as Will, with a dark face and the black eyes of someone who had seen death and had caused it. The man had spent more time in combat than even Will Parker had. He'd likely carried an AK as a child, certainly as a teenager. His reaction time would be sharp, quick, and deadly. But Will Parker was no less a warrior. He, too, had spent time in direct hand to hand combat with the enemy. And he had an advantage. Will knew who he was. Will knew he had killed some innocent young women. He only had a guess as to who Will was.

The man forced a smile. It was false and telegraphed a confirmation that he was who Will thought he was.

"Jamal."

"Jamal? A true traveler! You must have come a long way," Will probed.

"No, not really. Just Denver."

"I'll make rice." Merc reached for a pot and the salt. "Oh, I need water." She pointed to Jamal. "Any left in your water bottle?"

"No."

"Okay, we need to boil some snow." She took the pot and headed for the door.

"Where are you going?" Jamal asked.

"Just snow. Too far to go into Aspen to get some water." Merc gave a false laugh that Will knew was a sign of fear. He knew then that she understood the situation.

Merc brought in the pot stuffed full of snow and placed it on the burner. She turned it on high and watched as it started to melt. She glanced over to the corner of the room.

Will caught the glance. He looked over to the corner as well and saw a biathlon-style .22 rifle leaning against the wall. He knew that Jamal had murdered half a dozen people. And he knew that the bolt action, particularly if a round had not been chambered, would take too much time to get a shot off. If she missed, Jamal would be on top of her in a second. And if she hit him with a single shot, the .22 slug would not likely prove fatal.

Even with Parker's help, the odds were long.

"Is that an Anschütz 64?" Will asked.

"Yes." She didn't seem pleased at all by the question.

Will was playing the odds. The question had two benefits. First, it stopped her from trying to reach the gun. She would never get a shot off if she tried. Second, it served to put Jamal at ease as to Parker.

"We need more water." Will grabbed a large pot from the shelf, stepped outside, used his hands to fill it up with snow, and put it on the fire as well. The pot took much longer to boil as he couldn't use the salt.

They ate their rice and tuna in silence.

Each man was making his plan.

Jamal acted like he could not be sure of Parker and whether the move was to pull out his revolver and shoot both of them on the spot. But he wanted her to know why he came.

"Well, I'm going to get some sleep. I'll take this corner." Will pulled up next to the heater and seemed to doze off. His hand was at his back the entire time.

Jamal choose the other corner. He kept on his parka despite the fact that the hut, though not warm, was far from cold enough to keep on his parka, as he pretended to sleep as well.

Merc took the bunk and her sleeping bag.

No one got any sleep. Both Merc and Will sat awake in the dark, trying to plan. Will had to take down a killer without harming the woman. And he had yet to tell her the news that the man she expected to arrive never would. That he'd died worrying about her.

Chapter 49

Daylight

"Here, right here!" Kevin pointed to the side of Richmond Hill less than a half a mile from Barnard. A gully formed the path for what might be needed. The projection on the screen in Leadville from the MUX was crystal clear.

"This point?" The Marine operator used his mouse to pull a red dot over the spot.

"A little higher." Moncrief had something in mind. "Can we send this to his FiPad?"

"Sure," Hernandez replied as he pulled out another he was using to communicate with Will. "Not sure he's online."

"Just send it."

Moncrief stared at the image.

"Wait!" He pointed to an outcrop of rocks below. The MUX infrared showed the tramped down snow and an article of clothing that just barely stuck out from the overhang.

"He already knows it. Use that point on the ridge above the rock overhang."

The MUX was still on the airfield, finishing up its refueling. The aircraft sat in the center of the runway. No one was using the runway in this weather, so it didn't block anything. But Moncrief had another thought in mind.

"We need the Hueys to be ready."

"What are you thinking?" Hernandez asked.

"This may be the day. I may need you as well." Moncrief turned to Stidham. It wasn't ideal, his thinking that they might need the doctor, but he was covering all the possibilities.

"I'll get 'em going." Gunny Works had been sitting in the room with his YETI cup of coffee watching the operation unfold.

* * * *

The MUX's turbines could be heard spinning up, and with liftoff, a strong warm wind blew across the encampment. The drone turned toward the mountain and soon was well beyond the ears of the base camp.

Moncrief watched as the bird headed up the valley and then turned into the mountains.

The weather was clearing, but there was still a low-hanging overcast over the high-altitude valleys.

"We need this weather to stay calm a little longer." He sat on the edge of his seat as he watched the operator turn the MUX up the valley and past Twin Lakes. It could only be seen in fragments between the breaks in the clouds. Beyond, there was a layer of clouds that covered several thousand feet of climb. The clouds were dark and still a danger. The weather didn't affect the MUX, but it did stop the Venom Hueys from making the trip.

"You can take it higher." Moncrief wanted some distance between the aircraft and the ground.

The UAV broke through the clouds at twelve thousand feet. Above, the sun's brilliant, blinding light reflected off the tops. The aircraft turned to the northwest and as it made its turn Moncrief saw through the MUX cameras the peaks of several mountain tops poke through the cloud cover.

"That's Mount Massive and Mount Elbert." The pilot pointed to what the camera showed on the clear screen. He turned the aircraft to the west. "And that's La Plata."

Beyond La Plata a string of mountaintops protruded above the storm clouds.

"All fourteens."

"Meaning?" Hernandez asked.

"Fourteen thousand feet." The operator turned the ship back on course. "We're going just to the east of that one. Castle Peak."

"Stay as high as you can until you descend down to Richmond Hill. Can you get in and out quick?"

"Oh, yeah. You gotta watch this bird."

"Drop it right there. Right on top of that snow pack."

Chapter 50

The Hut

"Are you awake?"

Merc was so close to Will that he could smell the scent of peppermint from the Dr. Bronner's soap.

He was awake and hadn't slept all night. His one eye remained open to survey the room in the near darkness of pre-dawn light. He saw Jamal in the corner on the opposite side of the cabin. The man slumped awkwardly against the wall in the manner of one asleep who, when awoken, would complain of a crick in his neck. He had an object in his hand. Will didn't have to see it to know it was the revolver. He could tell it was a large caliber with perhaps a six-inch barrel. Parker knew that Jamal had spent most of his adult life in the front line of combat. If he weren't deeply asleep, he'd fire a shot before Will made it half way across the room. It was too great a risk. His primary mission was to protect Merc, after all. He didn't know her, but he had known Michael Kerr. He owed it to his fellow Marine to keep her alive. Which he couldn't do if he was dead or injured.

Will made a quiet hiss and put his finger to his lips. He pulled her up against him so that her lips would be as close to his ear as possible.

"Who are you?" she asked.

"Friend," Will whispered into her ear.

"That man is dangerous," she whispered back.

Will's guess when he saw her hesitate at the door turned out to be right.

"He has my friend's water bottle. No one gives up their water bottle in the backcountry."

"Right," he said.

"What do we do?" Merc's voice was full of fear. She had clearly come to the brutal realization that her whole plan for being in the backcountry had been a terrible mistake. Now she had to depend upon this other stranger that had showed up out of nowhere.

"The rock overhang?" Will smiled at her. It gave some sense of hope and security.

"Yes!"

"When it is time, run to it."

She slid back to her spot on the bunk and pulled the pillow into a tight wad below her head. It wasn't a comfortable way to sleep. It was a sleepless effort. She would wait out the minutes until the daylight broke through.

Will did the same.

* * * *

"Hello." Jamal stirred, stood up, and announced to the room that he was awake.

"Oh, morning." Will said as he sat up, stretched his arms and turned his neck from side to side.

Merc sat up as well, but said nothing.

"Going in today," Will announced as he looked out at the weather. "Looks like the storm's passed. Anyone joining me?"

"I'll go," Merc answered too quickly.

Jamal reacted to the speed of her response. It was undoubtedly a sign that she knew.

"What's today?" Jamal asked.

"The fifth," Merc answered, pointing to a training calendar on the wall marked through, daily, with the laps done, exercises, and the progress she had made.

"The fifth." Jamal seemed to ponder the date. "Today was my daughter's birthday.

"*My Lala*." He said the Arabic words in the Yemeni dialect of Sanaani.

"Her name?" Will responded in the same dialect.

It caused Jamal to stiffen.

"You know my language?" He continued the conversation in Sanaani. It was only spoken by a small segment of the country.

"I do. How old is she?"

The question threw Jamal off. It telegraphed that the man didn't quite know who he was or why he was here.

"She died. She would have been five." They continued their conversation.

"To Allah we belong, and to him we return." Will spoke with the perfect dialect of someone from Jamal's homeland.

"Do not confuse me." Jamal reverted to English.

"She did nothing to cause this." Will returned to Jamal's language.

"Nor did my child and wife."

Jamal sat on a bench. Now, he was holding the revolver on his lap, in the open.

The trio had reached a new level of confrontation.

"Sorry," Merc murmured.

"My wife too. And my friend. They were murdered as well." Jamal looked out into space as he said the words. Then, his tone suddenly changed. "Yes, let's go in. I'll join you."

* * * *

The three put on packs. This time Merc was more deliberate, thinking that packing all of her gear would send some signal of all being normal. It wasn't and she tried to breathe as calmly as possible, knowing that she was within a few feet of a killer.

How many are ever this close to an assassin? It seemed crazy. Not only was he a killer, he was clearly here to kill *her.* Television shows didn't capture the gut-wrenching fear of the thought going through her mind.

Likewise, Merc didn't have a problem doing the math. He was from the Arabic world, his daughter and wife and friend had all died at the same time, and her father had left office as president only a short time ago. The former president was known for prosecuting the War on Terror with a deadly drone force. She could imagine what had happened. Now, she could think only of escape.

* * * *

"Shouldn't take long to get in." Will made the statement simply to get a reaction. It seemed that Jamal's mission would not end here. Perhaps he thought there were too many weapons available in the cabin that wouldn't be on the trail. "Let me check the weather."

Will reached into his backpack and pulled out the FiPad. It had no markings of being military. The bullet he had swallowed with the password pill worked without hesitation. The screen opened up and Will saw a message from Moncrief. In the millisecond his glance took, he had a plan.

"What's that?" Jamal asked.

"An iPad. Got a great app that shows the weather radar." Will switched the screen and held it up for Jamal to look at. A weather app displayed yellows and some reds of a formation to their west. It appeared to be less than a mile and closing. "Best get going."

"Can I see it?" Jamal switched the revolver to his other hand.

"Sure, but a pistol?" Will forced the bet.

"Sorry, old habit." He took the FiPad and examined it. Once it left Will's hands, the screen went dark.

"What's wrong?" Jamal asked as he shook the tablet, somehow expecting it to come on with the shaking.

"It's temperamental."

"What's in your belt?" Jamal pointed his weapon at Will, using it to suggest he turn around. "Behind you?"

Will held up his hands and slowly turned.

Jamal pulled out the semi-automatic and took it. He directed with his revolver for Will to sit. Slowly, Will sat on the bench.

"Hands. Let me see them." Jamal slid back against the wall, protecting himself, and examined the H&K with its silencer. He dropped the magazine to the floor and pulled back the slide. A bullet bounced out onto the floor and rolled on the wood planks.

"U.S. military?" Jamal unscrewed the suppressor. "Well-made. We only had Chinese and Russian in Yemen. Not well-made, but they always worked." It was as if the two were soldiers meeting across the front line and talking about their wares of war.

"Yes, yours always worked."

"Are there others?"

"No." Will looked him in the eye.

"You know I was the one who did the *Cole*." Jamal was bragging.

"Seventeen killed. Some in their sleep." Will remembered the Cole well.

"Yes, it wounded you badly," Jamal said softly. "And your accomplishments?"

"I've been in battle." Will had killed, but only men he'd faced. And while returning fire. "Never killed anyone in their sleep." Will let his disdain for his enemy show. Early on in the War on Terror, the enemy had been cowards, wreaking damage disproportionate with their numbers.

"Her father did," Jamal shot back. "Wives, children, anyone."

"Perhaps peace would have been a better route." Will was making conversation, engaging his enemy in hopes of buying time.

"Peace will come when all infidels are removed from the Earth." Jamal didn't offer a middle ground.

"And this president?"

"Oh, Reet?"

"Was that his name?"

"He kept their attention."

"So, he gave his life as a diversion?"

"I needed the support. If I had told them I was going after some daughter they would have laughed at me."

"And this is simply revenge."

"Let's go."

Merc led the three out of the cabin. Will followed and Jamal came behind, pushing Will with the revolver in his back. It seemed clear that Jamal, like he had with the others, would kill them in the wilderness so that it would take time to find the bodies. Will had him profiled as essentially a suicide killer. He wouldn't hide their bodies because a delay would help him escape. It was a swipe at her father, who would be tortured further by his missing daughter, presumed dead. And all the while, Mother Nature would degrade their corpses. It would be fair payback for his own daughter's death.

"There," he told Mercury, pointing the way.

"You mean *that* way?" Will pointed toward Richmond Hill.

"Yes, this way?" She also pointed towards the opening and beyond the line of trees.

"Go!" Jamal just wanted them out, well beyond the cabin, so the search would be more difficult.

None of them wore skis or snowshoes. Merc made her way down the stairs.

The clouds suddenly became dark and foreboding.

"More snow," Jamal said. "Your bodies will not be found until spring."

Will was at the top of the stairs. Merc had made it to the bottom and started for the path. As the snow thickened, the wind picked up. As if orchestrated by Will Parker and his weather app, the flakes started to come down in droves.

And then it happened.

Whoosh...

A blast of hot air came from above.

Will didn't hesitate, turning and throwing a punch into the man's solar plexus. Jamal fell back into the hut's doorway, still holding the revolver.

The MUX drone hovered in the snow-filled air, blowing a blast of air from above.

Merc ran in the deep snow as fast as she could, lifting one foot out, as high as it would go, followed by the other. She fell, got up, ran more, and fell again. Her training gave her the chance. She moved quickly towards the tree line and Richmond Hill.

The revolver fired.

The bullet struck Will in the center of his chest and threw him back over the railing. He disappeared into the snow below.

Jamal stood up but lost his footing on the ice, falling to the porch, and with the fall, the revolver flew out of his hand and into the deep snow.

The MUX had kept the blast on them, but it seemed to hit an air pocket, and climbed out of sight.

Will stood, gasping for air. The round had hit the bulletproof sweater hard, not penetrating his skin but bruising the muscles beneath. As he moved to go after Jamal, the killer rose and slipped into the cabin. Will immediately knew what he was doing.

"Got to get to her!" Will turned towards Merc and began to run. He grabbed a pole as he went by where it was stuck in the snow. It was the only weapon nearby. They made it almost to the tree line.

Pow.

The small-caliber bullet from the Anschütz biathlon rifle struck the snow just beyond Will's feet. He moved to protect Mercury's back, his breathing still seized with pain from the big pistol slug.

Pow...

The next round hit Will in the neck. The searing pain burned like a red iron.

"Keep moving!" Will yelled as he fell to the snow. The rounds were getting closer.

Pow... Another round hit Merc in the leg.

Will grabbed her up, holding her in his arms along with the ski pole, and continued to run.

Jamal was following. Will moved forward, following Merc as his blood stained the white snow.

"Where?" Merc yelled.

"The outcrop of rocks!"

Will and Merc were well into the aspen grove now. It provided protection and bought time, but it also meant they were beyond the help of the air-blast from the MUX. They were on their own.

Will saw Jamal following and gaining ground.

Pow...

Another bullet struck the trunk of an aspen near Merc. Splinters flew up. Her startled reaction sent her sprawling in the snow.

"Come on." Will held on to her. "The overhang's just there."

It seemed to offer only a small reprieve from the inevitable.

They ran through the deep snow as best as they could, making easy targets. With a well-aimed shot, a bullet would strike them and end it all. It was, however, like the biathlon. The altitude, the running, and the deep snow all made it difficult for Jamal to take a well aimed shot. Merc slid under the overhang first. She pulled herself under the protection of the rock, but it offered little cover. Jamal would follow and the overhang would make the killing easier. They would be trapped.

Will stopped at the opening and turned with the pole in his hand. If Jamal gave him the chance, it would be a fair fight.

* * * *

Jamal came to the edge of the clearing on the other side. He wore a smile like the one he had when he'd seen, from a hill overlooking the harbor in Aden, the blast that had torn through the *Cole*. The ship that had the red, white, and blue flag on its stern. He slowly stepped out in the clearing to get a better shot, raised his rifle, and aimed.

Will looked him directly in the eye.

"You're a coward!" Will shouted in Jamal's own language.

Jamal dropped the rifle for a moment, then chambered another round. He moved further into the clearing so as to aim directly at his target.

"Come on!" Will taunted him.

Jamal stopped to laugh. To torture his prey, he moved forward a few steps and stopped. A ski pole versus a rifle. It was a joke. He raised the rifle for the killing blow.

Jamal looked down the sights to see Will smiling. He paused for a moment to comprehend the smile of a man who was within a trigger pull of death.

Crack...

The boom shook the earth. Suddenly, snow fell from the branches of the aspens.

Jamal looked in the wrong direction, his deaf ear turning him toward the downslope. The turn took away any chance of his seeking protection from what came next.

* * * *

A bolt of lightning came out of the sky and struck the hill above their location. It was followed by the thunder of what sounded like a thousand horses stampeding.

Will dove into the hole under the rock overhang with Mercury and held on as tons upon tons of snow tore through the trees, carrying with the avalanche rocks and other debris. Jamal disappeared, as did all the light under the overhanging rock.

It was over.

Chapter 51

The Slope below Richmond Hill

"Do we know where they are?" Kevin stood at the base of the destruction and next to the two helicopters. There were Marines working their way up the path of the avalanche in a line, using long probes to aid in their search for survivors.

"Yeah." Hernandez had his FiPad with him. "Over to the far left!" he shouted to the ones on the hillside. The rocky overhang had disappeared in the piles of snow. Hernandez was tied in directly to the MUX overhead and its thermal equipment, which had found a pair of warm bodies.

"That's it!" he yelled again.

"Let's get up there." Moncrief started to run in the direction of the marked location.

"Come on, doc!"

Kaili Stidham followed in their tracks with her medical bag.

The others had already struck the rock of the overhang and were working their way around it when they reached a hollow space in the snow. They were standing at the opening, ready to crawl in, when they saw movement.

Mercury was being pushed out from behind. She had a rough bandage on her leg made from the overwhites that Will had stored under the rocks.

"She's hurt!" Kaili said as soon as she helped Mercury from below the snow. The other Marines brough a stretcher forward and had her on the helicopter in a matter of minutes.

Kaili Stidham crawled through the hole and out of sight.

"My bag, quick!" Her voice echoed from of the space below the rock.

Moncrief started to climb into the opening, but Hernandez stopped him.

"Hold on. She needs the room."

"Get another stretcher." Kaili's voice again, muffled by tons of snow.

She pulled Will Parker, semi-conscious, to the opening and pushed him up. Two Marines grabbed him, pulled him to the surface, and placed him on the stretcher.

Kaili followed up from the hole. Somehow, she had already bandaged the wound and run an IV into his arm.

"Let's get him out of here," she directed Moncrief and the others.

The doctor had taken control.

Will tried to sit up on the stretcher, but fell back down. His sweater was covered in congealed blood.

"Hold on." Kevin kept his hand on Will's shoulder.

They boarded the Huey with Kaili Stidham on one side and Moncrief in the seat behind.

Will grabbed Kaili's arm and pulled her down to him. "I thought you didn't like to fly in helicopters."

She smiled. "Only in snowstorms."

"What about the target?" Hernandez had seen on the FiPad another, slightly cooler shape in the snow. The MUX scan revealed an odd outline, as if a man's body had been twisted in two. There was no movement and the color was quickly fading to blue.

"Log those coordinates," said Moncrief. "We might come back in the spring."

Chapter 52

Aspen Valley Hospital

"Can we take this out?" Will Parker sat up in bed as the on-duty doctor stood nearby. He started to yank at the IV.

"I guess so." The doctor had treated a lot of broken bones, but this was his first gunshot wound.

"Where's *my* doctor?" Will asked as Kaili Stidham walked into the room.

"Difficult patient?" Kaili asked.

"Most definitely." The doctor gave Will a look.

"You've got a visitor," Kaili said.

"Just need to get out of here. How is she?" Will started to sit up. "We need a lift back to Leadville to get Coyote Six."

"Fine: a grazing leg wound that shouldn't keep her down for more than a week, and a hell of a good story."

"The lift?" Will was ready to go.

"I think that can be arranged." Kaili smiled knowingly as Moncrief came in with Mercury and her father.

"Thank you for saving my daughter's life." The former president came into the room and shook Will's hand.

"Are you okay?" Will asked Mercury. She was standing on a pair of crutches.

"Yeah, not great, but okay." He knew she wasn't speaking of her near-death experience, or the death of her friends, but also about the loss of Michael Kerr. "He did save me. If he hadn't gone to you, who knows what would've happened."

"He was a Marine who needed help," Moncrief said with a nod.

"Thanks again. Oh." The former president paused. "I thought you might want no press around. There are none."

"Yes." Will smiled.

* * * *

"There is *some* press," Moncrief added after Mercury and her father left the hospital room.

"What?"

"Your man, Gill." Kevin showed him the FiPad.

Will saw two messages. One contained a draft of an article designed to appear on the front page of the *Boston Globe*. It covered the death of a Marine pilot killed due to a defective ejection seat. It went on to say that a past board member and major stockholder of the ejection-seat company happened to be the new chief of staff at the White House.

"Yeah," Will murmured.

"He's done," said Moncrief.

A congressional investigation will follow. Will thought. The visit to the chief of staff's office by the ejection-seat company officer would be easily tied to the order from the White House to describe Kerr's death as "pilot in command error."

Another article by Terrance Gill was destined for a back page of the *Globe*. It noted that the president had stopped the Secret Service from protecting the children of past administrations who were over the age of sixteen. This was done despite a known threat. A congressional hearing regarding this had already been announced.

Both article drafts had been sent, somehow, by Gill directly to Moncrief.

"They were at that airport when we were at Beaufort." Will realized now that Moncrief had stayed in touch with the reporter.

"DARPA wants to know how Nimbus worked." Moncrief was asking about the other weapon that Will had used to save their lives.

The avalanche had been man made.

The terawatt laser beam from the device dropped off by the MUX had shot up into a cloud, causing filaments to lead current through like a large lightning rod. DARPA had developed a small portable teramobile that caused lightning.

"Better than my H&K."

"By the way, I found this." Moncrief handed him the automatic pistol, back in its shoulder holster. He had its suppressor in his other hand.

"Hate to lose it."

"Figured you'd need it again."

Conclusion

Stewart County, Georgia

One month later

"How about Alaska?" Kevin asked as they sat around the firepit. The chill of winter had reached into Georgia and the warmth of the well-stoked fire kept them huddled near it. Moncrief had a glass of bourbon that he was nursing.

"With the grant, she's staying out in the field. Probably for some time." Will knew that the danger had become too much for her. It had become unfair. And she loved her work. What he wasn't saying was that on every mission, the weak link stood to be the one one cared for. He wasn't going to put her through the risk.

"I got a call," Moncrief said after a long pause.

"Yeah?"

"They want you back in."

"Langley?"

"Yeah. To quote them: you *and* your team."

Twenty-Two Miles east of Al-Mahfid, Yemen

The two Ospreys sat in the river bed in complete darkness. The new moon cloaked the Marine aircraft as they sat in the wadi waiting. The team had secured the four points of the compass and waited.

An SUV's lights penetrated the darkness and could be seen for more than a mile as it came up the dirt road that followed the wadi. Its lights bounced up and down as it hit the ruts of the road. As it approached, the chambers of the automatic rifles were loaded and the night vision scopes followed every turn and twist that the vehicle made. The drone stood watch overhead and followed the SUV. Simultaneously, it scanned the surrounding hills of the river valley, watching for the slightest movement.

As the Toyota Highlander approached the site, the turbines of the Ospreys spinning up broke the silence of the night. The aircraft had the cover of two F-35s sitting on top, ready to strike.

The SUV slammed to a stop with its front wheels on the edge of a drop-off. Its lights shined down on the two aircraft on the dry riverbed for only a moment. The suppressed zip of a rifle cracked the glass of the headlight, followed by another, causing the wadis to become black again. A baby's cry could be heard even with the turbines of the blades starting to spin.

"Come with me." A Marine in the full combat gear of a special operator pulled the door open and grabbed the man by his arm.

"My wife and children?"

"It was supposed to be only you." The well-armed combatant didn't care about the number of passengers as much as the fact that each had to be frisked, allowing no one on the aircraft who had even the smallest chance of endangering the bird.

"They would have been killed."

He was right. The man and his family would be killed once he was found out. His crime would result in the most painful of punishments—he would be held to watch as his wife was raped, then her neck opened with a knife followed by the murder of his children. He would be the last to die.

"Okay, let's go."

The man, his wife holding the baby, and two sons were led down the wall of the wadi, then stopped as every inch of their bodies was patted down. The baby screamed. The passengers were in the darkness, effectively blind as the soldiers searched them. The Marines, with their night-vision gear, saw every person. After one had performed a body check, they moved closer to the aircraft, and then another did a second frisk.

"Two cells." The Marine held up the phones as the mother and children boarded the aircraft. The team leader held out his hand and looked at both.

"I only need this Apple." The man pointed to the iPhone X.

The Apple cell held the numbers of the accounts of funds the treasurer had kept for the organization. The other phone was the one that the treasurer had left on for the meeting with Jamal, which had allowed the Pegasus spyware to be installed. Jamal had been doomed from the beginning.

Keep reading for a special excerpt of the new Will Parker thriller by Anderson Harp.

MISLED

Marine recon veteran and small-town prosecutor Will Parker became a bush pilot for two reasons: a love of flying, and Dr. Karen Stewart. Years ago, in Somalia, Will saved the dedicated CDC researcher's life. Now he may have to do it again, under even more challenging conditions.

Two Marines have died under suspicious circumstances, and Will is the only person who can get to the truth. Even if it means an off-the-books mission that will take him thousands of miles away to remote Russia. Both of the dead had in common a fellow student at the Maryland Cyber Security Center. He's missing, but his trail leads Will to a small village outside Moscow known for worldwide hacking—and ultimately to an American financial institution with a shady multi-trillion-dollar secret to which the Marines and their classmate held the key. That key compelled certain executives to unleash killers to ensure its concealment...

Because of her importance to Will, Dr. Karen Stewart is once again a target. The enemy knows if they get to her, they get to him. Now, with her research taking her into the far-flung Yukon, Parker's arctic-combat training and skills as a bush pilot will be his only hope of saving her, not to mention himself...

Chapter 1

Deep in the Yukon

The arctic fox did not move when the aircraft narrowly cleared the tree line and crossed the open field. The animal was caught in the open, far from the protection of the tall pines and spruce, paralyzed by fear and sickness. His nearly pure-white fur blended perfectly into the blinding sunlit snow of the Yukon. The air had a sting in it from the subzero cold. His breath caused the faintest vapor cloud to form as he panted, his white-frothed tongue hanging from his mouth. The exhaustion had overtaken him. He was dying.

In a daze, the animal tracked the airborne object above, head canting left and right as if he were drunk. As the engine's throaty sound grew louder, he jumped and fell back into the snow. He tried again to run, but at a tilt, stumbling as if his internal gyroscope were off. He recovered his balance and made a desperate break for the protection of the trees.

The DHC-3 Otter's pilot circled the field, lining up what had once been an Army runway, putting his flaps down, and landing softly on the single strip buried under the snow. The sleds of the aircraft barreled through the drifts as the aircraft's propeller churned the dry, powder-like snow into a cloud of white that followed the bright yellow Otter to the end of the runway.

A lone person waited next to the runway with a backpack and a rectangular object next to her feet. The shape of her parka gave a clear impression that this was a woman, petite, not nearly tall enough to reach up and touch the aircraft's wing. She held up an arm to shield her face from the blast of icy air from the propeller. A black, canvas-covered rectangular object near her feet shook as the aircraft approached, seeming to wobble on its own. Something alive inside moved the covered cage.

The aircraft stopped at the end of the runway near the passenger and her cargo. The old Otter had black oil streaks across its yellow engine cowling. The tall propeller blades came to a stop and the engine silenced. With the motor halted, the sudden silence of the outback weighed heavily until movement in the airplane broke the quiet. The sound of metal echoed as the door handle was turned. The pilot's door swung open and a man climbed down. Tall and built firmly, he jumped down from the cockpit with a subtle air of confidence. It didn't seem to be his first trip to the backcountry.

"Did you see that fox?" Will Parker glanced toward the other end of the runway.

"Did it have two tipped black ears?" the woman asked, carrying her backpack to the airplane.

"Yeah." He leaned against the cargo door. "Didn't think he was going to move."

"Surprised he moved at all. That's George." She took off her mitten and pulled the strings on her backpack at her feet to ensure it was closed.

"Another infected one?" He had already seen a few types of animal in the area infected with the rapidly spreading rabies virus. Mostly, the small varmints were the targets of the dreaded disease.

She nodded.

What a way to go, he thought. As a Marine who had served in special operations in some of the most dangerous places in the world, William Parker knew all about "ways to go." Having spent much of his time in the Arctic prior to leaving the Marines, he also knew that rabies was rare in such cold climates. Will had been a member of a small band of experts that instructed Marines in how to survive above the Arctic Circle. He knew what eighty-below could do to the human body. But brutal cold was an old and well-known threat up in the north. The rabies epidemic, on the other hand, was new. And growing.

To pick up his cargo, Will had flown to this remote, abandoned airfield in Snag, Canada, deep in the Yukon and well east of the Alaskan border. Snag was an abandoned outpost of the Royal Canadian Air Force from World War II and it no longer hosted regular visitors, instead becoming a backcountry ghost town.

Perfect for my Otter, Will thought as he walked around his aircraft, performing a post flight check. The Otter aircraft was designed to get down fast and land hard in a very short space. But flying in the Arctic required much of a bush pilot. Something as simple as a slightly damaged strut could, in extreme, subzero temperatures, easily snap off as the airplane landed. Yet the unusual demands of flying in the bush were what had brought Will here. He'd long ago passed the ultimate challenge for a bush pilot: landing a Super Cub on a riverbank no wider than the wheels of the aircraft. But winter was something else again. Regardless of season, though, Will had found no place on earth that had flying like the Yukon.

He had also come for the cargo.

Dr. Karen Stewart visited Snag on a regular basis. Lying to the east of the Saint Elias Mountains, the flatlands ranging north and south drew a variety of wildlife to the local habitat. Karen had left Médecins Sans

Frontières to take a position with the CDC's unit in Alaska, monitoring zoonotic infections. Zoonotic diseases followed the movement of animals, and the most dangerous of the zoonotic illnesses was rabies. Alaska and the northwest had gradually become warmer each year and, as they did, the rate of rabies had increased. The rabies virus burned through the brain and progressed relatively quickly. But as winters became milder, the sick animals were able to move farther north before dying, thus interacting with more animals and continuing the rapid spread of the fatal disease. In joining the CDC, Karen Stewart had followed in her father's footsteps, but by studying the spread of viruses among the animals of the extreme north, she'd blazed her own trail in this relatively new field.

She and Will Parker had some history—he had saved her from a kidnapping by Al-Shabaab in the western frontier of Somalia. The purpose behind the raid on the Doctors Without Borders camp had been simple: Capture those whose families could pay the ransom. Like her father before her, Karen had worked with Doctors Without Borders in the meningitis-stricken Horn of Africa until it and terrorism caught up to her. After her close call in Africa, she'd taken the CDC job and been posted to Alaska. That's when her father had called in a favor from Will Parker.

"Just keep an eye on her," was all Dr. Paul Stewart had asked after hearing that Will was flying as a bush pilot out of Anchorage.

Will had agreed gladly. He owed the man who had saved his life.

"Did you get one?" He hefted Karen's backpack and fitted it into the Otter's cargo space.

"Yeah."

He walked to the canvas-covered cage, slipping on his leather gloves. "This one have a name?"

"Juliet."

"She going to make it?" He managed to fit the cage in the rear seat of the cabin.

"No."

Karen had been in the backcountry for several days already. Parker had wanted to join her, but she'd refused. She was fiercely independent and he respected that about her. Having been a prisoner of a terrorist group in Somalia and living face-to-face with death every day, Karen had plenty of reasons to take a nine-to-five in Atlanta. But, like Will, she'd had enough of being walled in by an office.

"We need to get out of here." Will glanced west at the Saint Elias Mountains and the darkening skies above. "A bad one's coming."

She nodded, hauled herself up into the copilot's seat, and pulled back her parka hood. Her short, shaggy haircut and well-tanned face made for an attractive, athletic woman who could live in the outback with no makeup and look no worse for the wear.

He climbed into the pilot's seat, buckled in, and started running through his preflight checklist. "You know, that's a good name," he said as he worked.

"What?"

"Juliet."

She gave him a false frown.

"Dr. Juliet." Will smiled, knowing it was her middle name.

The Otter's engine roared with a throaty growl. Will spun up the turboprop to a deafening roar, turned the aircraft into the wind, and sped along the runway until the sleds started to leave the surface. As the plane lifted, he banked to the southeast, heading away from Anchorage.

"Why this way?" she asked through her mike.

She had donned earphones to hear Will above the guttural sound of the engine. The radial Pratt & Whitney engine on the Otter was as old as the 1967 aircraft, but more than once it had been taken apart piece-by-piece and rebuilt. An engine like this was meant to be overhauled. Its parts were made of heavy castings for repeated use until it ended up in a graveyard or short of a runway in a bad crash. No matter how it died, the Otter's body would be cannibalized for its knobs, handles, and gauges like a transplant donor. In that way, it would keep on living for decades. But for now, it had thousands of landings to go and many years of flying to come.

"We need to skirt the storm." He pointed to a dark line that crowded the tops of the peaks that stood between them and Anchorage. "There's a valley to the south that we can pass through." Some of the mountains in the Saint Elias range topped out at 19,000 feet. Will's Otter was not made for such high altitudes.

Suddenly, the cockpit's electronics panel shuddered. At the same time, the aircraft's engine sputtered.

"What?" Karen's voice betrayed her fear.

"We're okay."

Will knew immediately what had occurred: A solar flare. The weather report that morning on takeoff had mentioned a risk of the flare's arrival. The sun had unleashed a magnetic shockwave that had traveled millions of miles through space until it collided with the earth and overloaded the electronics of the airplane. Like being knocked down by a wave, the avionics on the cockpit's panel sputtered, then went black.

It shouldn't have affected the engine, Will thought as he loosened his grip. A nervous pilot only made matters worse. He kept the yoke steady and the wings level, going through the mental checklist that an experienced pilot would use to check each system quickly. He looked at the fuel gauge, then tried to turn the engine over, but the big radial simply coughed and went silent again.

Probably some bad fuel. Will scanned the panel again. He had landed at a small airport to refuel after crossing the mountain range. It didn't take much water in the fuel to cause havoc, especially when combined with an electrical failure.

Will Parker knew one thing about the Otter: It was made to land in any condition and on any surface.

Give me the space between home plate and first base...that's all I need. Ninety feet and he could put the airplane safely on the ground.

He scanned the terrain ahead for that much room, keeping the nose of the aircraft tilted down to maintain his airspeed. Without power, some airplanes can glide for miles as long as a calm hand can keep the nose down.

"Hand me that radio." Will pointed to a small handheld in a storage pocket next to her seat. The battery-powered radio was a must for flying in the bush. It could serve as a most important backup.

He radioed air traffic control. "Anchorage Control, this is November one-one-two." He hesitated to use the word *mayday*. A quick landing, with an equally quick passing of the solar interference, did not qualify for a mayday.

The SP-400 radio only crackled.

"We can land this...no problem." His voice was intended to calm his passenger—and himself. He looked straight ahead for a likely landing spot, as a turn would only cause the plane to lose critical airspeed. Air slowing down as it passed over the wing meant the loss of lift.

Easy, Will thought as he relaxed his hands again. It never helped to fight an airplane, even in a situation like this. He scanned his panel to make sure that something obvious was not missing. Engine failure in the Arctic didn't happen every day, but this was not Will Parker's first.

Nothing.

He looked across the horizon. A ridge stood in front of the nose. There was no telling what was on the other side. It didn't matter. Their situation required commitment without hesitation. He steered the plane steadily, holding on to as much altitude as possible and for as long as possible.

"Altitude is our friend." He spoke the words unconsciously, forgetting for a moment that he had a passenger. It was an old pilot's saying that went back to the most basic instructions and first flight lessons.

"What?" Karen was turning pale.

The Otter's sleds brushed the top of the trees at the crown of the ridge.

"There you go." He pointed to a small, ice-covered pothole lake just to the left of the nose. The pothole lakes of the Yukon were Mother Nature's version of the same small, deep holes found in the Yukon's road surfaces. These were filled with ice and water. If he could hold on to a gentle turn, they had a chance. The Otter slowly slid down the hill as it lost altitude. The crown of a pine tree brushed the strut. Lower, lower, finally reaching the lake.

The aircraft slammed down on the ice and snow, the banking turn having caused the airplane to lose all of its remaining lift. The speed rapidly bled off as the skids scraped across the frozen lake until Will saw a log sticking up out of the ice.

"Hold on!"

The crunch of metal echoed through the woods and all movement stopped. The right skid had been sheared off, and the remaining sharp point of the landing gear had gotten stuck in the ice. At least the airplane had come to a stop.

"Let's get out of here." Will pointed to the door on his side. The aircraft was tilted with her starboard side angled down, causing the cargo to slide to the right. He pulled Karen across his seat and helped her down onto the ice, which seemed more than adequate to hold their weight.

"You okay?" Will was still holding her on the ice. She'd felt so small and light in her parka as he'd helped her out. He'd forgotten what the woman he'd saved in Africa felt like.

"Yeah." Her face remained ash-gray, but she seemed steady enough on her feet. Suddenly, she jumped at a noise from behind.

The cargo door on the other side had popped open; they heard another sound.

"Watch out." Karen shielded him with an arm and backed away from the wrecked aircraft.

Will saw motion on the other side as a white form crawled out of the wreckage and scurried away across the ice and into the woods on the far side of the lake.

Juliet had escaped.

"This storm isn't going to be pretty." He looked back to the Saint Elias Mountains. "We need shelter."

He knew that the clouds would bring a blizzard; after that, the temperature would drop precipitously. The clear Siberian air that followed a major front could be deadly. He pointed to a space in the timberline on the other side of the aircraft across the lake. The gap in the trees made an oddly straight line from the edge of the lake deep into the woods. In the center of the timber cut was what appeared to be a rock formation covered in deep snow.

Will pointed at the outcropping. "Let's go there. We need to get out of this wind."

A cold breeze swept across the lake. The tail of the Otter squeaked as the rudder was pushed from side to side by the wind. It was the only sound.

"Whitehorse is south." He pointed in the same direction as the swath of broken trees. "But no one will come." He calculated the process. The airplane would not be missing for some time, and air traffic control was likely overwhelmed with others affected by the solar flare.

"Even though we crashed?" She looked up at him with eyes that seemed larger than normal.

"Not a crash." He smiled. "A landing." He looked back at the storm coming in. "Anything you walk away from is a landing."

"Great." Karen gave him a sarcastic smile like the teenager told about a curfew. But at least he got a smile.

They were several miles from Snag and a massive, thickly forested hill deep in snow stood between them and the airfield. Although the pilot-training strip had closed decades ago, pilots still recognized the name Snag. It had a distinction in Canada that Will didn't choose to share with Karen. Gasoline froze at forty below, but Snag was known for temperatures that turned oil into fudge. Metal would break off in your hand when the mercury hit seventy or eighty below zero, like stale icing falling off of a leftover cake.

"Follow me," he said, taking her arm. "We need some shelter, Dr. Juliet."

Printed in the United States
by Baker & Taylor Publisher Services